The Mistletoe Mix-up

The Mistletoe Mix-up

Codi Hall

Podium

For my bad boy–loving ladies who enjoy
watching the confirmed bachelor fall . . .
This one's for you!

Cover design by Wendi Chen

ISBN: 978-1-0394-7825-1

Published in 2024 by Podium Publishing
www.podiumentertainment.com

Podium

The Mistletoe Mix-up

Chapter One

Sam Griffin sprawled out on the couch with the remote in his hand, watching *Young Sheldon* after scrolling through all his streaming services and finding nothing that caught his eye. On a normal Friday night, he'd either be working or heading to the Wolf's Den or Brews and Chews for a drink, but tonight he'd taken his ten-year-old nephew, Jace, so his brother could have a date night with his pregnant wife, Merry. While Merry's parents would have been happy to have their adopted grandson, Jace had requested a guys' night with his favorite uncle.

Jace actually called Sam his original uncle, since he now had Merry's brother, Nick, but tomato, tomahto.

Jace had crashed out an hour ago and was soundly sleeping in Sam's room, and Sam was restless. Although he'd tried to get comfortable on the couch, he could not sleep. It wasn't only the lumpy, secondhand cushions under his back keeping him awake, but his mind wouldn't quiet. It wasn't an uncommon occurrence, especially late at night in the quiet of his one-bedroom apartment.

Sam climbed off the couch, groaning at the pull in his back. Although he was in great shape, his body was starting to feel all of its thirty-seven years. Knees creaking. Back aching. As he shuffled to the kitchen, a picture of an elderly Sam, all alone with a cane in his hand, popped into his head, and he grimaced. How was he three years shy of forty? He could still remember being twenty-five, doing backflips into the river and not having a twinge the next day. How had his life flashed forward twelve years?

He grabbed the milk out of the fridge and quietly opened the high cupboard where he kept his good snacks when his nephew visited. Sam loved the boy dearly, but there was no way he was sharing his Little

Debbie Christmas Tree Cakes with him. They were his guilty pleasure, a basic-bitch trend he could get behind, and they always ran out well before Christmas, so he made sure to stock up to get him through the holidays. No one touched these babies but him.

Sam returned to the couch with his milk and cake, placing the plastic wrapper between his teeth.

"Uncle Sam?" Jace's voice called from behind him.

Sam froze, opening his hands and mouth carefully to drop the cake to the floor and away from the prying eyes of ten-year-old boys. "Yeah, pal?"

"Jilly G wants to talk to you."

Sam twisted around, staring at his nephew for several moments before realization struck him like an eighteen-wheeler, and he asked slowly, "The . . . radio show host?"

Jace nodded, his expression wary.

Sam turned away briefly from the sheepish child to check the time before meeting the boy's gaze again. "Why is there a radio show host on the phone wanting to talk to me at eleven at night?"

Jace's eyes were enormous in his small face, but his voice came out steady. "I listen to her before bed, and she was doing a show about people who were alone, and I thought of you. So, I called in, and after I explained what was going on, she asked to talk to you."

Sam wanted to sink into the couch with a groan. "Who introduced you to the radio?"

"Dad. He always listens to it when he can't sleep."

Sam climbed to his feet and came around to take the cell phone from Jace. "I'm going to kick your dad's"—Sam caught himself before he owed Jace two dollars to the swear jar—"butt."

"Why?" Jace asked.

Sam covered the receiver. "For buying you a cell phone," he whispered. Sam heard a woman's voice calling his name, and he put the cell to his ear, scowling. "This is Sam."

"Hi, Sam. This is Jilly G at 103.2 FM. How are you tonight?" Her tone was sweet and soothing, almost distracting him from the fact that his nephew had called up the local radio station for Mistletoe, Idaho. Her tone would have relaxed him, except he remembered that even now he was live on the air, and people he saw every day were listening.

"You know, Jilly, I was doing great until this moment, so maybe we can cut to the chase?" Jace jumped up onto the couch, watching Sam, and he pointed at his nephew and mouthed, *You're in big trouble.*

Jace didn't seem disturbed.

"Well, Jace called in very concerned about you. He said you've been spending all your time alone, that you haven't had a girlfriend in years, and you've been binging sweets in front of the TV like Homer Simpson."

Sam's gaze skirted to the floor where he'd dropped his tree cake and grimaced. "My nephew doesn't know who Homer Simpson is, so I know he didn't say that."

"No, I inferred it from his description."

"I look nothing like Homer Simpson!"

"Of course not, Sam," she crooned gently. "He's a cartoon character."

"I mean," Sam ground out between his gritted teeth, "I'm not an overweight sad sack, eating in front of the TV! I like an occasional treat, and I'm fine being single. In fact, I prefer it that way. I don't have to worry about anyone else's plans or feelings—"

"You sound like a very . . . self-reliant and isolated person." Sam's jaw dropped at the dig, and before he could respond, she chirped, "Oh, we have a caller. Hang on, Sam. I'm going to loop in Molly in the Mountains."

"No, don't loop in—"

"Hi, Molly! This is Jilly G. You wanted to say something to Lonely in Mistletoe?"

"Mostly, I called in to warn anyone who has never dated Sam——" A loud beep covered his last name. "Run away as fast as you can! He is the most egotistical, selfish, pathetic—"

"Alright, Molly," Jilly G interjected, "I'm going to stop you right there and let some of these other callers get a few adjectives in."

"Other callers?" Sam whispered in horror. He couldn't place Molly off the bat, but if he'd burned that bridge to a cinder, how many more disgruntled women were waiting to read him the riot act?

The list could be massive. As much as he tried to be open and honest, some women didn't take the end of their acquaintance well.

"Sam, before I take our next caller, do you have any thoughts on Molly's warning to other women?"

"Do I have thoughts? On whether women should run from me? Many, but I'm a bit terrified anything I say will leave me roasted in the court of public opinion."

"Are you saying that Molly has the wrong idea about you?" Jilly asked sweetly.

"I mean . . . I'm not egotistical, I'm confident." A loud boo chorused in his ear. "Hey now, you wanted me to respond! I'm honest about what I'm looking for. Why does not wanting a relationship make me pathetic?"

"Maybe it is your delivery or reasoning that has Molly feeling this way. Let's hear from Jen in Sun Valley."

Sam found himself muted again, and a gravelly voice said hi to Jilly.

"Hi, Jen. I understand that you've also had a previous relationship with Lonely in Mistletoe. Care to share?"

The woman chortled, and he stiffened at the familiar sound. "Oh my God, not the hacker!"

"Sam is a jerk," Jen said, bringing back memories of the night he'd met her when he was passing through Sun. He'd been staying with a friend, and they'd gone out to a bar. He'd approached a gorgeous redhead, but the place was too loud to talk. They went outside, and the moment he'd heard her voice, he'd wanted to hightail it back inside. She sounded like a croaking toad, and while Sam thought he could get over that, kissing her had been like licking an ashtray. Before he could let her down easy, she'd started hacking against his mouth. When he'd felt the hunk of her spit tag him in the face and start sliding down, he was done. He'd told her he needed to pee, grabbed his friend, and rushed out the door.

"It sounds like you know that from experience. Do you want to elaborate, Jen?"

"I met him last year, and we were having a lovely time. Suddenly, he disappears. Sam specializes in blowing women off without any explanation. If he's alone, binge eating, it's his own *bleeping* fault!"

The line went dead, and Jilly laughed. "Apparently, she got what was needed said off her chest. Sam? Thoughts?"

Sam wasn't going to throw stones and humiliate Jen on the radio. "Yeah, I think I'm going to get off this phone call and discuss at length why boundaries are important with my nephew."

"Oh, Sam, don't leave! If you go, how will you respond to the dozens of ladies waiting in the queue to talk to you? Or at you, as was the case with Jen?"

"Naw, thank you, but this little experiment is over. You have a nice night now."

"Sam—"

He ended the call, tapping his phone against his thigh.

"You look mad," Jace said.

"I am, but initially, I was just confused." Sam kneeled in front of Jace, watching his nephew's downcast face. "What did you think calling a radio station was going to do for my love life?"

Jace shrugged. "Miss Jilly has helped lots of people! Listen, she gives great advice." Jace hopped off the couch, and Sam heard the telltale sound of plastic being crushed under his nephew's slippers, but Jace was too riled up to notice the cake he'd smushed under his feet. He took off down the hallway, returning with his tablet, and the first thing Sam heard was Jilly's voice.

"So, you disagree with the other ladies about Sam's qualities?" Jilly asked.

"Look, I'm not saying he can't be an insensitive turd, but he's smart. He's funny. Obviously good-looking, or women wouldn't line up to sleep with him, knowing what they do about him." Sam recognized Ricki's voice and groaned. His friend and occasional lover thought she was helping, but no doubt it would only fuel the hate fire the ladies of Mistletoe seemed to be stoking tonight.

"Are you saying they're asking for it?"

"Whoa, not the words I'd choose," the woman said. "Just that everyone involved is a consenting adult, and if they don't want him to continue perpetrating his man-whore ways, maybe don't answer the phone when he calls with sex on the brain."

"Thank you for your insights, Ricki."

Sam shot Ricki a text.

WTF? You getting involved in my public roasting?

At least I said something sweet about you!

Sweet my ass, you called me a man-whore.

"Our next caller is Sally's Life is Sweet."

"Oh no," Sam moaned, banging his face against the soft pillowy top of his couch.

"What's the matter, Uncle Sam?"

Sam looked up at Jace, his head already throbbing. He pointed to the tablet, but before he could tell him to turn it off, Sally started in.

"Sam is a fatphobic, scared little boy who wouldn't know a good thing if it bit him in the ass."

Sam groaned, thinking about that one time at Brews and Chews when Sally had offered to do just that, and he'd been horrified. Not that he didn't like a little rough play, but he didn't mess around with women who'd dated any of his friends. Or if not friends, people who hung around with him and his brother during social gatherings. While he might think Pike Sutton was a bit of a prissy prima donna, he was not going to fuck him over by sleeping with his ex.

And I'm not fatphobic! Big or small, I love them all.

Nope, that rebuttal would definitely get him killed.

Sam picked Jace up off the couch and shook his head. "Next time you're worried about my well-being, can we not involve the general public and some radio personality quack?"

"She is usually more helpful," Jace said, obviously disappointed.

"The lines are still lighting up, and I'm sorry to say the consensus seems to be that Sam isn't relationship material and is destined to die alone, but maybe I'm wrong. Next caller?"

Sam tapped on Jace's tablet, cutting off whatever new tirade was coming. Sam carried Jace into the bedroom and tucked him back in, giving him a reassuring smile. "Why don't you listen to something else, alright? I don't really want you hearing all that stuff about your uncle."

"It's alright, Uncle Sam. I hear a lot when Mom and Aunt Holly talk about you."

Sam groaned. "Uh, I'm afraid to ask what they say."

"Aunt Holly thinks when you meet the right girl, you will be an amazing husband."

Sam smiled. There was a reason Holly Winters held a soft spot in his heart.

"Mom doesn't think it will happen though. She says you're too set in your ways."

Sam ruffled his nephew's hair, ignoring the sting of those words. "I guess I'll have to prove your mom wrong, then, huh?"

"What do you mean?" Jace asked.

"Well, if your mom doesn't think I can get a girlfriend and your aunt does, I think we should prove Holly right. That I can be a good boyfriend."

Jace sat up so fast, their foreheads nearly collided. "Really?"

"Hey, if you think a girlfriend will make me happy, who am I to argue with a smart guy like you?"

Jace nodded solemnly. "It's true. I get A's on all my spelling tests."

"I've heard that about you." Sam hugged him and pushed him back onto the bed. "Now, get some sleep. We're making a donut run in the morning."

Sam got up from the bed but didn't make it to the doorway before Jace called his name. Sam turned, his hand on the frame. "Yeah, pal?"

"Are you going to share your secret stash with your girlfriend?"

Sam's eyes narrowed. "How do you know about my stash?"

"Dad said you always keep one. He told me to watch out for where you were hiding it so we could raid it when you weren't home."

"And did you report back, super spy?" Sam asked, quirking a brow.

Jace grinned. "I'll keep the location a secret, but only for the big bag of gummy bears."

Sam's mouth twitched, suppressing a smile at the little extortionist's cunning. "Deal."

Chapter Two

The town of Mistletoe was quiet at six in the morning, like a picturesque painting of a sweet, small mountain town. The sky was still dark, but Officer Wren Little's high beams caught the flash of buildings and lampposts as she drove down Main Street, making a left onto Spruce. She rolled down her window, ignoring the sting of cold air on her skin as she pressed in the code to get into the employee parking lot of the police station. The gate sprang to life with a loud screech as it pulled across the gravel, allowing Wren to pass through. She stopped just inside, making sure it closed without anyone sneaking through. No one had tried since she arrived six weeks ago, but that didn't mean someone wouldn't. If spending the last sixteen years in major cities had taught her anything, it was to always be on her guard. One wrong move and—

Four rapid knocks on her window before she'd even put the cruiser in park sent her nearly jumping through the roof. Her dog, Duke, let out a low growl from the back seat, his chin resting on her left shoulder, closest to the intruder. She turned to glare out the window at the dark figure, rolling down the window again.

"B, what are you doing out here?" she grumbled.

Officer Barret Hughes ducked down, grinning at her through the open window. The twentysomething officer was friendly and engaging most days, but scaring her to death was a good way to get tased.

"Sorry, but I saw you pulling in and wanted to tell you I got coffee and donuts." Barret reached in and rubbed Duke's head. "I even got one for you, boy."

Duke's tail thumped happily against the car's interior, and Wren rolled her eyes. The dog was a spoiled brat, but he'd been her faithful companion the last five years. She couldn't have asked for a better partner.

"Thank you, I appreciate the update, but I could have gotten that information inside."

"True, true." Barret fell back, allowing her to open the door and step out. "Sorry, I know I can be a bit much sometimes."

Wren smiled reassuringly at the younger man as she opened the back door to release Duke. The German shepherd mix hopped out of the SUV, his long tan and black fur creating tufts along his jaw and ears, which were flopped over instead of straight up. When she'd adopted Duke from a program out of Sacramento that trained shelter dogs, the other members of the Force had dubbed him Temu because he was smaller and fluffier than the Belgian Malinois the department liked to purchase. Her former chief had liked the publicity, though, and when Duke suddenly doubled in size around six months, her fellow officers stopped talking smack. Especially after putting on a training suit and getting taken down by the hundred-pound underdog.

Barret was a head taller than her and lanky like a track runner. It made him fast, but intimidating he was not. Especially when he squatted down and talked in a high-pitched baby voice to Duke. "Who's a good dog? Huh?"

Duke sat at Wren's side, his tail wagging frantically, but he didn't move otherwise. He looked up at her in the parking lot lights with dark, pleading eyes, and she sighed. "Play."

Duke bounded toward Barret, and the officer rubbed the canine all over, continuing to talk to him like he was an adorable toddler. When Duke was working, he was the best dog, but watching him relaxed and playful never failed to make her laugh.

"Alright, you two, that's enough. I'm just a cranky mess before I've had my coffee. Time to work."

Duke straightened up and returned to her side, panting with his tongue lolling out.

"Say no more," Barret said, holding his crooked arm out to her. "Let's go inside where I can get you caffeinated and tell you all about the happs last night."

Wren chuckled and looped her arm with Barret's, letting him lead her and Duke into the station. He punched in his code at the back door, holding it for them to pass through. The small station sported a front desk with no protective glass, which was so strange after working in Sacramento the last few years. There were security precautions everywhere at big-city stations, but in Mistletoe, the only secured doors were the front and side, and the gray door at the back of the room that led to the two holding cells. Desks lined either side of the room behind the door that separated the main reception area from the bullpen. The front lobby had two rows of blue chairs and a few side tables with magazines splayed across the tops. The walls had various posters about outreach programs and laws, including multiple that discouraged drunk driving, which was a massive problem in a town with nothing else to do during the long, cold months.

Compared to her time in larger cities, the most she'd had to deal with since being here were a few assault collars and a lot of drunk and disorderliness. Otherwise, Mistletoe was rather peaceful, and she was soaking it all in.

"Coffee and donuts are on the counter," Barret said, releasing her arm. "Case files are on my desk. Had one domestic out at the Reeds'."

"Uh-oh. What did old Lloyd do to poor Margaret?" Wren asked, her tone laced with sarcasm. She removed her coffee cup from the cardboard carrier, thinking about how quick the older woman was to throw something at her poor husband over the smallest slight.

Barret picked up the donut obviously made for Duke with dog bone sprinkles and waved it at her. "Can I?"

Wren nodded, addressing Duke, who sat patiently, but his eyes were locked on the pastry. "Eat."

Barret gave Duke the donut, which disappeared in two bites, and wiped his hands on a napkin before answering her question. "This time Lloyd had the nerve to complain that Margaret rearranged the furniture to try something new and he didn't like it. In return, she called him a host of names she didn't mean and chucked a lamp at his head. Luckily, it was still plugged in and didn't get very far. She eventually apologized to both her husband and myself, after telling me I needed to head back to the playground with the rest of the kiddies."

"Well, isn't that nice." The sarcasm hung heavy and thick like fog. "I'm actually Team Margaret on this one. If anyone tried telling me how I could decorate my house, I'd do more than throw a lamp."

Barret took a drink of his coffee, head cocked slightly to the side. "If two people live together and are partners, shouldn't they both get a say?"

Wren pointed her finger at Barret smugly. "And that's why I don't have a romantic partner. I like things my way."

"Well," Barret said, flashing her a sheepish grin that made her instantly suspicious, "if you change your mind on that front, I've had several inquiries about you."

Wren choked on the hunk of maple bar she'd just bitten off. "From who?"

"Guys at the gym. Kiss My Donut. Clive Ewan asked for you instead of me when I picked him up from the Wolf's Den last night. Apparently, you're prettier." Barret turned toward the glass window with his hand on his chin, studying his reflection. "I don't see it."

She snorted. Barret's delicate features, slim nose, and full lips were part of his youthful face, whereas Wren had started up a skin care regimen when she turned thirty just to keep her skin from turning to leather like her dad's had. Wren had no idea what her mom looked like now. Her dad put away all the pictures of her when she left, and Wren didn't care enough to look her up on social media.

Wren's jaw tightened. She didn't like thinking about her mother, so her thoughts circled back to Barret's offer to set her up. Dating and relationships were the last thing on her mind, but unfortunately, the one thing she wanted did require the participation of a man. Nothing like getting shot to make you start questioning your whole life's purpose and thinking about your biological clock.

Since her return to Mistletoe, men hadn't been shy about asking her out, but they were barking up the wrong tree. Love was a trap that destroyed lives, and there was no way she was falling into it again.

"I wouldn't trust Clive Ewan's beer goggles," Wren teased. "I think you're gorgeous."

"Well, thank you very much." He pursed his lips, moving his face back and forth like a male model. "Also, on the plus side, I didn't get punched in the face, so that is a win in my book."

"Ah, 'The Book of Fun Facts and Opinions According to Barret'!" Wren put the last of the maple bar in her mouth and clapped.

"Hey now, don't mock 'The book of Barret.' It's full of fun factoids, like how the chief comes in early to talk about what to expect during the holidays."

That made sense. Although Wren had been a decorated officer since she was twenty-one, this was her first year serving the Mistletoe

community, and while she didn't expect massive drug busts and mur-
ders, it was always good to be prepared. Especially with the holiday
festivities and how many tourists came through.

Barret had been a part of Mistletoe's finest for three years, and while
there were five other veteran officers on staff, Barret and the chief were
the only ones she cared to know. One of the guys had been her older
brother's friend since high school, and he was a bigger tool now than
he had been then.

The back door opened, and Chief Monroe stepped through the
doors, looking sharp in his uniform, his close-cropped gray hair standing out against his dark skin. He was a big man, well over six feet, and
had lived his whole life in Mistletoe. His dad had been a prominent
figure in the community, a member of the school board, and the chief
spoke about the man with reverence.

Wren wasn't one to sing the praises of anyone, least of all her dad,
who had been a county sheriff. God love the man, but he was a hard-
headed son of a bitch, and Wren had no plans to be anything like him.

Especially when she had a child of her own.

"Good morning. Are we ready for another fine day protecting and
serving?" Chief greeted Duke with a pat on the head. Duke leaned into
the affection so hard he almost fell over.

Wren shot the chief a wry smile. "Yes, sir."

"Ah, Wren, how you've grown," Chief said, his dark eyes twinkling.
"Six weeks ago, you would have looked at me with disgust for my
cheery demeanor."

"Only because I am not a morning person, sir, and prefer to be
sleeping when the hideous light of the day star is upon us."

"Only it's not out yet." The chief picked up the lemon-filled glazed
from the box and smirked. "And when she does come out, I'm not sure
how much sun we'll have today. Weatherman called for snow."

Barret laughed. "When are these guys going to learn that Idaho
does what she wants and there is no guessing what's going to happen on
any given day until you look up at the sky and say, 'Hey, it's snowing.'"

Wren waved what remained of her second donut between the two
of them. "Are we really gonna stand around and bullshit about the
weather?"

"No, we are not." Chief turned to Barret. "How were patrols last
night?"

"Nothing I couldn't handle," Barret said.

Chief shook his head. "Barret, you don't have to prove you have the mettle to do this job. I've seen it. I just want to know how it went."

"It went fine."

Chief nodded, turning his attention to Wren. "And you? Still pissed at me for pulling you off nights?"

"Absolutely not. That would be unprofessional."

He patted her shoulder. "I appreciate it, and I'm sure Johnson does, too. Being a new dad is hard enough, but also being on opposite schedules from your wife?" Chief shook his head. "I was lucky that we could afford for my wife to stay home with our kids and then go back to teaching when they were in school."

Wren's chest squeezed a bit. Over the last year, a slow, burning need had been brewing inside her, which became excruciating every time someone brought up kids. Having a family had always lingered at the back of her mind, but after growing up in her father's home with three older brothers and then working in a male-dominated field, she'd given up on dating a long time ago. Sex, absolutely not, but trying to make a relationship work? Men either grew to resent her long hours or were initially turned on by what she did, then looked for ways to challenge her at home, like they were in some kind of dominance struggle.

If she wanted to have kids, Wren knew she'd have to get started soon, but after she'd watched that documentary about the man who'd fathered a thousand kids, artificial insemination was off the table, at least from a donor who was a stranger. The last thing she wanted was her child to accidentally date their sibling when they reached maturity and end up on some weird TLC show.

She'd posted a profile on a local dating site, marking the "casual" box, and her inbox had been flooded with responses from eager men. She'd looked through their profiles and set up a few informal dates with some who looked promising, but she needed a nondisclosure agreement signed before she discussed what she was looking for so that rumors wouldn't fly. The last thing she wanted was for information to get back to her dad. No need to have that fight with him until there was something to fight about.

It was crazy to think that she was a grown woman of thirty-five, still worried about what her dad would think. She knew he'd be against her being a single parent. Maybe not to the degree when she'd been sixteen, but he had old-fashioned ideas about how people should live their lives. People went to college or trade schools, built up their career, then got married, and, finally, had kids.

It was funny to think she was so desperate to start a family now, but if life had taken a different route when she was sixteen, Wren would have a nineteen-year-old kid right now.

She sighed heavily. Some things just weren't meant to be, and God had been looking out for her. Wren had obviously dodged a bullet by not running off with Sam Griffin when she was a teenager. From the way the women of Mistletoe had roasted him last night on the radio, he'd turned into a philandering dog in his middle years.

Of course, she couldn't blame them for falling for his charms. Although she hadn't spoken to him since coming back to town, Wren had seen him around, and damn if he hadn't aged like fine wine. His blond hair swept back off his face, which was all high cheekbones and angles. Combined with a leather jacket, white T-shirt, and loose boot-cut jeans, he was pure sex walking. In high school, he'd been less lean and his face was softer, but that was a long time ago. People changed.

"Wren?" Barret asked, dragging her out of her head.

"Sorry!" Wren gave him a thumbs-up, even though she had no idea what they'd been talking about. "We're good."

"Alright, over the next few weeks we're going to rotate shifts patrolling events. I'll have a schedule uploaded Friday." The chief grabbed one more donut and said, "As for today, Wren is going to start in town and work her way outward, Barret is going home, and when the rest of the guys trickle in, I will give them their assignments." Chief picked up his coffee and held it in a salute. "You two have a nice day now."

"You, too, sir," they said in unison.

Once the chief shut the door to his office, Barret grinned at Wren. "Want me to bring dinner at shift change?"

"Sure. But I'm buying since you provided the hearty breakfast."

"Oh, you are on! Food always tastes better when I don't pay."

Wren hip checked him as they headed for the door. "Mooch."

Chapter Three

Sam scowled at his younger brother, who was bent over and laughing uproariously at the events of the previous night. Jace had relayed a portion when they arrived before running off to his room, leaving Sam with the proverbial bag.

"So, my son good-naturedly tried to help you get a girlfriend and instead made you the town pariah?" Clark's dark eyes danced, his neck-length brown hair bouncing with his guffawing. Sam had taken after his mother in coloring, while Clark looked more like their dad, and the difference in their personalities was still a mystery to Sam. Their parents were cold people with a sense of humor as dry as toast.

"You're an ass," Sam said, dropping Jace's backpack on the couch. "Has anyone ever told you that?"

"Not lately." Clark Griffin grinned at his older brother, holding on to the back of the couch for support as he wiped tears of mirth from his eyes. "Then again, we haven't spent much time together, so that makes sense."

"Come on, man, lay off. I had a hell of a night."

Clark's eyes widened. "Please tell me you didn't listen to the rest of the show."

Sam avoided his brother's gaze. "I caught a little bit here and there. It was hard to ignore it once I knew it was happening."

Clark grimaced. "How bad?"

"Like a train wreck that explodes and body pieces fly everywhere. Then zombies come and pick apart the flesh."

"Sorry I asked," Clark said grimly, patting his brother on the back.

Merry came out of the back room, glowing and smiling. Her pregnant stomach preceded her as she shuffled across the room to hug him. "Hello, Sam. How was your guys' night in?"

"Eye-opening," Sam deadpanned, and when Merry's curious gaze swung to her husband, he shook his head.

"Don't ask."

"Alright, I won't." Merry released him with a comforting arm squeeze and headed to the front door.

"Where are you off to?" Clark asked.

She grabbed her purse and jacket off the hook before kissing Clark in a long, lingering meeting of lips. "I'm going to meet up with all the businesses participating in this year's Christmas activities. I'll be home this afternoon."

Clark brushed her hair back, his expression etched with concern. "If you get tired, come home. Make one of the other committee members set things in motion."

Merry laughed, a light tinkling sound that matched her angelic blond beauty. "You know I'm a control freak and I could never leave this to anyone else."

"I do know this, but I don't like to see you stressed." Clark kissed her again. "That's all."

"Thank you for your concern, but I will be fine." Merry pulled away from her husband and leveled Sam with a heavy stare. "Since I have you, I need bachelors."

"What?" Sam asked.

"We are having a bachelor auction in a few weeks, and I need all single, non-douchebags on deck."

Sam snorted. "Haven't you heard? I'm the biggest douche in Mistletoe."

"I have no idea what you're talking about, but I need you." His sister-in-law watched him with big, pleading eyes. "You just have to offer goods or services from your business and a few hours of your time for a short date. Make her smile, maybe share a few laughs, and you can walk away knowing you've done your civic duty."

Clark cleared his throat. "He's concerned that the ladies of Mistletoe may not find him appealing anymore."

"Huh? That's stupid," Merry said, pointing at Sam. "With that jawline and those pecks? He'd have to be carrying around a serious STD to repel the horny ladies of this town."

"That is the most horrifying thing I think has ever come out of your mouth," Clark said, blinking at her. "I'm stunned."

"Believe me, I've said worse, but I know there are little ears down the hall." Merry took a deep breath and hollered, "Bye, Jace! I love you!"

Thundering boy feet preceded the blur of Jace's body as he hugged Merry and ran back to his room. "Love you, too!"

Merry watched him retreat with a soft expression, which melted into a serious, I'm-not-taking-no-for-an-answer look when her gaze returned to Sam. "I'm going to include you in the auction, even if you only bring in a small amount. Everything helps."

Sam scowled at Clark. "Your wife is mean when she's prego."

"Don't blame my pregnancy. My fetus is not the reason you lost your appeal. Women get tired of looking for men and only finding"— Merry glanced down the hallway and lowered her voice to barely above a whisper—"fuckboys."

"Merry," Sam said, his voice dangerously calm despite the fury raging below the surface, "I love you as my sister-in-law, but I'm no one's fuckboy."

Clark wrapped his arms around his wife's shoulders and started ushering her toward the door, an apologetic expression directed at his brother. "You should probably get going, babe. Don't want to keep all the Mistletoe residents waiting."

Merry stalled in the doorway with a sigh, giving Sam a small smile over her husband's shoulder. "Sorry, Sam. I know you don't lead women on. I'm just worried the dating pool in Mistletoe is going to be so low that this whole event is going to flop."

Sam shook his head. "I'll do it, but I think you're selling the men of Mistletoe short. There's some prime beefcake in this little town."

"Why do you have to objectify them?" Merry griped.

Sam threw up his hands. "I give up!"

"Alright, honey, let's give Sam a break this morning. Our son kind of set him up for a rough one last night."

"What are you talking about?" Merry asked, but the door shut before Sam could hear Clark's response. He could just imagine Clark relaying last night's events, chuckling up a storm. Sam waited several moments until he heard his sister-in-law's car start and then he pulled open the door just as Clark was coming back inside.

"I'm going to take off," Sam grumbled.

"Hey, man, are you okay?" Clark took hold of his arm before he could get past him, closing the door so they were standing face-to-face on the porch. "I know Merry was giving you a hard time, and last night sounds like a barrel of laughs, but you're not one to let shit like that get to you."

"I'm fine, bro." Clark continued to watch him skeptically, and Sam admitted, "I'm just tired of everyone writing me off because I haven't wanted a relationship. Some men are just late bloomers, you know?"

"Late bloomers?" Clark repeated, oblivious to anything else Sam said.

"Stop acting like you can't understand what I'm saying!" Sam crossed the wood planks, gripping the railing as he stared off toward the trees and mountains. "I don't want to be this guy who bounces from bed to bed. I think I want something real."

When his brother didn't respond, Sam turned to see Clark's mouth open and close several times. Sam rolled his eyes and leaned back against the railing with a grunt. "What? Is that so crazy?"

"Huh? No! It's just surprising." Clark cleared his throat, hesitating before he asked, "Have you ever been serious about anyone?"

Of the handful of women Sam had dated more than a couple of months, he could honestly say he'd never been tempted. If he went further back to his last year of high school, there was one girl he'd been willing to give up everything for and almost had.

If she hadn't ripped his still-beating heart from his chest and stomped on it.

He would have given up anything, even his freedom, to be with Wren Little. She was beautiful, strong, funny, and challenged him. Back when he was a romantic fool, she had been the highlight of his youth, and he thought they would be together forever, but that wasn't the case.

It was bad enough that Wren's father hated Sam and had threatened to throw him in jail if he didn't stay away from her, but for her to tell him they were just kidding themselves about how they felt? That they would never have made it in the real world?

Maybe not, but they'd have been happy. Whether it would have lasted months or years was anyone's guess, but he'd been willing to go for it.

He'd seen her a couple times around town since she'd returned, that dark uniform hugging hips and thighs, which were fuller than he remembered. He hadn't gotten close enough to really study her, but that tight bun secured at the back of her head was a far cry from the wild curls that used to hang down her back as she straddled his motorcycle, lips cherry red and begging to be kissed.

That was the Wren from his past, not the uptight cop strutting around town like she had a bug up her butt.

"Sam?" Clark asked, driving away thoughts of Wren. "What are you up to today?"

"I'm going to head into work and then probably hit the Den afterward."

Clark shook his head. "I can't believe you like that dive. Aren't you worried about getting busted in some raid on the place?"

Sam snorted. "The place is hardly a criminal enterprise. Nothing illegal is happening at the Den."

"Still, it's suspicious with those rooms in the back and the rough crowd," Clark said, frowning. "Just don't get caught up in anything I have to bail you out of."

"No worries, little brother. I can stay out of trouble for a night or two and give you peace of mind. However, if I should end up in a situation where bail money and a lawyer are needed, you're my first call."

Clark's mouth kicked up in the corner, giving Sam a small smile. "I'm flattered."

"You should be. You're the only person I can count on."

"Now, come on. Chris and Victoria treat you like family."

"I know, but I would never call them to save me from the drunk tank." Sam glanced at his smartwatch and shrugged. "Guess I better be taking off. Just a few more months of working my tail off, and I'll have enough to open my own tattoo parlor."

"That's great, man," Clark said, following him off the porch. "You think there's enough business in town to support two tattoo parlors?"

"I don't know." The possibility that Sam would have to set up somewhere else had been weighing on him, but owning a business and calling the shots had been his dream since he was a kid. "I would have had my own place a long time ago if I hadn't been betrayed by a snake."

"I know," Clark said softly.

Although Sam's brother knew some of what happened, he didn't know the full story. How he'd looked up to his boss, Ray Kilpatrick, and when the older man talked about retiring, Sam offered to buy his tattoo parlor. When he couldn't get a loan through the bank, Sam had given Ray his savings and agreed to continue making payments to Ray—what the older man called carrying the loan—until the building was paid for. It turned out that Ray had gotten behind on some payments of his own, so he sold the business out from under Sam and ran off with Sam's money.

It was the main reason Sam had come back to Mistletoe. That and to be close to Clark and Jace, the only family he cared about.

"Whew, how did we get stuck on such a bummer subject?" Sam asked.

"We were talking about dreams, and sometimes that can bring up things we would rather forget." Clark's expression pinched, pain etched in his eyes. "Remember, I had to put my life on hold when Jace's mom left and I was trying to figure out how to raise him and finish school."

"I'm sorry I wasn't there for you, bro," Sam said.

"You did your best, but it was my responsibility, and we did alright. Even after I finished college and got a great job, it wasn't until I took the job here that I realized my true calling was woodworking. Like I finally found my place in the world." Clark smiled softly. "And the woman I love."

"That's what I want," Sam said, pushing off the railing. "To find my passion and maybe even someone to share my dream with."

Clark shook his head. "I can't believe you're talking like this. Do you have anyone in mind?"

Sam shook his head. "No, but I've got time. Been waiting around for thirty-seven years. What's a few more?" Sam stared out into the trees, his jaw stiff with determination. "When I do find someone who gets me, everyone in this town who said I wouldn't commit is going to eat some serious crow."

"Falling in love shouldn't be about proving people wrong."

Sam shrugged. "Why can't it be both?"

Chapter Four

Wren drove through downtown, slowing to roll down her window and holler at a couple running across the road. "Use the crosswalk!"

If she wasn't on her way to another call, Wren would have stopped and given them each a ticket. Why couldn't people follow simple rules? It was like people thought that breaking laws meant to keep people safe were no big deal, but people died every day speeding and getting hit by idiots because they crossed roads willy-nilly like a bunch of headless chickens.

She parked the SUV cruiser in front of the Wolf's Den, studying the dark building with a rush of nostalgia. This was the place she'd snuck into with Sam as a teen, barely old enough to drive. She should have been home watching TV or studying, not sneaking into the bar with her fake ID or letting Sam take her into one of the back rooms to show her a new way he could make her body tingle. While things could have taken a bad turn any time she visited the Den, the bar owner, Quint, had always kept an eye on her because he knew she was underage. He'd told her once she was safer drinking in his bar than getting drunk at the lake or some house party with a bunch of idiots. He'd taken a risk letting her hang around, but Wren's rebellious years had been safe.

Well, except for the whole broken heart and pregnancy scare.

Wren climbed out of the SUV, looking into the far back where Duke sat watching her. "I'll be right back, possibly with a friend."

Wren headed around to the front, nodding at the man guarding the door. He took one look at her uniform, and his lips twisted in disgust. Wren couldn't blame him. Mistletoe police and the crowd at the Den had never been on the same page, but Wren was only there because an old friend called about a disturbance.

Wren took a deep breath, trying to calm her racing heart. Although she'd attended department-mandated therapy after her shooting last year, Wren fought back a rush of panic every time she went to a disturbance call. Even in Mistletoe, where violent crime was minuscule, the anxiety always hung in the back of her mind.

She stepped into the bar, smiling as she stared up at the dark chandelier that disappeared into the high ceiling above. To the right and against the far wall was a stage, where a black karaoke machine was tucked in back against the wall. Tonight, a live band played a lively rendition of "Can't Buy Me Love," while the dance floor was packed with couples bouncing along to the beat. There were several tall tables scattered among shorter ones, but the biggest crowd was by the bar, waiting to get the attention of the two bartenders on duty. Wren knew that the back area would have one man on the door, taking passwords from bikers who needed a little R & R before they got back on the road.

For Wren, those private rooms had been a safe place to be with Sam, to experiment with the first boy she'd ever been with. At the time, she'd been swept up in being in love and experiencing passion. It had been nearly twenty years since she'd been back there, and Wren had no plans to revisit and drag up old memories.

"Wren, darlin'!" A booming voice hailed her from over the Beatle's song. Quinton Gains was average height and barrel-chested. His dark, silver-streaked hair was pulled back in a short ponytail, and his Fu Manchu was salt and pepper, perched happily above a wide, welcome smile.

"Quint!" Wren found herself enveloped in a bear hug and returned it as best she could with her shorter arms. "You look good."

"I look like grizzled jerky, and you know it." Quint stepped back and gave her a once-over. "You're a stunner, though! Has Blondie Boy seen you yet?"

Wren's cheeks warmed at the familiar nickname for Sam. "I'm sure in passing."

"Never could figure out how he let you get away, but I'm glad to have a friendly face on the Force." He nodded his head toward the back. "Disturbance is back this way."

Wren trailed behind Quint toward the private rooms in the back, passing by the other bouncer without issue. The hallway was dimly lit, with a red light overhead and numbered doors on either side. They stopped in front of number eight, and Quint opened the door.

A man sat on the chair in the middle of the room, holding his eyes and wailing.

"What happened to him?" Wren asked.

"Apparently, old Dan has been coming here for two weeks, creating his own little peep show on either side of the room and cleverly hiding his peepholes from us. But today the guest next door spotted the holes in the wall, and when she realized those were eyes staring back at her, she poked him."

"She poked him in the eyes?" Wren nodded her head approvingly. "Good for her."

"Yeah, except now Pervy Boy here is threatening charges against her and to sue me." Quint folded his arms over his chest, scowling at the whimpering man. "I want him booked for trespassing, destruction of property, and anything else you can throw at the little weasel."

"I need a doctor!" the man hollered, covering his eyes with both hands. His balding head was bent over, obscuring the rest of his features. "I think I'm blind!"

"Doc already looked at you and said you were fine!" Quint growled.

The man removed his hands for a split second and blinked at Quint before slapping them back over his face. "I want a proper examination."

Wren pressed her lips together disapprovingly when Quint took a step toward the man. "I'll give you an examination, you little—"

Wren stepped between Quint and Dan, shaking her head. "If he's injured, Quint, I have to take him to the hospital."

"Oh, come on, Wren!" Quint objected, pointing at Dan over her shoulder like he was stabbing the air. "He's full of shit."

"I still got to take him." Wren pulled her cuffs out and asked, "Where is the victim?"

"She had to split," Quint said, his gaze steady.

"Uh-huh." Wren went around the back of Peeper and secured his hands. When he started to whine, she said, "You're lucky all she did was poke your eyes. Knock it off."

The guy grumbled as she read him his rights and helped him to his feet. Shooting Quint a dry look, she pulled her card out of her pocket and handed it to him. When he took it, Wren said, "Let her know I'll need her to come in and make a formal statement as soon as possible."

"Sure thing, Wren." Quint pocketed the card and led her and Peeper out of the room and down the hall. As they reentered the bar area, a familiar head of blond hair arrested her in place. Sam was leaning against the bar, chatting up a brunette who didn't seem as enthralled with him as Wren would have expected. Then again, after the things she'd heard on the Jilly G Show, it seemed the entire female population of Idaho wanted a piece of Sam and not in a good way.

Tonight, he wore a red bomber jacket, the tips of his hair brushing his collar, and she could only see his profile. His jawline was tense, and she wondered if whatever the girl was talking about had to do with his on-air roasting last night.

"Well, look what the cat dragged in," Quint called loudly, most likely for Wren's benefit, and she could have cursed the big man for trying to play matchmaker. That time had long passed.

Sam turned around, flashing a wide, crooked grin at Quint before he appeared to politely excuse himself from his companion and cross the floorboards to hug Quint. There was a lot of back slapping and manly guffaws, which made Wren want to gag.

Wren cleared her throat. "Excuse me," she said, hauling Peepers around them.

She hadn't taken two steps toward the exit when Sam's deep voice called out, "No hi for me, Birdy?"

Wren grimaced as the old nickname stirred something warm and sensual inside her, swirling like a tornado straight to her pussy. Even with nearly two decades between those intimate moments and now, that name took her back to that time. To the frantic last kisses before curfew. Their first time next to the river. The last—

"Hey," she said curtly, refusing to go back there. She'd left that girl behind a long time ago.

She continued past the dancing patrons and those lookie-loos watching her and her charge. Once they stepped outside, Peeper really started blubbering.

"Officer, you got me all wrong. I found those holes in the wall and was just curious what they were! I had no idea—"

"Sir, do you not understand your Miranda rights? Because being silent is the first one."

"I'm just trying to explain," he whined.

"Let me give you a rundown of what's going to happen. I'm going to take you to the doctor's office in town, who will check you over after hours. When he gives you the okay, I will take you to the station for processing. At that time, I'll run your fingerprints, and I'm going to guess this isn't your first offense. So, I suggest you keep your excuses to yourself and wait to unburden yourself to your attorney."

Wren opened the back door of her cruiser and ducked his head with her hand on top of it, helping him onto the seat.

Duke pressed his nose against the metal barrier, and Peeper leaned forward, releasing a panicked yelp. "I'm allergic to dogs!"

"Womp, womp." She shut the door with a thud and took a deep, searching breath. Why was the last call of her shift the craziest? The chief wasn't going to be happy about the overtime, but unless she wanted to call in one of the other guys to take over, there was nothing for it. Besides, she was curious to see what other crimes this slimeball had in his past, and if her victim called, Wren wanted to be the first person she talked to.

"Hey."

Wren closed her eyes at Sam's low greeting and knew he was standing behind her, probably with his hands shoved in his pockets.

She turned slowly to face him, giving herself silent kudos for being right. He stood a few feet away, looking like a lost little boy.

"You're looking well," she said.

His lips quirked up in the corner. "High praise. I was thinking the same."

"I take my vitamins." Her fists squeezed when he chuckled, and she tried to ignore the tight tingling of her nipples. "You leaving already?"

"Seems I've earned myself a reputation, and all women in Mistletoe think I'm scum. Might as well head home and do something productive like clean my apartment."

"I heard a bit about that. You called into a radio show looking for relationship advice?"

Sam shook his head. "My nephew called. I was innocently sitting on the couch, snacking and watching TV when he came out and let me know Jilly G wanted to talk to me."

"That sucks. I'm sorry it went south for you." She patted the top of the cruiser. "I should probably get him seen, or he's going to slap a medical neglect suit on the department."

"Wait—" Sam stepped forward, taking his hands out of his pockets, and her breath caught in her throat. What was he doing? He wasn't going to hug her or something, was he?

God, I bet he smells fantastic still— No, stop! It didn't go well the first time around. There's no need for a repeat.

He didn't come any closer than that, and she waited silently for him to finish, ignoring the voice in her head arguing that they'd been kids. That if he wanted to get coffee or something, they were older and wiser now. They could be cordial. They could be . . .

Friends?

"What is it, Sam?" she said impatiently, the thought of being Sam's buddy, listening to all his conquests and mistakes, made her stomach twist in disgust.

Sam swallowed, his gaze sweeping over her face before he shrugged. "Be safe out there."

"Thanks. You, too."

As she was climbing into the cruiser, he called out, "I'm glad you got everything you wanted."

Wren reeled back like she'd been slapped. "Everything I wanted?" What was he talking about? She'd wanted to go to college and get her criminology degree, maybe go into the FBI. She hadn't wanted to jump around to different states, starting over at each precinct. She especially hadn't wanted to get shot and end up alone, back in Mistletoe.

"How do you figure that?"

Sam held his hands up, taking a step back. "Whoa, why are you jumping on my ass for being friendly?"

Because when I was sixteen, I saw my future with you? Perhaps 'everything I wanted' was a career and a life with the guy I loved? Instead, I'm back in my hometown, the one thing I want within my grasp, but I'm unable to take the leap.

Not that Wren was going to pour her soul out about her childlessness to Sam. He'd probably gag like a teenager who heard something distasteful.

Wren snorted. "Maybe because I can't figure out whether that was sarcasm or an accusation."

"It was neither," he said, cocking his head to the side. "You're here in Mistletoe, following in your father's footsteps, just like you—"

"I'm in no way like my father, but obviously the rumors about you are true," she snapped.

He crossed his arms over the red of his jacket, the white T-shirt poking through. "What rumors would those be?"

"That you're a world-class jackass that deserves to be alone." Damn, she'd really come out swinging on that one.

Sam nodded, a bitter laugh escaping him. "Well, if that's my issue, what's your excuse for being single?"

Wren didn't answer, wanting to escape the escalating situation, which was bringing too many unresolved feelings to the surface. She unlocked the car door and climbed inside.

"You're just going to bail without finishing this conversation?" Sam called out.

Wren didn't bother rolling the window down to respond. "No point in rehashing something dead and buried," she said before putting the car into gear and pulling out of the parking lot.

"You know, that was unfair of him," Peeper said from the back seat. "Many women are alone by choice—"

"Not. Another. Word."

"Roger that."

Wren let it go. There was no law against being annoying, unfortunately.

If there was, Sam would be sitting in the back next to Peeper. He didn't know her, hadn't spoken to her in almost twenty years, and she was damn sure there weren't any rumors racing around town about her.

She really should have stuck to her initial instincts and stayed the hell away from Sam.

Going forward, Wren would do just that.

Chapter Five

"Ouch, man!" Mitch Denton glared at Sam from his prone position in the tattoo chair. "Are you okay?"

"Yeah, I'm fine, why?" Sam placed a hand on Mitch's shoulder, but his friend refused to go down.

"Because I feel like you're pounding me with the tattoo gun."

Sam snorted. "Maybe you're getting soft in your old age."

"Ha, don't you mean 'our old age'?" Mitch hiked a dark eyebrow, grinning. "You've got a few months on me, if I remember right."

Sam's mouth flattened into a thin line at the reminder. "And yet, I'm not whining about a little discomfort. Don't you know what they say? No pain, no gain?"

"That's in regard to bodybuilding, not tattoos!" Mitch said, lying back again. "Besides, it was your technique I was concerned with. You're usually a gentle hand at this sort of thing."

Sam bit his tongue, unsure of what to say to Mitch. They hadn't gone to school together, as Mitch had moved to Mistletoe in his early thirties from Montana. When Sam had come back to town, they'd started working at the shop together and bonded over their love of art. Mitch's work was flawless and intricate, and Sam had several of his tats across his back and shoulders. They were late-in-life friends, without the shared history, and talking about Wren seemed out of bounds somehow.

"I've been a little preoccupied lately, I guess. Getting my name dragged through the mud will do that to a person."

Mitch winced, his blue eyes watching him sympathetically. "Oof, I'm sorry, man. When I heard about what happened, I'll admit, I laughed a little and thanked the Lord that it wasn't me."

"Understandable," Sam mumbled.

"However, it isn't fair of women to drag your name without taking responsibility for their part in the situation."

Sam stopped buzzing and looked up. "What do you mean?"

"Well, you were honest and forthright about what you were looking for. If someone thought they could change your mind, they didn't listen, and their heartbreak is their fault."

"That's great. Wanna go on air and tell them that?" Sam asked dryly.

"No, thank you. I'm just showing support for you, my guy," Mitch said, grinning. "From the safety of the sidelines, of course."

"Right." Sam went back to shaking for several moments, but when he felt Mitch jerk under his hand, he sighed, talking over the gun. "Why don't you talk about something that will calm me down, then, and maybe I'll stop drilling you?"

"I can do that. Oh, have you seen that new female cop? She is fine— Ow! Fuck!"

"Shit, sorry. Not her either," Sam growled.

Mitch studied his shoulder before turning his attention back to Sam. "Damn, dude, is there any woman who isn't on your bad side?"

"My sister-in-law and Holly."

"Oh yeah, pretty little Holly Winters."

Sam caught Mitch's grin before his friend turned away, letting him get back to work. He knew what that look meant and braced himself for the questions that came up any time one of his friends mentioned Holly.

"How come you didn't snatch that girl up when you had the chance?" Mitch asked.

Sam had answered this question a hundred different ways, but people still didn't seem to understand that Holly was the one woman he'd never wanted to sleep with. From the moment they met, they understood each other, had connected like they'd known each other for years, and even if he had been interested, he'd never have ruined that by sleeping with her.

"Because I didn't. Have a chance that is. She was hung up on Declan for years." Sam added with a chuckle, "Besides, she's the Garcia to my Morgan."

"What in the hell are you talking about? Who is Garcia?" Mitch asked.

Relaxed now, Sam went about his work as he explained, "From *Criminal Minds*. Derek Morgan and Penelope Garcia have incredible chemistry, they're always flirting, but they both know they are better off as friends."

Mitch stared over his shoulder at him like he was speaking a foreign language, and Sam realized how he sounded. He'd started watching the show with Holly a few months ago at her place, and apparently her thoughts and insights were rubbing off on him. Maybe that was why she was in a functioning relationship and he was single.

"It's a TV show," Sam grumbled.

"I've never seen the show, but I'm not sure I agree. If you've got chemistry, that should always be explored."

"Not if the chemistry is just going to fizzle out and destroy what you have."

Mitch scoffed. "How do you know if you don't try?"

"Trust me, man. I can tell when something isn't meant to be." Of course, Wren's face sprang to mind, and he kicked himself for letting his emotions get the better of him. What happened nineteen years ago was ancient history and had no bearing on his life today. And yet the minute he'd seen her, Sam couldn't help following her outside just to see . . .

If what? That overwhelming need for each other still exists? Safe to say that it doesn't, especially after her reaction to my snark.

He hadn't meant to come off like such a dick, but come on! Wren acted like Sam was the one who gave her up, when actually she'd told him to go. She'd said they didn't have a future because she'd wanted to stay in Mistletoe and he'd wanted to find a fresh start for them both. Only she hadn't stayed. After graduation, she'd left for another state, and he'd never heard from her again. What else was he supposed to think except that she'd always wanted her freedom from him, her father, and this town, but she hadn't had the guts to tell him?

The fact that she'd come back after all these years was insane to him, but he should have just let her go instead of trying to engage with her outside the Den. Maybe if he had, there wouldn't be a knot of irritation and regret twisting him up on this gloomy Monday afternoon.

"Are you about done?" Mitch asked tightly, breaking Sam out of his melancholy.

"Yeah, I've just got this small section left."

"Thank God. When you're finished, go get a Snickers or something. You better hope I don't remember this experience the next time you want something inked."

Sam bit back a laugh as he finished up the skull and blue flames Mitch wanted in honor of his dad. He'd passed away a month ago, and Mitch had chosen his motorcycle club's symbol as his latest tattoo. Sam and Clark's dad was enjoying life in Florida, away from his sons, while he and his wife sipped drinks on the beach and forgot they ever had children. He'd never inspire the kind of sentimental honor Mitch's dad did.

"You're probably right. I need a candy bar to stop being so stressed and frustrated. Chocolate fixes all."

"According to my sister, it does," Mitch said.

Sam turned off his tool and started cleaning up. "You're finished."

"In all seriousness, Griffin, maybe it's time to turn over a new leaf."

Sam glanced up from his task, frowning. "In what sense?"

"With women? Show them you've changed and are looking for something more." Mitch frowned. "That is what you want, right? That's why you're upset? You're finally looking to get serious, and no woman will touch you with a ten-foot pole?"

"That's not what I said." Although it was exactly what he'd been worried about.

"Then why does it bother you?" Mitch asked, climbing off the stool and stretching. "There are plenty of women who won't care about your reputation and will let you tear their clothes off."

Sam wasn't sure how to explain it, and that got him really thinking about Mitch's suggestion. Was Sam ready for something more than just a short-term arrangement?

Sam grabbed the plastic to cover Mitch's tattoo, securing it in place. "All set."

Mitch slipped his flannel over his arms, watching Sam. "Just so we're clear, you're not interested in the lovely Officer Wren Little, right?"

The question sucked the air out of Sam's lungs for a moment, leaving him breathless. His first reaction was to tell Mitch *Hell yes*, because they had history and even if there wasn't going to be a repeat between them, he didn't want his friend going after his ex.

But that would require a whole conversation about their past, which was something he wasn't itching to talk about.

"No, of course not. Go nuts," Sam mumbled.

"I plan to." Mitch chuckled, working on the buttons of his shirt. "Dad would have loved this. Thanks for squeezing me in."

Sam almost laughed. Usually, Mitch and Sam would be too busy to tattoo each other except on rare occasions, but a Monday before a major holiday was slow. They hadn't had a call in hours, and both their shifts were nearly over when the owner, Astrid, and her husband, Sven, came in. Although the sound of their names automatically made Sam think of Vikings, he knew they'd both grown up here. They were just blessed to have been christened with those names.

"I'm gonna step out to get some air, if you're good here?" Sam posed it as a mix between question and statement, knowing that he was going to take a walk whether Mitch agreed or not. He needed to clear his head.

"Sounds good." Mitch patted him on the back. "I appreciate you, even if you did borderline assault me today."

"Assault my ass, drama queen."

They both laughed as Sam headed out the door, breathing in the crisp winter air. Sam popped out of the alley onto the sidewalk, passing by a few people who smiled and said hello. Even though he wasn't part of the mainstream crowd that everyone revered, like his brother, Clark, people were still polite.

He'd never been good at fitting in, even as a kid, and had found his people among the loners, the kids who chose art over grades. He'd barely graduated high school, not because he couldn't do the work, but because he was so done with all of it: his parents, who put on a big show of caring in public but privately treated their two sons like a burden; the teachers, who didn't care if someone needed extra help with a concept; the cops, who had looked at him like any minute he was going to detonate and take the whole town with him.

Although he was an adult now, Sam still had his own crowd away from the masses. He'd gotten to start over after his world fell apart in Oregon. He got to be with his brother and watch his nephew grow up. All these things were in the plus column for him.

Sam rounded the corner and almost doubled back when he spotted Sally and her friend Tara walking toward him. The door to Kiss My Donut was between him and them, which meant they were going to reach it at the same time. Sally had upgraded her wardrobe since she'd started dating a doctor, her full figure wrapped in a navy pea coat and brown knee-high boots on her feet. Her light brown hair was cut below her chin, curled, and bouncy. Choosing not to date her had nothing to do with her appearance. Sam had the sense that hooking up with her would have caused mountains of drama.

After Sally's scathing call-in, it seemed either way Sam chose, he had to deal with the fallout. If he'd hooked up with her and walked away, she would have had something to say anyway.

Since when does Sam Griffin run from a fight?

Sam reached the door first and held it open. When Sally caught sight of him, her face paled. She slowed down a bit, and Tara's brow furrowed until she followed Sally's gaze and saw him. While Sally was classy in fall colors, Tara wore purple lipstick, her dark hair loose around her shoulders under a black fedora hat. Her black leather jacket, tight jeans, and boots gave off "mess with me, and I'll put a spell on you" vibes, and Sam put on his difficult-customer smile and nodded. "Ladies. Are you heading in?"

"Uh, yes." Tara glanced at Sally, who still seemed stunned. "Come on, Sal."

"By the way," he said, leaning against the edge of the door. "Thanks for all those honest opinions about me on Friday, Sally. It really opened my eyes to my character's shortcomings. Especially all those times when I *kindly* told you I wasn't interested. I guess I would have been better off sleeping with you and rejecting you afterward instead of being honest about how I didn't want to tangle with you because I smelled your crazy from a mile away."

Tara gasped while Sally's jaw flapped open and closed like a fish without oxygen. Sam released the door, and Tara caught it before it smacked her shoulder, glaring at him. He wouldn't be surprised if she asked Merry for one of her famous plush voodoo peens later. His sister-in-law's crafty business venture of adult knitted items included some quirky things like holiday-themed penis-shaped plushies. Holly had an elf one she kept on her shelf in the living room, and the thing creeped him out, its beady eyes seeming to watch him.

"Have a great day, ladies. Stay real."

Tara dragged Sally inside, and Sam grimaced. He knew it was a dick way to handle things, but women talked all the time about how men couldn't handle rejection. That rejecting the wrong man could turn out dangerous, and yet, women could tear down not only a man's reputation but his life.

"Look at you, making friends everywhere you go."

Sam groaned as he turned around to face Wren, who stood behind him in full uniform with her arms crossed over her chest. A big black and tan dog sat by her side, watching him with—Who knew it was possible?—a matching expression.

Sam imitated her stance, looking down at her from his height advantage. "My friends don't lie and try to ruin my life."

"So all those women who called in were lying about your horndog ways?"

"No," Sam admitted sheepishly before pointing to where Sally had disappeared inside, "but that one was. I politely rejected her last year, and apparently she's still sore about it."

Wren frowned. "That's not okay."

He shrugged. "It's over now and not worth any more energy."

Wren cleared her throat. "About the other night. I'm sorry I made assumptions about you. It's really none of my business."

"You mean like me asking why you're single?" he asked ruefully.

"Maybe we just let sleeping dogs lie and start over?" Wren asked.

Sam nodded toward Duke. "Speaking of dogs . . . Who is this?"

"Duke, but he's working right now."

"So, no kneeling and giving him belly scratches?"

"I'm sure he'd love a rain check on that." Wren's lips twitched. "As to the lady in question, I'd be angry, too, if I'd heard all the rumors about how good you were in bed, but I didn't get to find out."

A surprised chuckle escaped him before he could catch it. "Maybe if she'd had the chance, she'd have been disappointed."

"Nah," Wren said, her gaze sweeping him from head to toe. "You were pretty good at eighteen, and I'd imagine you've learned a few tricks since then."

"Pretty good? That's not exactly high praise."

"I can only base your score on my limited experience back then. Now, it's a little different. I've learned a thing or two over the years, too."

Sam took a step closer and placed his hand on the wall, leaning over her with a devilish grin. "Care to share?"

Duke growled at Sam's proximity, and Wren reached down, touching his ear. "Relax."

Duke settled, and Wren grazed Sam's chest lightly with the tip of her finger, dark eyes flashing with heat. "I don't think you can handle it."

Chapter Six

Wren had no idea what she was doing.

Saturday night she had been furious with Sam and had gone home to take her anger out on her punching bag, then engaged in a little stress release in the shower. After overhearing his interaction with one of the women who had dogged him on air, Wren wondered if perhaps his reputation wasn't exaggerated. Was he getting a bad rap from women who were jealous that he'd never given them the time of day? Or was he really the dirtbag they'd made him out to be?

Either way, Sam's leaning was seriously going to her head, especially as the scent of his musky cologne assailed her nostrils. She took a deep breath, breathing him in. This cologne was different from the Nautica one he wore in high school. She'd loved that one, too, and she remembered burying her nose in the front of his T-shirt, the same impulse she was experiencing now.

Sam dipped a little closer, that crooked grin doing unspeakable things to her insides. "If you're up for it, we can always find out," he murmured.

Her gaze settled on his mouth, and she wondered if he still kissed with the same deep urgency that came from knowing that each moment was timed and could be their last, or if he took things slower now, lingering with an expertise born of years of conquests.

This was dangerous. *He* was dangerous to her peace of mind. Here she was on a city street, in full uniform, wondering what he kissed like.

What was she thinking? She'd set up a date tonight after work to meet with a potential donor, and here she was, being taken in by her ex-boyfriend.

Wren took a deep breath and a hesitant step back. "Unfortunately, I'm on duty."

"When do you get off?" Sam asked with a deep rumble that made her shiver.

"Not until six, but I have plans."

"Some other time, then?" he asked.

"Even then, we shouldn't do this." Her cheeks burned with embarrassment and regret. Being near him was like experiencing a roller coaster of emotions. One minute, her blood pressure rose with anger, and the next, she regretted not taking him up on his offer.

"Too bad," he said, pushing off the wall with a sheepish smile. "With everything going on, and you being newly returned to town, I thought it might be fun for us to stave off the holiday blues."

Wren laughed. "The holiday blues? What are those?"

Sam shrugged. "I don't know, but I'm sure some people have them."

Wren thought about meeting up with him and at the very least, enjoying his company, but Wren hadn't come back to Mistletoe to start things up with an old boyfriend. "Well, my holidays are going to be low-key this year."

"What about New Year's?" Sam asked.

"I haven't figured out yet," she said.

"No one to kiss at midnight?" he teased. "That's kind of a sucky feeling. If you're cool with me standing in, I'm more than happy to take the bullet."

Wren laughed. "That is sweet. I'm not really looking for anyone to dodge or take a bullet for me."

"Really," he said, stroking his chin. "Most women, especially women over—"

"Careful," she drawled warningly.

"What? Ladies over thirty seem to be looking for someone to settle down with—"

"And I am not," she said flatly. "I am looking for a little peace and quiet and possibly to take other steps in my future, but settling down with a man isn't one of them."

"Other steps?" he asked.

Why had she even alluded to her desire to have a child? "It's nothing." She glanced over his shoulders, eyes narrowing when a group of teens bypassed the crosswalk and ran across the street. "I should probably get back on patrol. You know, lots of people shoplifting toothpaste and jaywalking."

"Yeah, you should get right on that."

Wren and Duke walked around him, but they only made it a few steps before he called after her.

"Before you go . . ."

Wren stopped and turned. "What?"

"You know what, never mind." He backed away from her, hands in the air. "It was nothing."

She started to move but hesitated, swallowing hard. "Sam?"

He paused, watching her expectantly. "What's up?"

"I really am sorry about last night." Her stomach twisted painfully, and Duke, as if sensing her discomfort, nuzzled her hand. "You know I didn't come back to town to wage war with you over things we did when we were both kids. I'm just trying to find somewhere I belong."

Sam nodded. "I understand that. We should just chalk it up to being two young people, wrong place, wrong time. Romeo and Juliet. Not meant to be."

"I get the picture," she said softly.

"There is one thing that's always bothered me," he said, watching her so intently that she started to squirm. "When your dad showed up at my house and threatened to have me thrown in jail if I didn't stay away from you, I was willing to go against him and take the chance. Why weren't you?"

Wren swallowed. "I guess I thought what we had wasn't worth you going to jail for. I didn't want to put you through that, especially when the whole reason he came after you was my fault."

"What do you mean?" he asked.

Wren couldn't tell him she didn't want to go back to that moment. It was over.

"He read my diary and found out we were sleeping together," she lied. "If I hadn't written about it, then he wouldn't have been able to use it against you."

"If it's any consolation, I don't think your diary would've held up in court, especially considering we're only a year and eight months apart in age."

"It didn't matter. My dad would've figured out some way to punish me if he couldn't get to you."

"That sounds healthy," he muttered.

Wren shrugged. "He loves me, but he wanted me to make the right choices." She tapped her shield with a smirk. "I got one thing right."

"How is your dad doing?" Sam asked, his eyes sparkling. "Still hate me?"

"I don't know, you've probably seen him more than me, but if I had to guess, no. I doubt he hates you. Hell, he'd probably be thrilled if I brought you home."

"Why is that?"

"He hasn't quite gotten used to the new me. Single. Independent. Back-talker."

Sam grinned. "Ah, gotcha. Now I understand his loathing for me. I always talk back, even when I shouldn't."

"Shocker," Wren deadpanned.

"I know, right? As far as seeing him, he mostly keeps to himself since he's retired."

"I see." Wren could just imagine her dad hanging out on his property in the woods like the Mountain Man of Mistletoe, hiding away from the world. He didn't used to be so bitter, but after her mom took off and all his kids left home, he'd seemed to withdraw from everyone, even Luke. He was her oldest brother, who'd followed in her father's law-enforcement footsteps, except he became Idaho State Police instead of a county sheriff. While Wren had gone off and taken positions in big cities, Luke had stayed in Idaho and made his career here. Wren assumed her father had heard about her sporadic visits over the last two decades, but besides a hug and a "glad you're home," he barely strung a few sentences together, even during their family lunches on Sunday. She'd made it to nearly every one, and they hadn't seemed to get any less strained.

"Well, my dad's always been kind of hard to read," Wren said.

It was true. Her dad kept his feelings close to the breast, but he hadn't treated her differently than any of her brothers until high school, when she met Sam. It seemed that having a boyfriend had finally woke him up to the fact that she was a girl, and that's when their relationship changed. Wren had left after high school in hopes that time and distance would heal the rift between them, but as more time passed, the harder it was to come home. It wasn't until everything in her life had lost meaning that she'd finally tucked tail and dragged herself back home. Even then, it had been less like the prodigal daughter returning and more like an inconvenient truth.

"How are your parents doing?" Wren asked.

"They're doing fine, living in a warmer climate, and forgetting they have any children or a grandchild," he said.

Wren frowned. "I'm sorry, that sucks."

"It is what it is. Life can't be perfect, right? If it was, nothing bad would ever happen, and we'd never grow and learn."

"What did you learn from having distant parents?"

"How to not be like them?" Sam shook his head. "Life can still be great. My brother and I had each other, and with Jace and Merry . . . we built our own family."

Wren's heart squeezed. That is what she wanted. To have a child and to create a life for the two of them. To be the kind of mother she wished she'd had.

"I'm glad we talked," Sam said, his expression somber. "When I heard you were back, I wasn't sure if you'd even want to talk to me."

"I figured the same. We didn't exactly end on the best of terms."

"Maybe we can start over on better ones?" Sam said.

"I'd like that," she said.

Sam chuckled. "Although, if you're ever looking for someone to do a lot less talking with, I'm here for that, too."

Wren smiled. "I'll keep that in mind."

"I better let you go protect the masses." He gave her a little salute. "Enjoy the rest of your day. Nice to meet you, Duke."

"You, too, Sam."

Chapter Seven

Wren stepped into Brews and Chews with her shoulders back, ignoring the nervous fluttering in the pit of her stomach. Her gaze searched the modest crowd of patrons inhabiting the rustic bar and grill, pausing on a smiling man in the corner booth. A trophy moose with large antlers hung on the wall above the secluded table, and as she approached, he stood up and she got a look at him. His picture online was accurate, give or take a few years, and Wren appreciated the honesty. While they'd exchanged pics, she hadn't gotten a full body look.

Handsome, check. Takes care of himself, check.

"Hi, Steve," she said, holding out a hand to him. "It's very nice to meet you."

"Likewise," he murmured.

Wren could feel his appraising gaze drifting over her as she removed her jacket, revealing her black cowl-neck sweater and jeans. She hadn't had a lot of time to primp between getting off work and their meet-up time, so her only makeup was a coat of mascara and a touch of lipstick. She'd released her bun and let her long blond hair fall around her shoulders in loose waves she'd tried to fluff up.

"Sorry about being a little late."

"Not an issue. I ordered us drinks and a basket of Idaho nachos."

"Thanks," Wren said, sliding into the booth across from him. She set her bag and coat on the bench next to her and folded her hands, leaning onto her forearms as she turned her brightest smile on him. "I appreciate you coming to meet me here. I can give you gas money."

Steve chuckled. "That's not necessary. I'm a grown man who makes money; I can pay for my own gas."

"I'm sure. I was just saying I appreciate you making the drive. I couldn't find a place where we could meet halfway, and by the time I got out of work and drove to you, it would have been almost eight thirty . . ." She trailed off, realizing that she was rambling. "Anyway, we're here."

"Yes, we are." His eyes sparkled, and Wren could admit that if she was looking for someone to date, he wouldn't be a bad candidate. He seemed sweet, and his background check came back with all green flags.

"Before we get started, I have something I need you to sign." Wren opened her satchel and pulled out a short stack of papers.

"What's that?" he asked, his green eyes following her motions with interest.

"It's an NDA."

"A what?"

Wren glanced up at him, frowning. "You're in finance, and you've never heard of a nondisclosure agreement?"

"I have, but why do I need to sign one to have drinks with you?"

A server brought over their drinks and the Idaho nachos, which was a basket of French fries covered in nacho cheese, meat, beans, sour cream, guacamole, and salsa.

"Thank you, Larry," Wren said, then turned back to Steve. "Because some of the things we may talk about during dinner are sensitive information, and I'd rather go into this without any worry or stress."

Steve picked up the papers, flipping through them until he reached the back page. "Are you a former CIA agent or something?"

Wren laughed. "No, but my job is another reason why I want to keep my private life private."

"You know that to make this legal, you have to have it notarized, right?" Steve asked.

"That's why Larry is still here. He works at the post office during the day and at Brews and Chews on weekends."

Larry nodded grimly. "Child support, man."

"Alright, do you have a—" Wren held out a pen to Steve before he could finish, and he signed the document, setting the paper and pen off to the side. Her breath whooshed out with relief as she took the pen and the contract, handing them to Larry.

"I'll be right back with this," Larry said, leaving her alone with Steve again.

Steve released an awkward chuckle. "Well, now that we've gotten all the legalities out of the way, are you ready to tell me your deep, dark secrets?"

"I really don't have any," Wren said, nodding at him. "You?"

"No, not really."

"That's good. Have you ever donated sperm?"

Steve was taking a drink when she asked, and he spewed the liquid back into the glass and down his chin.

"Oh, sorry! I guess I should have waited until you finished drinking before I dived right in." Wren twisted her hands in front of her on the table. "I'm a little nervous."

Steve grabbed the napkin she held out to him and wiped his chin. "No, I haven't donated sperm before."

"That's great, because I saw this documentary about a guy who donated so much sperm that he fathered over a thousand kids, and it grossed me out."

"I haven't fathered any children, through donation or otherwise," he said slowly, as if trying to figure out where she was headed with this conversation.

"Would you be open to private sperm donation?" Wren asked, tapping her pen on the tabletop.

"This is a strange line of questioning for a first date," Steve said, spooning out a section of Idaho nachos onto his plate.

"Oh, this isn't really a date."

Steve quirked a brow. "Okay, whatever you call it, I thought you were interested in something casual."

"There isn't exactly a category for what I'm looking for, but casual seemed to be the closest."

Steve frowned. "I thought you were looking to hook up."

"Mostly, I'm looking for sperm." At his horrified expression, she continued, "Not for anything weird! I want to have kids, but not necessarily be in a relationship, so I am looking for professional men between twenty-five and forty who would be willing to donate and sign over their parental rights. There is a clinic in Sun Valley—"

"Whoa!" Steve held up his hands, waving them in front of him like he was surrendering. "Are you being serious right now?"

"Yes."

"You—" Steve laughed, the sound ending on a high, panicked note. "I have been out on some weird dates, but this is the first time I've had anyone ask for bodily fluids." Steve leaned forward, smirking.

"You know, you could have just taken me home and gotten it the old-fashioned way?"

"Only twenty-five percent of men don't use condoms during one-night stands, and the chances of conception are twenty percent during ovulation." She realized that she sounded like an encyclopedia, but there was no way an arrangement like that would be feasible. "We would have to continue the arrangement until it took, which increases the likelihood of feelings developing, and I'm looking for a detached arrangement."

"So, you want me to hand over my DNA to a clinic so that they can use it to impregnate you? Exactly what do I get out of this?"

Wren cleared her throat. "I am willing to compensate you for expenses, like mileage when you go to the clinic."

Steve grabbed his drink and downed the rest of it before he took a long, bracing breath. "As interesting as this has been, I was just looking for a little dinner conversation before getting laid. This is a bit"—he paused, as if searching for the least insulting word—"much for me." He pulled out his wallet and dropped a fifty-dollar bill on the table. Once he was on his feet, he gave her a rueful smile. "Good luck with your quest, though."

Larry came back to the table with the contract. "Do you need a copy of this NDA?"

"Believe me, friend, I'm not telling anyone about this," Steve said, shrugging into his jacket and heading toward the door.

Larry set the contract and receipt down on the edge of the table. "Here you go, Wren."

"Thanks, Larry. I have one more coming in about fifteen minutes. What time are you off?"

"I'll be here until ten, so don't worry."

Larry walked away, leaving Wren to play out the exchange in her mind. Maybe she should try a one-night stand and roll the dice. She'd never have to talk to the man again or tell him that he had a child.

Wren shook her head. She wasn't going to lie to anyone, even a lie by omission. Plus, at least the clinic would check for any STDs. She wasn't about to trust the word of a man if she didn't know that he was clean.

She pulled up her dating profile, which was a picture of her from behind in a boudoir shoot she'd done for her thirty-fifth birthday. The black negligee she wore was backless with strings crisscrossing along the open back. She had her feet crossed under her butt, and she lifted her blond hair so it appeared to be falling from her fingers.

It was tantalizing and sexy, and it had worked to get the attention of plenty of men on the site. Poor Steve probably felt like he'd gotten the old bait and switch. Maybe talking about her needs in person was a bad idea, and she should lay it all out on her profile? It had crossed her mind, but she was afraid of getting a bunch of weirdos reaching out and messing with her. Plus, she didn't want anyone to recognize her and talk about it.

Wren read over her profile, starting with the tagline. *Thirty-something professional seeks unique agreement with open-minded individual.*

Wren didn't think that sounded misleading. She glanced over her main profile and wrinkled her nose. Maybe she should just lay it all out and see what happened.

She highlighted and deleted everything, typing, *Hi, I'm just looking for an absent baby daddy with healthy sperm and good genes. Must be educated, gainfully employed between the ages of twenty-five and forty. I am not seeking a partner but someone who will be willing to donate to a clinic of my choice, sign over parental rights, and never speak of this again.*

Wren took a deep breath and hit submit, her stomach twisting in knots. This was the right thing to do. Better to not waste anyone's time.

"Hello," a man said, and Wren glanced up as he came up alongside her table. He had dark, curly hair and a fluffy salt-and-pepper beard.

"Hi."

"I'm Carl Bevin. We were supposed to meet at eight, but I got here a little early."

Wren quirked a brow, pulling out the background check and social media dive she'd done on him. Although there was a resemblance, the Carl Bevin she pulled was marked as six foot on his driver's license, topping this man by several inches, and probably a good ten years younger.

"Really? You don't look much like your pictures, *Carl.*"

"So, it's a bit outdated." He took the seat across from her, grinning. "Damn, you're gorgeous."

"May I see your driver's license?" Wren asked.

"What for?" Faux Carl asked, reaching for the appetizer Steve had left and popping a hunk of fries and toppings into his mouth.

"So I can verify you are Carl, since I pulled his background check," she said, taking the folder with Carl's information out of her bag and setting it on the table, "and some things don't add up."

Faux Carl's eyes widened. "You did a background check? What are you, a cop?"

"Yes."

Carl stilled with his hand hovering over the fries. "Really?"

"I am. Would you like to see my badge?"

"Honestly?" Carl cleared his throat before bailing out of the booth with a "bye" over his shoulder.

"Someone should let Mr. Bevin know that his identity's been stolen," Wren muttered.

"What did you say to him?" Larry asked, coming up to the table.

"Politics, Larry. Never discuss politics or religion on a first date. Doesn't end well."

Chapter Eight

The next few days flew by for Sam. The holidays were filled with nostalgia, and people used it as an excuse for new tattoos and body piercings. It was their gift to themselves. Something they felt they deserved. While he wasn't sure that was true, Sam wasn't going to argue with them. He was so close to having enough money for his own shop, after nearly five years of saving. After he'd been screwed over by his former boss and had his savings stolen from him, he was nearly ready to follow his dream and have it realized.

Although other businesses were closed on Thanksgiving, Sam planned on going in to work later, after he finished dinner at the Winters' house, to handle a couple of his regular clients who wanted some work done. Thanksgiving had never been a big draw for him. He was more of a summer holiday guy. Give him Memorial Day weekend and the Fourth of July where there was outdoorsy fun. Christmas wasn't so bad, especially since his nephew had come along. He loved to go overboard for Jace, because kids were what made Christmas magical: their belief in the fantasy, and the joy and excitement on their faces.

Soon, he'd have a new little niece or nephew to spoil, and then, when his other friends started having babies, he would get to be the fun uncle to them, too. The cool one.

Why did that sound like such a lame prospect? When they became teenagers, would he still be cool? Or would he be the weird uncle who couldn't find a girlfriend?

It wasn't that he set out to avoid relationships. In his early twenties, he'd had a couple of good ones, but he was still figuring out who he was, and the women had been ready for next steps. Suddenly, he was in his thirties and trying to get his dream off the ground before he added anyone else to the mix. When his chance at owning a business crashed and burned the first time, he'd had tunnel vision about getting back on track, and now . . .

He was the relationship pariah.

Sam sat off to a corner of the Winters' living room with Pike, drinking a beer and watching the happy members of the Winters family laugh and talk together as they set up for the Thanksgiving meal in the dining room. Although he wasn't directly related to them, the family had opened their guest house and home up to him with open arms. They were some of the kindest, most empathetic people he'd ever met, and he was thankful that his little brother had found a wonderful wife who made him happy with a supportive family that would make all the difference in his life.

"Oh, I almost forgot," Victoria Winters said, gathering a second plate in her hands. "I promised I would deliver dinner to the station for the officers on duty. It stinks to have to work Thanksgiving." Victoria looked around the room and asked, "Would anybody be willing to drop these off at the police station for me?"

Maybe Wren was working, and they could chat a little more about what she'd been up to. Plus, seeing her pretty smile would bring a little sunshine to this average day.

"I'll do it," Sam called, getting up off the couch and taking the leftover three-quarters of his beer to the sink to dump.

"Great! Thank you, Sam." Victoria pointed to the beer bottle in his hand. "That's your first, right?"

"Yes, ma'am. I don't drink and drive."

Victoria gave him a hug. "That's because you're a smart man."

"You are the only woman who thinks that, but I appreciate it just the same."

"Oh stop. You just haven't met the one yet, but when you do, she is going to see all that good stuff you bury under that devil-may-care charm. Do not sell yourself short."

"Victoria, if you don't stop flirting with that man, I'm going to run him out of here," Chris Winters said, standing over the beautiful, brown turkey with a carving fork and knife in his hand.

"I am not flirting with him. I am bolstering his ego after that late-night radio show trampled all over it."

Sam winced. "You heard about that?"

Chris scoffed. "Course we did. However, Sam's confidence is bulletproof, so you can stop laying it on so thick. Bad enough I got to deal with him buttering you up all the time."

Sam chuckled. "You sure you don't got another single daughter hanging around here, Chris? Because having you for a father-in-law is at the top of my bucket list."

Declan Gallagher moved his girlfriend, Holly Winters, behind him, fixing Sam with a menacing scowl. "Nope."

Holly peeked around Declan's shoulder, her brown eyes sparkling as she kissed his arm. "Declan, are you still worried Sam is going to steal me away?"

"Of course he isn't," Sam said, winking at her. "He knows I'm not surly enough for you, but he continues to pretend he's jealous because it makes you smile."

Holly smacked Declan's arm. "Is that true?"

"No! The man is full of bullshit!" Declan's lips twitched slightly, as if he were fighting a smile.

"Declan, would you be open to being brother husbands?" Sam held his hand out to the other man, waggling his brows. "I'll marry Holly so I can have Chris and Victoria for parents, and you can have all the benefits."

"Sam, you do not need to marry into this family to be one of my children." Victoria finished wrapping the plate she was working on and pointed toward the living room. "Look at Pike and Anthony! They just showed up one day, and suddenly, I had two more boys to love."

"I love you, too, Victoria!" Pike called out from his perch on the couch.

Chris shook his head, grumbling, "She keeps bringing home strays, and I keep feeding them. Something wrong here."

Victoria ignored him. "I'll get these fixed up and covered and you can drop them off."

"How come you volunteered?" Clark asked Sam, popping an olive from the hors d'oeuvre tray into his mouth. "Does it have anything to do with Wren Little?"

Sam narrowed his eyes at his loudmouthed little brother. "No."

"Who is that?" Jace asked.

"She was your uncle's first girlfriend."

A dozen eyes swung his way, and a few voices whispered, "Girlfriend?"

Sam huffed. "It was high school. No need to make a case about it."

"How long did you two date?" Holly asked.

"A little over a year," Sam said.

"I liked her," Clark said, leaning against the counter. "She bought me this great Spider-Man comic for my birthday."

"Yeah, you used to follow us around when she came over," Sam grumbled.

"I guess you got your revenge when Merry and I started dating," Clark said, wagging his finger at his brother. "Always hovering and making little comments."

"Hey," Sam said, holding his hands up. "I was just sticking around to make sure you didn't screw it up."

"Gee, thanks." Clark made a face at his brother while a laughing Merry snuggled into his side, her pregnant belly between them.

"He did kind of help," Merry teased.

"Don't encourage him, please," Clark said.

"I can't see it," Holly said, studying Sam like he was a research specimen. "Wren is straight as an arrow. She hollered at Delilah for crossing the street outside of a crosswalk."

Sam smirked. "Yeah, she wasn't like that in high school. She liked to break the rules."

Shit! He could tell by Holly's wide-eyed gaze she wanted to ask more, but luckily, he was saved by Victoria.

"Here you are," Victoria said, handing off the stack of plates to him with a smile.

"Thanks, Victoria. I'll be back in a bit."

"Do you need some help?" Pike asked, and Sam felt bad because he was the only other single guy in the room, but he didn't need a wingman for this.

"I'm good, bro. Thanks."

"You won't escape that easily next time, Griffin!" Holly hollered after him.

"I'm not escaping, Hol. I'll be back in a bit."

"Hmmm, good, 'cause I have questions."

Sam rolled his eyes as he walked out the front door with the stack of plates in hand, imagining how they were all speculating about his relationship with Wren. Even he could admit that if anyone had been watching them the other day when they stood on the sidewalk outside of Kiss

My Donut talking, they would probably assume she was questioning him about something. While he hadn't been in legal trouble since he was a teen, Sam didn't make a habit of hanging with cops. Partly because the ones he'd met on the Mistletoe force were just this side of douchey.

He climbed into the car and started it up, thinking about Wren walking down the hall of their high school the first time he'd noticed her, wearing a pair of high-waisted jeans that hugged her hips as she swayed by. The square neckline of the black tank top she'd worn showed off a deep V of cleavage, and he remembered thinking she had to be at least a D cup. She was cursing down the hallway with a female teacher walking behind her, speaking in a low, calm manner that did nothing to stop Wren's ranting.

Why am I getting dress coded when half the girls in school are wearing the same thing or worse? Just because I have bigger tits—

Miss Little, there is no need to be vulgar.

No, screw that. You're enforcing an oppressive dress code that punishes women for being tall, curvy, or stacked. You need to ask yourself, Mrs. Pillier, who are you protecting?

As she'd passed by him, Sam couldn't help giving her a once-over, and she'd returned his perusal with a middle finger.

Take a picture, perv.

Not another word, Miss Little, or we'll call your father.

Sam took the long driveway out to the main road and turned left toward town, lost in his memories. He'd spent the last week of his junior year asking about Wren, balking slightly when he found out her dad was a cop. Was the tough-girl thing all an act to piss off Daddy?

He'd spotted her that Friday, sitting on top of a street bike parked next to his rebuilt chopper.

I heard you've been asking about me.

What can I say? Sam had stopped alongside her, crossing his arms over his chest. *You made an impression.*

She'd swung her leg over and faced him, her band T-shirt stretched across her impressive chest. *Me? Or my body?*

Are you going to slap me if I say both?

Wren flashed a grin. *Maybe. I guess you'll have to take your chances and find out.*

That was all it took for him to ask Wren Little out, and for the next year, he'd realized that she was more than just the girl who fought the dress code on a weekly basis. She was a complex person who would organize a food drive in the morning and drag him under the bleachers during seventh period. She was as sweet as honey with a fire that could scorch everything around her. The closer Sam got to her, the harder he fell.

When his senior year ended, Sam knew he wanted a fresh start, and he begged her to come with him. She was a month shy of seventeen, and even though she had a year of high school left, he tried to convince her to get her GED and leave everything behind. It was a stupid plan, but he was willing to take on her dad and any legal hassles Sheriff Little threw his way if it meant keeping Wren in his life.

Sam could still remember his body shaking as he stood under the old pine at the *Welcome to Mistletoe* sign, away from the prying eyes of people driving past. Wren stood quietly, listening to his plan with silent consideration until he finished.

Sam, if I go with you, it will ruin your future. He'll make sure whatever you're charged with sticks. I can't have that on my conscience. Staying together isn't worth the price.

Those words shattered something inside him, and he'd taken off on his bike before she saw him cry. He'd left a few days later, but by that time, he no longer believed that she was as resolved as she pretended to be about their separation. He ended up hiding a note for her in their spot. He'd told her that he'd be back in a year, right after her eighteenth birthday, and if she wanted to leave with him then, there was nothing her father could do.

Sam had kept his promise and came back, but she hadn't been here. She'd already left for college in Arizona. There was no goodbye note in their tree. Not a phone call or explanation. He'd realized that what he'd built up in his head as this epic love was just infatuation on her part. She'd moved on with her life without him. So, he'd returned to Oregon, determined to put Wren in his rearview.

Until he lost his savings, and Sam decided to join his brother and nephew back in Mistletoe to start over.

And now Sam and Wren were in the same space again. Was it a second chance for the two of them to, at the very least, have closure?

The police station was at the edge of town, just to the right after the stop sign, and Sam passed by the gated parking lot with an *Employees Only* sign. Sam took one of the parking spots out front of the station and jogged around to the other side to gather up the plates. His heart pounded a rapid tempo as he drew closer to the front door, wishing he wasn't so nervous. He carried the plates inside to the police station steps and into the front lobby, where an old guy with glasses hung out behind the reception desk, reading a John Grisham novel. George Willers set his novel down, plastering a welcoming smile over his face when he recognized Sam.

"What can I do for you, Sam?" George asked. He'd been the head of the Agricultural department at the high school when Sam was a student, and while he hadn't been a part of Future Farmers of America, Sam had loved the welding program the FFA offered.

"I just got some food here for you and the crew," Sam said, holding up the stack of plates, "if you're up for it."

"Well, that's mighty nice of you. Let me buzz you in," George said, pressing something under his desk and then climbing to his feet slowly. Sam thought he could hear the old man's bones creaking and grinding with every step.

"It's actually from the Winters," Sam said when George finally opened the door, letting Sam pass through.

"Please give Victoria and Chris my best and thank them." George waved to a counter on the side of the room with a coffeepot, fridge, and microwave. "You can set them there."

Sam did as George asked, glancing around the back, but all the desks were empty. "Anyone else here with you?"

George cocked a bushy eyebrow. "That depends. You looking for someone in particular?"

Sam chuckled. "I am, actually. Your only female officer."

"Of course you are," George said, wagging his finger at him. "I remember the two of you playing kissy-face before my class and showing up late."

"Can you blame me, sir?" Sam asked, leaning on the counter.

"No, I don't. Lovely girl, inside and out." George pointed his thumb behind him. "She's just in the back. We had a fight break out over who could cook the Thanksgiving turkey at the Marksons'. She had to separate Tony and Troy Markson, so it might take a few more minutes if you want to have a seat in reception."

"I can do that." Sam figured that George couldn't let a civilian wander around with sensitive case files and such, so he took hold of the door and went back out into the lobby to wait.

"I'll let her know you're here." George shuffled out of sight, and Sam awkwardly paced in the reception area. Would she be irritated about him bugging her at work? Sam figured since he was already there, they could at least have a conversation.

Sam discreetly blew into his hand, smelling his breath. Maybe he should pop into the bathroom and make sure he didn't have anything in his teeth.

Sam laughed, rubbing his hand over his face. Shit, where was the confident ladies' man Mistletoe kept talking about?

George reappeared and sat down at his desk, picking up his book. "I let her know."

"Thanks, George." Sam sat down, pulling his phone out. He scrolled through his apps, tapping on a dating one he hadn't checked out in a while. He swiped his thumb through the newest profiles closest to him, and his gaze lingered on one of a woman with her back to the camera in a little nightie, her blond hair falling like a waterfall down her back. He barely got through her tagline before he heard a thump and looked up.

Wren appeared at the back of the room, shutting the jail cell door with a thud. She was heading toward George, releasing a heavy breath.

"I swear, George, the things men choose to compete over is wild."

"Hmm, don't throw all men under the bus. Those two have never had a lick of sense."

Wren laughed. "I believe it." She finally caught Sam's gaze, and her face broke into a wide smile. "Hey!"

"Happy Thanksgiving," Sam murmured.

As she stepped through the door and into the lobby, Sam's gaze trailed over her blond hair swept back away from her face in a tight bun, drawing attention to her flushed, round cheeks and pointed chin. Her face was fuller now, more mature, but her skin was still smooth, her brown eyes large and luminous.

"Happy Thanksgiving," she said, stopping in front of him with her hands holding on to her vest. "What are you doing here?"

"I brought food for everybody from Victoria and Chris Winters."

"And then he asked for you specifically," George said.

Sam's face burned. "Thanks, George."

"Just delivering the message." George picked up his book and called out, "I'm going to grab a plate and take my break. You got the front?"

"Sure, George." George waved at Sam with his book, and he spotted the old man's wink before he disappeared.

Sam pointed after George. "That is a good man."

"He is." Wren shook her head with a smile. "I don't know how he reads those crime novels working in a police station."

"Makes him feel like he's a part of the action?" Sam suggested.

"Maybe. Thank you for bringing us food."

"Sure," Sam said, shrugging. "I was at the Winters' house, and they asked someone to drop the food by."

"Well, George and I appreciate it." Wren waved toward the receptionist window. "Want to come back here and sit with me while I eat?"

"I figured civilians weren't allowed behind the glass curtain," he said, grinning.

"Usually not, but you're with me. Plus, I figured if you try anything hinky, I'll take you down and cuff you."

"Hmmm, don't tease me now," he said, catching the door when she opened it.

She paused and looked up at him with a straight face and heat in those dark eyes. "I wasn't."

Sam's heart kicked up, staring down at those full lips that curved in the corner before she turned away from him, heading around the corner to the receptionist desk. He dropped the door and followed behind, his imagination running wild as he thought about how much fun getting in trouble with Wren used to be. Would getting in trouble by her be better, especially if it involved handcuffs?

"I was gonna go to my brother's once I got off," Wren said, oblivious to the train of his thoughts as she sat down in George's chair, "but he's not a great cook. He tries, but I'd rather eat a meal prepared by Victoria."

Sam took the seat next to her, leaning over her shoulder as she removed the clear wrap. "What if I'd said I made the meal?"

Wren turned, grinning sheepishly. "I may have been a little more skeptical about the edibility of the food."

"Whoa, why?" Sam asked, aware that their mouths were mere inches apart. "Because I'm a man?"

"Well, my experience and everything I've seen on TV tells me that Thanksgiving meals are made by women."

"You shouldn't believe everything you see on TV." He tsked, disappointed when she faced forward to take a bite of her dinner. "That's just marketing."

Wren snorted, pointing her plastic fork at him. "No offense, but I trust a woman who's won at least ten pie contests in her lifetime over a man who used to burn his campfire hot dog."

"First, I like them well done," Sam said, remembering that first camping trip when he'd cooked their hot dogs over the fire, and they'd been black on the outside and cold in the middle. They'd both tried gagging them down and eventually gave up, making a meal out of s'mores and each other. "I am highly offended by your assumption that I can't cook. People can change."

"You're right, but I'm not sure you can," Wren said, taking another bite of the potatoes.

Sam crossed his arms over his chest. "I am gonna have to prove you wrong, now."

"Oh, was that an offer to cook me dinner?" Wren asked. Her eyes were sparkling, her voice pleasant and even as she added, "If it was, I might just have to accept it, but if you give me food poisoning, I will tase you."

Her straight expression was so unreadable, Sam couldn't figure out if she was serious or teasing him.

"No contaminated food is on the menu."

"Then I'm willing to take that chance." She spun the chair toward him, leaning on her knees until he had to widen his to make room. "Your place?"

Sam's stomach flipped with excitement. "Sure. Any food allergies?"

"No, but I'm not a big Chinese food fan."

He laughed. "Duly noted."

"Alright," she said, those beautiful, full lips spread wide into a joyful smile. "Do you need my phone number? That way you can text me your address."

"Sure." Sam pulled out his phone and put in her information as she recited it to him, texting her the address before slipping it back in his pocket and meeting her gaze again. "Would seven tomorrow night work?"

"Yeah, I'm off tomorrow, so that will be great."

"Awesome," he said, watching her tongue run along her fork, cleaning up the remaining mashed potatoes before she started in on her turkey. "I can't believe you still eat one thing at a time."

"I like to enjoy the individual flavors."

He chuckled at the same time the phone rang. Wren picked it up, pausing to swallow. "Mistletoe Police Department."

Sam stood up, and when she looked up, he mouthed, *I'm going to go*, motioning with his thumb.

She nodded and mouthed, *Night*.

Sam gave her a little wave and walked through the exit, crossing the lobby to the sound of Wren speaking calmly to whomever was on the other end of the line. He had no idea what had made Wren change her mind about him, but he wasn't going to question the hands of fate.

Sam bounded out of the station with a hop in his step he'd never experienced before. Well, that wasn't exactly true. He remembered this feeling when he was just a kid any time he got to see Wren.

He couldn't wait to see if the feelings stuck.

Chapter Nine

"Am I overdressed?" Wren asked her brother Pete as he lounged on her couch, eating a bag of Dynamites and watching *Law and Order*. Duke was curled up on top of her brother's feet, watching her with interest.

Pete glanced away from the TV, his face covered in red dust from the chips, and when he opened his mouth to speak, Wren saw the semi-chewed chips lingering inside.

"Nah, you look good," he said, smacking and chewing.

"And you're disgusting." She stepped into a pair of simple black boots, shooting him a dry look. "Seriously, how are we related?"

"You want me to explain the birds and the bees to you, little sis?" Pete grinned, holding up his hands, pressing his red fingertips together. "You see, our mom and dad decided to—"

"Nope, stop." Wren shook her head. "If you do not learn some manners right quick, I'm going to boot you out of my place."

"Nah, you love me. Warts and all."

Wren laughed because he was right. Of all her brothers, Pete was her favorite. He was a year older than her, and her constant playmate when they were kids. Although Pete had his own place, he had two roommates and had taken to hanging out at her house on Friday nights when his roommates had company over. She had an extra bedroom but hadn't furnished it yet, so he'd taken over her plush gray couch as his bed.

When Wren had sold her house in Sacramento, she'd also sold all the furnishings inside except for some of the more sentimental items because she didn't want to pay the exorbitant fee to move her entire house. It was how she'd handled every move over the last nineteen years. Everything went except for what she could fit in a small U-Haul, which was usually just her mattress and bed frame. She always bought her furniture used from thrift stores or online marketplaces because she hadn't planned on staying in any place too long.

Here, it was different. This was home, so she'd gone to Boise and splurged on a new living room set, but it was going to take her a while to refurnish her home if she bought all new furniture.

"Don't get any of that red stuff on my new couch," she called, heading to her room where she slipped her coat off a hanger in her closet. Combined with the knee-length simple black dress and waves in her hair, she turned in front of her closet mirror and smiled.

"Oh, I look good."

While Wren wasn't the same hard body she'd been before her injury, she didn't hate the fuller, softer figure she presented in the mirror. If getting hurt had taught her anything, it was that being in shape didn't stop a bullet.

Besides the humiliation, the events that led to her leaving Sacramento could have been worse. They'd saved the girl, caught the bad guy, and Wren had gotten a brand-new scar.

Her recovery had been longer than expected, and although they would have welcomed her back on the force with open arms, the time on the sidelines had given Wren a chance to think about what she wanted.

Turned out, being pushed into high-stress situations didn't do it for her the way it had in her twenties.

The thought of elevated stress reminded her of the explosive results the changeup to her online profile had brought about. While there had been a few responses that seemed genuinely interested in meeting her and taking next steps, most of them had fallen into two categories: obnoxious jerks treating her desire to be a mom as a joke, or a slew of nasty messages she'd deleted after reading the first lines. Neither camp had left her feeling hopeful, and she had decided to give it until Monday, but if the pattern continued, she was going to delete the profile. While it would mean reconsidering online sperm donors, Wren was willing to take the chance of her kid dating their half-sib in the future if it meant getting this over with.

Instead of staying home and weeding out the weirdos, Wren was about to have dinner with her high school boyfriend after having a chill day shopping Black Friday sales online. Working in the city, she'd rarely had a Friday or Saturday off, let alone a holiday. And while she'd been looking forward to this dinner, a tiny voice in the back of her mind kept asking why she was bothering if she had no plans to date. Taking a trip down memory lane with her first love seemed like a fruitless venture.

It's just dinner and an excuse to dress up, something you haven't done in a long while. Don't be so serious.

Wren walked out of the bedroom, her trench coat swinging around her legs. "What do you think of this?"

Pete lifted his head to give her a once-over and flopped back, eyes fixed on the TV. "You look like you're ready to slay him."

"Aw, that's the sweetest thing you've ever said to me."

Pete snorted. "Don't make it weird."

Wren paused near the doorway, purse in hand, then suddenly sat on the coffee table next to Pete, panic gripping her chest. "Am I making a huge mistake?"

Pete stared at the TV as he said, "You mean having dinner with the guy that Dad hated and the rest of us wanted to pound in the tripe many years ago?"

"Yes, and just . . . moving back here."

Pete paused the show and licked his fingertips as he wrestled his limbs out from under Duke, who didn't budge or get down to check on his mistress. Once he was free of the dog's weight, Pete swung his legs off the couch to sit up across from her. He reached for her hands, and she wrinkled her nose, holding them away from him. "You were just licking them like a toddler."

"Fine, pretend I'm holding your hands when I tell you this." Pete leaned in, looking into her eyes. "This is your home. No matter what. You belong here with us."

"Tell that to Dad," she mumbled.

"Dad's a grumpy asshole. He just got mad because he couldn't control any of us once we left home. When you took off, it was his last tie to Mom, and he was kind of twisting in the wind." Pete grinned. "He just needs a hobby. Or a girlfriend."

Wren laughed. "Oh yeah, I could just see dad signing up for online dating. Full background check and the third degree. They'd all take off running."

"Maybe, but I think he's lonely." Pete's serious expression made her stomach bottom out as he added, "I know the last few years with him were hard for you, especially before you graduated."

"That's putting it mildly," Wren scoffed.

"He was worried about you," Pete said, ticking off her behaviors on his fingers. "Getting in trouble. Buying a motorcycle. Dating."

"Dating Sam, you mean?"

Pete sighed. "Wren, it wouldn't matter who you chose as your first, Dad would have flipped out regardless. You were the only girl, and when he couldn't ignore it any longer, he tried to protect you."

Wren wasn't sure that was the right word, but she understood what Pete was saying. It was why she hadn't held a grudge against her dad for threatening Sam. While he may have gone through with it and maybe never had forgiven her, Wren knew that he always acted the worst when he was scared. And finding that pregnancy test in the bathroom nineteen years ago must have rocked him to his core.

"I guess everything worked out the way it was supposed to." Wren got up with her purse in hand. "Have a good night."

"Have fun recycling your exes."

Wren flipped him the bird before heading for the door.

"You're kind of mean when you've got a date," her brother called after her.

"No, I'm always mean to you." Wren stopped with her hand on the doorknob, giving him a cheeky grin. "That's what sisters are for."

"Yeah, right," he scoffed. "What time are you coming home?"

Wren opened the door, tossing him a dark scowl. "What, like I have a curfew?"

"Or an estimate so I don't think you've been murdered and dumped somewhere," Pete said.

"I guess it depends on how dinner goes."

Pete twisted around on the couch and pointed at her. "If you don't pull a walk of shame by eight tomorrow morning, I'm calling in reinforcements."

"Don't even think about it, Pete," Wren said, hovering in the open door. "I am a grown woman, and I carry a weapon."

"I'm not scared of you. Besides, you'd never risk the felony."

"You never know what a woman is capable of until you put her in a position where her brothers or her father are being idiots." Wren closed the door on his response and headed down the walkway to her Nissan Rogue, tugging her jacket closer as the cold found its way up her skirt. Gooseflesh popped up all over her legs, and she almost wished she'd worn a pair of leggings underneath, but it would have ruined the outfit.

Since when did she choose looks over comfort?

Probably about the same time Sam Griffin gave you a once-over that nearly incinerated your panties.

How long had it been since she'd hooked up with a man? Nine months? Time really flew when you weren't getting any.

Wren set up the GPS to Sam's home once she was inside and then turned up the heat, watching her windows defrost. Girls in high school used to tell her how lucky she was to have overprotective brothers, but those same girls were the ones who never spent a Friday or Saturday night at home the way she had her senior year.

Her father had barely looked at her after he found the test, even when she told him it was a false positive. She'd thought it was because he was ashamed of her, but she'd said a lot of harsh things to him when he'd delivered his ultimatum about Sam.

Either cut him off, or I'll make a phone call, putting him in a cell for five to ten years. Which one will it be?

She followed the directions on the GPS, memories overwhelming her. Of course she'd told Sam to go, that they had no future together. She'd expected him to argue, to fight her resolve, but in the end, he'd walked away.

That had been her first lesson on the fact that love had limits. The stories of men slaying dragons, of sacrificing themselves so that their significant other could live, were just fantasies. Even her mother hadn't loved her children enough to stay. She'd wanted a fresh break and her freedom more than she'd wanted to watch Wren and her brothers grow.

That betrayal was something Wren couldn't forgive.

Wren had tracked down her mother a few years after leaving home; she was remarried and living in a big, beautiful house in Texas. Wren had sat across from her in that picture-perfect living room, searching for the right thing to say. After a few minutes of small talk and comparing the weather in Texas to Idaho, Wren had asked, *I understand that you didn't want to stay married to Dad, but why didn't you want us?*

Her mom's brown eyes, the same shade as her own, dropped to her lap, and she answered softly, *I just needed to find myself. Without the ties of my old life dragging me down. I found what was missing, and I was so happy, but I— I couldn't find a way to make you kids fit in it. I'm sorry.*

That was the last conversation she'd had with her mom. There was nothing more she could say after that anyway. Any apology would fall flat. Wren knew where her priorities were, and Wren told herself when she became a mom, her child would never feel less than total and complete love and security.

Only the mom part hadn't happened yet.

Wren didn't want a relationship, and it seemed like Sam didn't want one either. Did he think tonight they might get some closure? Or was he hoping to rekindle things between them?

Sleeping with Sam would be a bad idea for several reasons, first and foremost being that letting anyone into her life, even as a friend, meant one more person she had to explain her choices to. How would Sam react if Wren told him she wanted a baby but not a man?

Wren shook her head, completely blown away that she was even thinking about this. It was bad enough reading the reactions from strangers, but people who knew her? Wren could just imagine how her dad would react if he knew, which was why she planned on being discreet until after she was pregnant. He didn't have to know what she was planning.

Just like she'd never told Sam about the pregnancy scare, which ended up being for the best.

I need to stop obsessing about this. Tonight is about having dinner with an old friend.

She parked in front of a small house on the older side of town and spotted Sam when he stepped out onto the front porch, the light illuminating his tousled blond hair like a halo. Wren got out of the car and noted that he was wearing a black button-down and blue jeans, so she didn't feel overdressed anymore.

"Am I late?" she asked, coming up the walkway to the front step.

"No, I was just going to watch for you. Make sure you found the place okay."

"I recognized the address," Wren said, nodding her head toward a blue house across the street. "They like to party."

Sam chuckled. "Yes, they do. I've been invited but never joined in."

"How long have you lived here?" she asked, stepping up onto the porch.

"About a year. I used to live in Merry Winters' tiny house behind her parents' place after she moved in with my brother," he said, holding the door open for her so she could walk inside. Wren took in the clean, simple space with a small sectional, side table, and entertainment center on the wall with video game consoles and a large TV.

"Why did you move out?" she asked.

"It helped me save money, but it felt weird bringing women back to sleep in my sister-in-law's former bed. Even though she didn't say anything, I think she felt that way, too."

Wren laughed. "Yeah, I probably would've been uncomfortable with that, too. Although, I'm surprised you didn't pick a better neighborhood."

"Eh, I like it here. Rent is still low enough for me to keep saving, and our neighbors look out for each other."

Most of the crime that occurred in Mistletoe happened in this area and at the two bars, but Wren didn't mention that. "What are you saving money for?"

"I want to buy my own tattoo place," he said, shutting the door. He helped her off with her coat, and Wren warmed at the appreciation in his eyes. "Damn."

"Well, thank you. This is my first dinner in a long time with someone other than my family, so I wanted to look my best."

"Mission accomplished."

Wren hung her purse up on the hook with her coat and cleared her throat. "So, what made you want to come back to Mistletoe and start your business here?"

"The fact that my life savings was stolen," he said with a bitter laugh.

Anger rushed through her. "No. Seriously? Who?"

"When I lived in Oregon, my boss was planning to retire, and we set up an agreement where I paid him to carry the loan to buy his tattoo shop since I didn't have the credit to get one through a bank. I gave him my savings and another year of payments before he took my money and ran." Sam held out his hand and she took it. "Come on, I'll give you a tour before dinner."

Wren let him lead her into the small dining room and kitchen, but she needed to know the rest of the story. "Was he ever prosecuted?"

"Nope. As far as I know, he is living large somewhere sunny. Our agreement was a gentleman's one, so I didn't have anything in writing. I didn't have a dime to my name when I showed up on my brother's doorstep with my tail tucked between my legs, but he welcomed me without any recriminations." Sam took her down the hallway and flipped on the light in the bathroom. It had a simple, silver-framed mirror and a gray and white checkered shower curtain with matching gray bathroom rugs on the floor in front of the tub and sink. "It sucks being such a sorry excuse for a big brother."

Wren squeezed his hand. "I'm sure Clark doesn't feel that way."

"He'd never say so out loud, but I think it."

"How close are you to being able to buy your own shop now?"

"Couple months maybe," he said.

"Well, you always were artistic, so it makes sense you'd make a career out of it."

He chuckled. "It was art or mechanics, and I don't like to get my hands dirty unless it's my own bike."

"Oh boy," Wren laughed, opening the door at the end of the hall. "I forgot what a prima donna you could be."

"What are you talking about?" he asked.

"I remember camping with a group of friends, and you and I had our own tent." Wren released his hand as she stepped over the threshold into his bedroom, lost in the memory as she looked around. It was as neat as the rest of the house, the black and white plaid bedspread turned down, revealing shiny black sheets. Wren smirked, tempted to ask if they were satin.

"And what, I snored?" he asked, leaning against the doorframe.

"You really don't remember?" Sam shook his head, and she continued, "A spider climbed inside with us, and you made me kill it."

Sam pushed off with a huff. "Not liking spiders doesn't make me a prima donna. That makes me honest and complex, instead of conforming to toxic masculinity."

"All I hear is that I'm"—she pointed to her chest—"the spider killer when we're together."

Sam reached out, running his fingertips along her cheek. "Thanks for keeping me safe."

Wren's stomach flipped at his soft tone. His touch continued down the side of her neck and down her arm, leaving a trail of warmth in his wake.

"I noticed you're still not sporting any ink." He grinned at her, taking her hand again and spinning her in a circle, as if searching for some hidden tattoo. "What happened to all that big bad talk about getting sleeves and maybe a neck tattoo?"

Wren smiled at his teasing. "I went with some friends in college, but I chickened out. There wasn't anything I loved enough to permanently put on my body."

"I understand what you mean. All of mine have special meaning to me."

"Really?" she said, reaching for his right arm. "May I?"

Sam grinned devilishly. "You don't ever have to ask permission to touch me, Birdy. In fact, I insist."

"Stop," Wren murmured, ducking her head so that he wouldn't see her blushing as she studied the colorful designs on his arm. They connected naturally, like puzzle pieces placed perfectly.

She pointed at a storm cloud with dark and light outlines to the blended layers. "What's the significance of this one?"

Sam turned his other arm, putting them next to each other so she could see the beautiful watercolor sun that seemed to line up like it was peeking out of the cloud. "It was a reminder that there is always sunshine after the rain."

Wren's brow furrowed as she traced the outline of the sun. "I feel like I've heard that before."

"I have no idea what you mean," Sam said innocently, but when she glanced up at him suspiciously, he looked ready to burst out laughing.

Suddenly, it hit her, and she snapped her fingers. "It was a song from one of those cringey boy bands you secretly loved."

Sam scoffed. "I didn't like boy bands."

"It may have been like a deep dark secret that you didn't tell anyone, but I remember stumbling onto your playlist." Her fingers traced the outline of the sun, smiling at his sheepish expression. "Who was it? Backstreet Boys?"

"Again, I wouldn't know, because I listen to hard-core rock music," Sam said, returning her smile before adding, "but if I was a boy band fan, I would correct you that the lyrics you are thinking of are from the 98 Degrees song *Because of You*."

"Aha," she said, poking him lightly in the chest. "I knew it!"

Sam took her hand and flattened it against his chest, electricity sizzling across the palm of her hand. She could feel the hard muscles of his pecks through his T-shirt and the racing of his heart, making her own kick up speed. She stared up into his twinkling eyes, admiring his full lips twisted in a rueful smile.

"You'll keep my secret safe, right?" he asked softly, stroking her chin with his other hand. "After all, players like me can't have a boy band playlist."

"I'm not going to tell anyone, but only because you asked so sweetly." Her fingers started to curl against his body, resisting the urge to pet him, and she dropped his hand, taking a step around him. "You have a nice place. Mine isn't nearly this clean."

She caught his shrug as he followed behind her. "It's just me, so it's easy to keep it up. Turn on a little music and go at it for a couple of hours a week. It decreases stress to come home to a clean house."

"Hey, I think it's cute that you have all these little quirks that make you more than Mistletoe's favorite fuckboy."

Suddenly, Wren found herself spun around with her back against the wall and Sam staring down at her with an intense frown. "I do not like being called a fuckboy."

His hard tone took her by surprise, but it was the way he loomed over her, framing her with his forearms against the wall that brought back intense memories of being pressed against any surface they could find. Of Sam's body plastered against hers and the thrill of arousal radiating from between her legs.

"I'm sorry," she whispered, aware of his warm, minty breath inches from her mouth. Even wearing that thunderous expression, Wren recognized the way his blue eyes darkened to the color of the sea during a storm, smoldering and raw, and holy hell, she wanted to reach up and drag his mouth down to hers.

That's not what you're here for! The tiny voice in her head continued to list all the reasons why she shouldn't kiss Sam, why pressing her body into his and climbing him like a tree was a very bad idea, but it was hard to focus over the loud blood drumming in her ears.

Sam took a deep breath, pushing off the wall and leaving her bereft. "No, I should be the one apologizing. I guess everything that was said on Jilly G's radio show really got to me."

Without thinking, Wren took ahold of his waist, keeping him close, and when his gaze met hers, she said, "I only meant that it is nice to get a peek behind some of those walls you put up. I get the feeling you've used your reputation to keep people at a distance."

Sam took a step into her body, and Wren sucked in a breath, the throbbing between her legs intensifying with him pressed against her.

"Maybe you're right, but it beats getting close to someone and finding out it was never real for them."

Wren stiffened, wondering if that was a dig at her or if he was making a general statement about relationships, but he backed away from her, dragging both hands through his hair.

"And this is why I don't let anyone behind the walls," he said with a dark laugh. "I let my emotions get the best of me." Before Wren could respond, he waved a hand toward the dining area, adding, "Why don't you come sit down, and we'll eat? I promise to be the charming philanderer that the ladies of Mistletoe love to hate."

Wren swallowed, acquiescing with a nod, but in her heart, she didn't want the Sam everyone else got.

She wanted him to be real.

Chapter Ten

Sam returned from the kitchen carrying several plates, balancing them like a circus performer. He'd grilled steaks, made garlic mashed potatoes and green beans, and cut up warm, buttered French bread, all to impress the beautiful woman watching him with expressive brown eyes and a wry smile.

His body still pulsed with the chemistry between them. The rush of heat being pressed against Wren lingered like an imprint on his body. While he hadn't reacted well to her calling him a fuckboy, Sam recognized that hitch in her breathing as he leaned over her, the dazed look in her eyes as she stared at his mouth. She still felt it, too, but was holding back.

It turned out Wren had erected some walls of her own.

Wren clapped for him as he set each dish down. "Very impressive. Where did you pick up that skill?"

"Which one?" he asked, waggling his eyebrows and lowering his voice suggestively. "I have so many."

Wren rolled her eyes. "Where did you learn how to carry plates like that?"

"Oh that," he teased, setting the steak plate down last. "When I moved to Oregon, I didn't have much to recommend me to most employers, but I got two jobs waiting tables in restaurants right off the bat. I learned how to do some fancy juggling . . . after a lot of broken plates and docked paychecks."

Wren laughed. "They didn't just fire you?"

"Hell no." Sam gave her his best smolder, pursing his lips and raising one eyebrow. "I was too pretty to get fired."

She made a disgusted noise in the back of her throat.

"What? You don't think so?"

"Oh, no. You're definitely pretty, but I don't know how you walk around upright with that big head of yours."

"It's called confidence." Sam pouted as he took a seat across from her at the square kitchen table. He reached across for her plate. "Here."

"I can serve myself," she murmured, but at his insistent hand motion, she passed him her plate, watching him take a bit of everything and fill it up with way more food than she could possibly eat.

Her stomach growled, as if to argue, *Are you kidding me? Bring it on!*

"Thank you," she said, taking it from him and setting it down in front of her, admiring the little details like the dollop of butter on the steak. "It smells amazing."

"I'll be expecting that apology once you've had a taste."

"Hmm, I would take a bite, but we seem to be missing something important from the table," Wren said, glancing down and back up again with a sly grin.

Sam realized he'd forgotten the silverware in his rush to make everything else perfect. "Whoops! I'll be right back."

As he got up from the table, Sam shook out his hand and took a deep breath. Man, he was nervous around her, which was ridiculous. He wasn't nervous around women, especially women he'd had previous relations with, but there was something about being in the same room with Wren, alone and aware of her subtle perfume, the way her makeup made her doe eyes wider. Her glossy red lips were lush and tempting him to kiss her, to find out if it was still as electrifying between them as when they were kids.

Sam laughed, dancing back into the dining room. "You're telling me you didn't want to eat with your hands?"

"Not particularly!"

"Alright, I got you covered." Sam set down the two forks and two steak knives he'd grabbed from the kitchen. He danced his way over to her, holding out her utensils with a flourish. "At your service."

"Thank you."

Sam watched Wren delicately cut her steak into small pieces, keeping it separated from the sides on her plate. When she slipped it between her lip and let out a little moan, Sam's cock twitched below the surface of his jeans.

She swallowed, opening her eyes and shooting him a blissful smile. "I apologize. You are quite the chef."

"Thank you. I used one of those food services that sends all the ingredients, and then I just have to prepare it."

Wren's eyes narrowed. "I feel like that's cheating."

Sam laughed. "How? It's just following a recipe."

"I don't know, but part of cooking is actually going to the store and selecting the ingredients, picking out the menu, not being spoon-fed everything by an online program."

"Tomato, tomahto," he said, pointing to his chest with his fork. "I cooked it." He pointed at her with his knife. "You liked it." Finally, he grinned at her, ignoring her sardonic expression. "Apology accepted."

"Mmm," she said, taking another bite of her steak, "you're lucky this is really good, or I'd throw some potatoes at you."

"Thanks for the restraint," he said, digging into his meal.

They sat in silence for a few beats, the sound of utensils and chewing the only noise, and finally, Sam asked, "You mentioned that you'd gained new experiences since you left home?"

Wren paused with her fork poised a few inches from her mouth and arched one of her dark brows. "Is this your version of polite dinner conversation? Asking how many men I've slept with?"

"Not what I asked," he said dryly. "I wanted to know about your new experiences. They don't have to be sexual."

"But you're not going to be upset if they are?" she teased.

"Well, you did insinuate."

Wren's eyes sparkled, and he almost cursed himself. She probably thought he was jealous or something.

"And you've been dwelling on it, huh?"

"Only because I want to know everything about you. Who you are now, I mean." Sam suddenly pushed back from the table, asking, "Do you want some wine? I feel like we may need wine for this conversation."

"I'll take water," she said, grinning at him. Was she getting a kick out of how discombobulated he was?

Sam got up from the table and filled two glasses with ice water, wondering why he was so jumpy. Wren was an old friend over for dinner, not a date.

Maybe that's what was off. If this was just a hookup, he'd already have his next move planned. They'd finish dinner, and after a quick trip to the bathroom to freshen up, they'd move to the sofa. From there, it would just naturally progress to sex.

With Wren, he hadn't been thinking about getting her into bed when he'd offered to make her dinner, but about catching up. Finding out who she was now. It was different than their first go-round, when he'd asked her out for burgers and they'd ended up making out by the lake. They hadn't been able to keep their hands off each other, just two horny teens letting their libidos run the show.

There had been more though. So much more. When Wren's best friend had rolled her truck and needed to be LifeFlighted to Boise, he'd held her all night while she cried as they waited for news. When he'd thought, for just a moment, that college might be for him, she'd been there to open his rejection letter. He'd brushed it off like he didn't care, but she'd railed against the school and what a bunch of idiots they were. Sam remembered smiling so hard his face hurt until he pulled her down into his arms and told her he loved her for the very first time.

Then tonight, as he'd leaned over her in the hallway, watching her pulse jump in her throat and the way her eyes locked on his mouth, that rush of need hit him like a ton of bricks.

"Are you okay in there?" she called.

"Yeah, I'm coming." What was going on with him? Why was he hung up on whether what he had with Wren in high school was real?

Maybe because of the handful of women I've lasted longer than a night with, she is the only one I never stopped thinking about? And having her in my home is bringing up all kinds of unresolved emotions?

Sam carried the glasses back to the table, tamping down the tiny voice in his head.

He settled in across from her and set her glass of water to the left of her plate. "There you go," he said.

"Thank you." She took a drink of her water and set it down with a smile. "Back to my experiences . . ." She tapped a finger against her mouth and shrugged. "There's been a lot. I've worked in five major cities, and I've been punched, kicked, stabbed once, and I got a bullet in the butt during my last job in Sacramento."

"Pause," he coughed, having inhaled a mouthful of wine when she'd gotten to *bullet in the butt.*

"Sorry, I know," she said, smirking, "that last one catches everyone by surprise."

"How did that happen?" he wheezed, still trying to get his coughing under control.

"My partner and I responded to a robbery in progress, and while I was chasing the first suspect, I missed the second guy. He had a gun and caught me in the left butt cheek as I was hopping a fence after his buddy." The way she relayed it, her tone a mix of cheerful humor and anger, made her voice thick, almost trembling. "My partner managed to tackle him, and another uniform grabbed my guy around the corner. I don't know which hurt more, the bullet or hitting the sidewalk below."

"Damn. I'm so sorry," he murmured, trying to put himself in her shoes.

She shrugged, taking another drink and setting it down. "It took me a while to heal, and when I did, I froze the first day back. There were horns blaring and people talking everywhere, and I couldn't handle it. That night, I decided that I didn't want to work in the city anymore. I wanted a quiet beat and to live in a place where the crime rate wasn't insane." She smiled a little too brightly and added, "Now, I'm here."

"Sounds like you have been through a lot and deserve a little peace."

"You aren't kidding. What about you?" she asked, her expression shifting to flirtatious. "Any experiences you want to share?"

Sam chuckled at her singsong tone. "Like I told you, I was living in Oregon. I'd worked my way into a spot at a local tattoo parlor, and my boss and I had a great relationship." His jaw muscles tightened when he thought about what he'd lost. "I trusted him, and turns out I made a mistake. So, I came back here, where I get to be with my brother and my nephew, and it's great for the most part."

"Do you ever miss Oregon?"

"Sometimes," he said, thinking about the music and art scene where he'd spent most of his weekend nights during his twenties. "There's not a lot to do in Mistletoe except hit one of the two bars in town. But here, at least I have family. Clark and Jace, plus the Winters, who have become a surrogate family to me. I have fun messing with Chris and teasing Victoria. They welcomed me into their home. I can never repay that."

Wren took another bite from her plate before responding, "I think that's sweet. I've always liked the Winters. They're good people."

"Yeah, they are. The Winters even threw me a surprise birthday party a couple of years ago. They're a lot warmer than my parents ever were," Sam said bitterly, thinking about the time they'd left on a trip the week before his birthday and hadn't come back until four days after.

They hadn't even called him to wish him a happy birthday. For some people, that wouldn't have been a big deal, but it was just further proof to Sam that he and Clark didn't matter to them.

"I remember." Wren reached across for his hand and squeezed. "One of my favorite memories is of you, me, and Clark going camping for the weekend to celebrate your birthday and my brothers crashing our bonfire. You were so freaked out at first, but it ended up being a blast."

"Says you!" Sam protested, setting his fork down to cover his heart. "Every time I glanced their way, they would send me threatening gestures. I figured I was going to wake up being dragged into the lake!"

Wren snorted. "My brothers could be overbearing and controlling like my dad, but they warmed up to you, and the point is, you had a great birthday despite your parents being jerks."

"How did you manage to escape after graduation? I expected to find you off in a tower somewhere, being guarded by a dragon."

She shook her head, taking his joking in stride. "Nothing that dramatic. The day after graduation, I just left." She paused briefly, swallowing as if it were painful to talk about. "That last year was pretty strained as it was."

"Because of us?" Sam murmured.

Wren sat solemnly for a few moments without answering, playing with her potatoes. "Partially, but it went both ways. We were like passing ships, barely communicating except to give each other our coordinates."

"That sounds . . . fun," he said.

She shrugged. "It was better than screaming at each other and throwing accusations. When I got a scholarship and left the state to go to college in Arizona, my dad didn't say much about it. When I graduated from Arizona State, I got a job on the police force, and I stayed there for a few years, but it was too hot for me."

Sam could imagine, having been to Vegas a time or two. "That was one nice thing about the Oregon coast. The weather was usually amazing."

Wren laughed. "Why didn't I ever check the climate of a city before I moved there?" She smacked her forehead playfully. "Stupid."

Sam chuckled. "Where did you go after Arizona?"

"Houston. That was fun. Lots of great bars and music places. Still hot though." Wren paused, taking another bite of her food. "After that,

I just kept moving any time I got antsy, until I guess I just decided there was nowhere else I wanted to be but back in Mistletoe."

"Well, I'm sure your dad is glad you're back."

"I think so, but he's not exactly the warm and fuzzy type." Wren placed her forearm on the table, cradling her face in her palm, and fluttered her lashes at him. "So, what new experiences have you discovered?"

Sam chuckled. "I thought we were gonna talk about yours first."

"Oh no, I figure if you're curious about mine, then you should give me some dirt first. Gotta give it to get it!" She picked up her fork and pointed it at him. "Plus, I get the chance to maybe finish my food."

"Ah, I guess I can hang with that."

She lifted her face off her hand and waved it as if to say *Get on with it*, and he decided to give her the biggest, juiciest experience he'd ever had. "Fine, we'll just dive into the time I learned that pegging was not something I was into."

Wren dropped her fork onto her plate with a clatter, potatoes flying as laughter bubbled out of her. "Holy hell! How did that even come about? Were you dating someone, and things escalated to that point?"

"Haven't you heard I don't date?" he joked. "No, she was a pretty girl I met in a bar and had a few drinks with. She asked me to go back to her place, and then we were fooling around in bed. The clothes came off, and she reached into the drawer of the nightstand, and I thought, 'Oh great, she's got a condom; she's prepared,' but nope, she pulled out this belt and gave me this eerie smile as she asked, 'Have you ever been pegged before?'"

"Oh my God, she just said it like that? And you agreed, like, 'I'm gonna let a stranger put something foreign in my butt?'"

Sam shrugged. "I am an adventurous guy, and I'm willing to try everything once, but yeah, I learned that that was not my thing. Plus, I think she pulled the old switcheroo when I said to use the small purple one."

"What were your other choices?" she asked, voice shaking with mirth.

"Mama Bear, which was this pink one that was about six inches, and Big Daddy, which was as big as it was round."

"Noted. No ass play for Sam."

"Your turn," he said before putting a slice of steak in his mouth.

"I learned that you can make a man pass out by sitting on his face," she deadpanned.

Sam's eyes widened, and he slammed his fist into his chest when a piece of steak got caught in his throat. Wren got up and went around, banging on his back. "Are you alright?"

"Yeah," he croaked, the steak flying back out onto his plate.

"Gross," Wren laughed.

"Maybe you shouldn't share that kind of stuff after I've put something in my mouth. Just to make sure I'm safe from unexpected choking hazards."

"Should I not finish the story then?" she asked, taking a bite of potatoes.

"No, I'm invested now." While he didn't relish hearing about her with other men, this sounded too good to pass up. "You didn't kill him, did you?"

"Obviously not since I'm sitting across from you and not in jail on a manslaughter charge," she said, smirking, "but he was a scrawny guy, who swore he wanted me to sit on his face. And when I did, he apparently hadn't taken into account how thick my thighs were and couldn't breathe. But his tongue kept doing this incredible thing, and I didn't realize when he was gripping my thighs, he was screaming for help."

Sam guffawed, his eyes watering. He wiped at them, trying to get his laughter under control. "Holy shit, that is crazy. When did you realize he was in danger?"

"Um, after I orgasmed, I realized his tongue had stopped moving."

"Jesus, you're a regular manslayer." Maybe it was cockiness on his part, but Sam was positive he could handle Wren sitting on his face. In fact, he'd love the fuck out of it.

"At least you got yours, right?" Sam asked.

"He got his, too, eventually"—the mischievous look in Wren's eyes captivated him—"but it took him a moment to recover."

"Alright, I think that's all I want to hear on that subject." Although the story was funny, the fact that another man had gotten his rocks off with Wren left a nasty taste in his mouth. He set his fork aside, done with his dinner.

"Oh, come on," she cajoled playfully, "you're Mistletoe's Casanova. I'm sure you've got some more great stories to tell."

"Not compared to attempted homicide," Sam said, wanting to shift the topic to something less titillating, especially on Wren's end. Thinking about her naked and writhing on top of him, his tongue tasting her pussy was creating an issue, and he wasn't sure he'd be able to stand up. "Most of my stories are boring."

"So? I still want to hear them."

"Fine." Sam sighed, pulling out one of his least favorite stories, but maybe Wren would get a kick out of it. "I'll tell you about the time I was handcuffed and left in a woman's apartment until I was able to get Siri to call Clark to come rescue me."

Wren slapped a hand over her mouth, her question coming out muffled. "Why did she kidnap you?"

"We'd been hot and heavy for a few weeks, but the relationship had run its course. I told her it was time to call it. She seemed fine, even said we should get together one last time—"

Wren dropped her hand, revealing her mouth twisted in disgust. "And you, being a man, thinking with your dick, thought, 'Oh yeah, this is gonna be great?'"

"Whoa, no need to be judgy, Miss Waited Until She Came Before Checking on Her Partner."

"Valid point, continue," she said magnanimously.

"Anyway, I fell for it, and it didn't end well for me."

"It could have ended worse. She could have hobbled you."

Sam reeled back in horror. "Jesus, that's dark."

"It's *Misery*. The book by Stephen King."

Sam shook his head. "Never read it. Your turn."

"Another funny sex story? Hmmm, have you heard of Badge Bunnies?"

"No?" Sam noticed her plate had been pushed aside, her attention completely focused on their conversation topic. Should he be scared she seemed to be soaking in all these sexual misadventures with gusto?

"It's usually women chasing male police officers, but I was lucky enough to meet a dude who loved female cops. I didn't realize this at first and thought he actually liked me. The first time we're about to have sex, he wanted me to wear my uniform while I'm going down on him, and I said, 'Okay, fine, whatever.' Then he starts talking all this shit, like, 'Oh, you're not so tough when you're on your knees, baby.'"

Fury shot through Sam like a torpedo, sending shock waves through his nerve endings. "What the fuck?"

"Oh yeah. It got worse, so I stopped and said, 'What did you just say?' He spluttered and stammered, saying it was all role-play, but by then I was pissed."

Sam realized his hands were so tightly fisted, his nails were digging into his palms. "I hope you left him hurting."

"Not quite. Instead of leaving him with the worst set of blue balls, I decided to let him finish. The minute he got close, I pushed his dick up, and he got a face full of his own come." Wren shook her head, chuckling. "I got up while he was still cleaning gunk out of his eyes, told him I never wanted to see him again, and left."

Sam sat back in complete awe, his fists relaxing. "You're tougher than me. I would have decked his ass first."

"No way. I'm not losing my job over some insecure douche with small-dick syndrome." She scoffed before adding, "Your turn."

"I gotta say, I don't have any stories like that in my repertoire." Sam racked his brain for something humiliating or hilarious, and finally, he snapped his fingers. "There was the time I thought it would be a good idea to break into the high school pool with a woman I met at Brews. We were in the shallow end when the cops showed up and hauled us in. They didn't press charges, but they replaced the locks after that."

Wren rolled her eyes. "How old were you?"

"It was last year," he said.

Wren shook her head. "You're lucky you didn't get charged with breaking and entering."

"Funny, that's the same thing the chief said." Her expression was so disapproving, he scoffed, "Oh, come on! You're telling me you never do anything stupid for kicks anymore? You've gone that legit?"

"If you're asking if I've broken any laws in the last fourteen years of being a police officer, the answer is no." She hesitated and added, "Except for a few speeding incidents."

"Oh, how many are we talking?" he asked.

Her expression turned sheepish. "Enough to where I almost got suspended and lost my license."

"Yikes, should we change your name to Flash?" he teased.

Wren lost her smile. "I don't know. Maybe we should we change your name to Peter Pan?"

Sam stiffened at her cutting tone. "What's that supposed to mean?"

"After I almost lost my job, I got my shit together and stopped speeding. I realized how dangerous and reckless I was being. Yet, here you are, still breaking into schools and bouncing around from girl to girl. Seems like you haven't grown up at all since high school."

Sam stood up and grabbed his dish from the table, hurt and anger stirring in his stomach like a twister. "You know, I thought that maybe you were saying all that stuff outside of the Wolf's Den because you were angry about how we left things. But don't come back here and act like you know who I am or what I've been through." He scraped off the leftover food into the trash and set the dish on the counter with a clack, stomping back into the room to grab her plate, adding, "One conversation over dinner isn't going to change the assumptions you've made about me, so why are we even here?"

Wren seemed to recoil at his anger, her eyes narrowing as she stood up, and she yanked her plate out of his hands. "I know you. You're the same guy who said he loved me, that it was you and me against the world, and then when things got scary, you took my word at face value and left."

"Oh, rehashing this now?" Sam snapped, memories of that day sweeping through him and dredging up all the humiliation and heartbreak to the surface. "I thought we were just gonna leave everything in the past and forget how we ended."

"You're telling me how much you've changed, but all I've seen is a guy who doesn't want complications." Wren stomped past him, cleaning off her own plate in the garbage and setting it on top of his before facing him again. "A man who doesn't want commitment. Just like when I gave you an out, and you took it like a scared little boy."

Sam took a step toward her, closing the distance as he stared down at the stubborn tilt of her chin and blazing eyes.

"You were the one who said we should end it because your dad wasn't ever gonna leave either one of us alone," Sam said softer, trying to get a handle on his temper even as his voice trembled with emotions he'd thought long dead and buried. "I knew that was true, at least while you were seventeen and under his roof, but I thought when I came back, you would be there waiting."

Wren stilled. "What do you mean, when you came back?"

Sam hesitated, watching her eyes narrow. "Didn't you get my letter?"

"No, I didn't get a letter," she whispered.

"I left it in the tree trunk. I thought you'd find it after I left, but when I came back and you were already gone, I just assumed you made your choice."

Wren's eyes shimmered in the kitchen light, never wavering from his. "I went back to that tree more than once before I left, and I never found anything."

Sam released a bitter laugh. "Well, that's that, then. Believe me or not."

Sam went into the other room to gather the rest of the dishes, and when he came back, Wren was leaning against the counter, wiping at her cheeks. The pain on her face ate at him, and he set the remaining cleanup on the counter and approached her slowly.

"Hey, I'm sorry I snapped at you—"

"What did the letter say?" She sniffled.

Sam released a heavy sigh, placing his hand under her chin and lifting her gaze to his. "That I'd come back the next July when you were eighteen and graduated. When there would be nothing to stop us from being together."

Wren's eyes widened. "And did you come back?"

"Of course I did. I always keep my promises."

Wren sat silently for several moments, staring at him. "I wish . . ."

"What?"

"I wish, knowing what we do now, we could go back to that day and handle things differently."

Sam cradled her face in his hands. "I know."

He started to lean in, but her hands came up between them, pressing against his chest.

"Sam, I have to tell you something—"

"Wren," he whispered, rubbing his thumb across her lower lip. "Can I kiss you first?"

Chapter Eleven

This *wasn't the plan*, Wren thought as she nodded, sinking into Sam's warm touch as he cradled her face. His mouth covered hers, spearing his tongue into her mouth, and she met his thrusts with eagerness, her hands curling in the front of his shirt.

She had every intention of telling him about the pregnancy scare, about her fears that if her father didn't ruin his life, trapping him with a kid would. Every worry she'd had at almost seventeen erupted into one choice, and it had changed the course of their lives. If she'd told him, and he hadn't left, would they have stayed together once they found out she wasn't pregnant? Would he still have asked her to leave with him?

There were so many what-ifs that didn't matter because they were here, now. Nineteen years later, they'd found their way back to each other. This wasn't what she'd come home for, but as his hands slid down her neck, circling it as his mouth devoured hers, Wren couldn't come up with a single reason why they should stop.

"Fuck, Birdy," Sam murmured against her mouth, his thumbs tracing the column of her throat and making her shiver. "I missed you so God damn much."

The raw need in his voice and the familiar nickname shook her to the core. He'd said it once as a goof, teasing her, but Wren discovered she loved it. A special name only the two of them knew about, intimate and sweet as teens, fueled the fire spreading from her core. He spread his fingers, dragging his hands along her shoulders. His touch found the bare skin of her arms, leaving a trail of heat in its wake.

Wren forgot how Sam's kiss could obliterate her knees, something no man had ever accomplished, and as she struggled to stay upright, her fingers worked the buttons of his black shirt. They trembled as she desperately pushed each button out of its hole, frustration tightening her core as she exposed his chest several inches at a time. Wren wanted to see him, all of him, and feel every part of his body connected with hers. Tonight was supposed to be about closure, but instead, the man had opened a whole-ass can of feelings she'd thought were long buried with her youth.

Someone else might think Sam was lying about the letter, but Wren believed him. There was no reason for him to tell her about it unless he thought she'd read it. Her heart had been broken when he'd walked away and left her behind. As much as she tried to push down the bitterness and pain, that wound had become infected and destroyed every relationship she had after. She never got over him not fighting for her, and it turned out, he had just been waiting in the wings, hoping for them to be together. They missed their chance at a life together, but at least they had tonight. Maybe this moment could heal old hurts, and they could finally move on.

Wren pulled the last two buttons hard, and they popped off the shirt. She mumbled under her breath, "I'm sorry."

"Don't worry about it," he said, his hands traveling along her back to grip her butt in his big hands, drawing a moan from her as his fingers squeezed. "It's just a shirt."

Her hands spread over his abs, longing coiling inside, her pussy throbbing with anticipation as his fingers flexed mere inches from her center. Last time they'd been together, he'd been a lean eighteen-year-old with slightly defined muscles, and now he was a man, all hard angles and planes. In contrast, her body was softer now, fuller, with stretch marks from too many "heal up soon" casseroles and bed rest after being shot. Would he note the differences and be turned off by them?

Sam spun her around roughly, and she grabbed hold of the counter as his hands skimmed all over her back. His touch felt so good through the fabric of her dress, she let him linger for a few moments before whispering, "If you're looking for the zipper, you just pull it over my head."

"Thanks for the heads-up," he said, kissing her neck as he reached down, grasping the hem of her dress. As he pulled it up over her head, his fingernails skimmed over her legs, hips, sides, breasts, and she shivered at the light graze, her panties soaked with desperation. She was glad she'd picked one of her sexier lingerie sets, since the fluorescent lights of the kitchen shined brightly, illuminating every flaw, and for a second, she almost balked at being so naked. The white lace panties were cut high in the back, exposing her butt cheeks, but by the way his hands caressed them, rubbing the globes of her ass with reverence, she figured it was the right choice.

"You're so fucking gorgeous, Birdy." His fingers traced the backs of her thighs, so light Wren barely felt his touch until he flattened his palms against her skin. "I want to explore every inch of you."

"There's a bit more of me now," Wren whispered, her insecurities bubbling to the surface. "I haven't been working out the way I . . ."

His hands wrapped around her thighs and squeezed, cutting off her thoughts as he rubbed and massaged her muscles, his lips leaving kisses across her back. "This body is fucking perfect. Do you understand?"

Sam's teeth nipped at her shoulder blade, and she nodded.

"Lean over the counter," he ordered, his voice a deep grumble in his throat, like the purr of a motorcycle engine. Wren did as he asked, her heart hammering against her breastbone as she pressed her chest against the cold counter. Her nipples hardened into peaks against the cups of her bra but she barely had a moment to adjust before the weight of his body disappeared and his warm breath rushed between her legs. It barely registered that he'd dropped to his knees behind her before his mouth covered her aching pussy.

Wren gasped, her hands clenching into fists as he licked her through the barrier of her panties, teasing her with his tongue. His fingers brushed against her swollen labia as he moved the panties to the side and sucked the delicate folds sharply, rolling them between his lips. Wren's eyes rolled back, closing them against the intensity when his teeth grazed her soft flesh, soothing the sting with his tongue. She whimpered as her pussy's throbbing intensified when his fingers found her clit, pressing it like a detonator before rubbing it in a rough, circular motion that sent frissons of electricity sparking to her core. When his tongue thrust inside her rapidly, the pressure built, her feet elevating her onto tiptoes as she sought relief. Her clenched fists opened, her fingers digging into the countertop, searching for something to hold on to as the pleasure took her higher.

Her orgasm burst over her like a waterfall cascading over a cliff, soaring to the bottom where she landed, her body trembling as she clung to his kitchen counter.

"Still so fucking responsive," he murmured, dragging his tongue along her seam, and she jerked, moaning as her sensitive flesh quaked with need. The orgasm had been wonderful, amazing in fact, but her body craved more. Knew that it could get better with him inside her, and when he sucked on her swollen clit, she pushed back against his mouth, rolling her hips.

He released her with a loud pop, her body pulsating as his hot breath rushed out across her exposed labia. "I could eat this pussy all fucking day, but I know you need more." Before she could agree, he pushed two fingers inside her slowly, working them in and out in shallow strokes, and her muscles clamped down, leaving her panting. "You need my cock, don't you, Birdy?"

Sam curled his fingers inside, stroking her G-spot, and she gasped, "Yes!"

"Hmmm, that's what I thought."

Wren was still trying to catch her breath when Sam slipped out of her and took hold of her panties, pushing them down to her knees. She stepped out of them with trembling legs, and as his hand rubbed over her, squeezing her flesh as he worked his hands back up to the apex between her thighs, she sank onto the cool countertop with a sigh.

"I wanna see this wound on your ass."

She laughed softly. "Left cheek. You can't miss it."

Wren sensed the moment he found it, his finger dragging along her scar lightly.

"You could've been killed."

Wren closed her eyes, not just because of the intensity of his words but the truth in them. It was something she'd struggled with after going back to work, the fear always lingering in the back of her mind. Although she pushed back the anxiety, her heart raced with every burglary call, memories flooding her.

One suspect. That's what the dispatcher had said, but she was wrong.

"I know, but I'm okay." Wren tried to turn, but Sam placed a hand on the small of her back, keeping her in place.

"Be still," he said, and she relaxed, letting him unclasp her bra and pull it apart. Sam kissed her shoulder, and as he slid the straps down her arms, she lifted enough to let her breasts pop free from the lace cups. He climbed to his feet and curled against her, as if shielding her from danger, and Wren hummed in pleasure at the warmth of him surrounding her.

God, I forgot how fucking good this feels.

Being held by Sam, spooned by him, was like being wrapped in her favorite loungewear in front of a roaring fire at Christmas. Happiness bubbled in her chest, and suddenly, she stiffened. This wasn't about comfort or reconnecting, but getting closure. This was too much, too intimate.

Sam didn't seem to notice her shifting mood and sucked sharply on her neck, chasing away the fear with a shock of pleasure. Wren gasped, instinctively closing her eyes as a quiver raced down her spine and settled in her lower back, tingling there.

"Do you remember the hickeys we'd give each other?" he murmured, his mouth closing over the space between her neck and shoulder blade, gently drawing her flesh between his lips, and she tilted her head to give him better access.

"Yes," she whimpered.

"Never where anyone could see them, but you used to shake under my mouth as if you could come apart from just that."

Wren remembered the marks peppered across her breasts, how she'd run her fingertips over them as she stared into the mirror, the sensation of his mouth on her skin like fire licking across her body.

"We're grown-ups now. No hickeys."

"No promises." He kissed his way down her back, along her spine, until he hit the small of her back and sucked right there. Her knees buckled, but he cupped her backside, keeping her pinned.

"Hmmm, still the spot, huh?"

Wren felt him reach between them and she pictured him unbuttoning his jeans, listening to the sound of his zipper opening with a *rrrffft*, her stomach fluttering. She leaned on her forearms and turned to watch him over her shoulder as he kicked off his boots and jeans, his hard-on straining against his boxer briefs. When Sam pushed those down, releasing his turgid cock, Wren licked her lips as it bobbed up in down with every motion of his body.

"Mmm, all that for me," she said, greedily watching him straighten up, noting the hunger in his eyes that matched hers.

In a blur of motion, he reached for her, tangling his fingers in her hair, giving it a gentle tug. "Every bit of it."

His mouth slammed down on hers at a slant, releasing his grip on her hair to circle her throat in a loose hold. She could feel the tip of his cock rubbing between her legs, sliding along her seam, and instinctively rocked back into him. The head of his hard length slipped inside, but he held himself away, refusing to give her more even when she arched her back. Her teeth bit his bottom lip in frustration, and Sam broke the kiss, nipping her ear with a growl.

"Such an eager little bird." His hand squeezed her throat gently, while his other hand gripped his cock. When he used the tip to circle her opening, she moaned.

"I'm clean," he whispered, his breath fanning the shell of her ear, "but if I need a condom, tell me now."

Wren opened her mouth to say yes, but his dick slipped between her folds against her clit, bucking against the sensitive nub, and her mind went blank.

"Birdy, answer me," he growled, his length gliding over her in several swift thrusts. His mouth closed over the side of her neck and sucked on her skin, hard and fast, and her thighs clenched together around his cock like a vise, holding him so she could think.

"We're good," she breathed, ignoring the guilt clawing its way up her throat. This wasn't anything but wanting the sensation of Sam's bare cock inside her, and one time wouldn't make a difference.

"Relax, baby." Wren's thighs fell apart, and Sam adjusted his angle, pushing into her with slow, steady thrusts that sank him deeper inside every time. Filling her, stretching her. Her channel burned, and she bit her lip against the ache.

"Shit, you're fucking tight," he grunted when he finally made it all the way in. "You okay?"

"Yeah, it's just been a while." She laughed breathlessly.

"How long?"

Wren felt his hand between her legs, slipping between her pussy lips and finding her clit again. She shook against the first stroke of his fingers, her body spasming around his cock, and she sucked in a breath.

"Hmmm, how long has it been, baby, since somebody's made this pretty pussy come?"

God, his mouth had always been dirty, but instead of making her giggle, her body quaked with arousal.

"Nine months, give or take," she murmured.

Sam clicked his tongue. "That's a fucking travesty. I could fucking live inside you forever."

He ground his hips into her as he continued to rub her clit, his mouth resting against the sensitive skin under her ear. His hand on her throat held her as he kissed her pulse, fucking her in a slow, steady rhythm that built like a balloon inside her ready to pop. Sex in their teens had been hard, fast, and hurried. Even after months together, learning each other's likes, they were always on a timeline. Curfews. A quickie during lunch. Someone else needing the room. Plus, their youthful eagerness to get to the good part usually made their connections a blur.

The fact that he remembered she loved being held, needing the press of his body against hers, his hand holding her throat softly. Wren wanted to be caged against him, his body like steel bars keeping her safe as he slipped in and out of her, picking up speed. His mouth, God, the sensation of his lips leaving kisses and gentle suction across her skin every time he slammed back in, and the pulse between her legs drummed faster, harder until a sweet rush of bliss bloomed.

When her orgasm finally burst, she pushed back into him, her hips jerking with the aftershocks of pleasure rocking her body. Instead of letting her come down from the high, he took her hips in both hands and gripped her tight as he pulled nearly all the way out before driving back into her. Her breasts slid over the counter, the smooth friction teasing her nipples to hard peaks, and she leaned on her forearms, cupping them in her hands as she played with herself. Wren moaned as she rolled her nipple between her fingers, and Sam ground into her, looking over her shoulder at what she was doing.

Sam groaned. "Fuck, Birdy, what are you doing to me?"

"I thought I was touching myself," she murmured teasingly.

"And it's hot as hell. Don't stop." Sam slipped almost completely out of her and dived back in, wringing a scream from her. "Don't. Ever. Fucking. Stop." He drove each word home with a hard thrust, and Wren's cries grew louder with every plunge of his dick.

"Oh God, fuck, yes, oh!"

"Good fucking Birdy." He pumped her so fast their bodies slapped together in a rhythmic beat that ended with Sam pulsating inside her, his cock jerking as he came. Wren turned her head, kissing wherever she could reach, which happened to be his neck.

"Wren," he groaned, shaking against her, their bodies slick with perspiration. She licked his skin playfully, sucking it between her lips, until he gave one last shuddering moan.

When he slumped over her, his arms curling around her middle, Wren took a deep, shaking breath. Her body was weak with satisfaction, and as she turned to look at Sam over her shoulder, studying the flushed cheeks and messy hair, she smiled softly.

"I guess you did learn a thing or two, huh?"

Sam shot her a tired grin and kissed her, hard and fast.

"Baby, you ain't seen nothing yet." He kissed the side of her neck, and when he stepped back, she started to move but found herself swept up in his arms.

"What are you doing?" she squealed.

"Taking you to my bedroom. I just need half an hour, hour tops, and I'll be ready to go again."

Wren swallowed hard, gripping Sam's shoulders in a panic. She'd been so caught up in how amazing it felt to be touched and taken by Sam, she hadn't thought ahead on what her exit strategy would be.

"Sam, I can't stay," she said.

Sam stopped and frowned, his eyes shuttered. "Why?"

"Duke. My dog. He's in his kennel, and I need to let him out to go to the bathroom."

Sam relaxed against her, his face softening. "Of course," he said, dropping her legs slowly so her body slid down his until she could touch the floor. He kissed her forehead, his hands rubbing up and down her back. "I hate to let you go. Any way you could let him out and come back?"

Wren's body warmed at his eager expression, hating that she was lying to him, but sleeping over meant a level of intimacy she wasn't looking for, even with Sam. "I have to be up for my shift at six." His expression was so boyishly crestfallen, Wren couldn't stop herself from adding, "But what if I came over tomorrow after work?"

"I work until nine," Sam said.

"That's perfect. Gives me enough time to feed Duke and take a shower."

Sam kissed her again, lingering over her lips. "Alright, you better get dressed and leave before I lose all sympathy for your dog and haul your ass back to my bedroom."

Wren kissed him back before stepping out of his embrace to search for her clothes. Sam made a noise deep in his throat, and Wren blushed when she caught him staring at her ass.

He blew out a breath and rubbed his hand over his hair, gloriously naked and beautiful. "I'm going to clean up. I'll be right back."

"No problem," she said, returning to the kitchen to gather her clothes. She finished getting dressed right as he came back in a pair of pajama pants with no shirt.

Wren headed for the front door and grabbed her coat and her purse off the hook.

"Text me when you get home," Sam said, helping her into her jacket.

"I will," she said, wrapping her arms around his shoulders when he leaned over to kiss her. Their mouths moved in tandem, drinking each other in until Sam finally pulled away and jerked the door open for her.

"Good night, Birdy."

"Night." Wren could feel Sam's gaze on her as she walked down the sidewalk to her car and climbed inside, locking the doors. He closed the door while her car was warming up, and she pulled out onto the street and then made the left toward the highway and her home. Although her house was only a mile outside the city limits, Sam's neighborhood felt like a completely different area, as there were hardly any houses around her place.

Wren's thoughts drifted to Sam and what had happened between them. She felt bad, leaving the way she did, but she wasn't quite sure what to say at this point. When he'd told her that he came back for her, she'd been overwhelmed with an emotion she hadn't been expecting. A joyful warmth spread through her, and she couldn't help jumping him. Which is how they'd ended up here. Wren let her emotions run away with her, and it could not happen again.

Not if she wanted to start a family.

How would she explain to Sam that while she enjoyed sleeping with him, she was looking for a sperm donor to have a baby with? Better to just cut ties and forget the whole thing.

Except they'd made plans for tomorrow night.

Wren shook her head. She could easily get out of that. Shoot him a text about how great the sex was, so why mess with perfection? Flatter him while she broke things off.

She snorted. "Yeah, that will go over well."

Her mind occupied, Wren crested the hill no more than a quarter mile from her house. Blue and red lights lit up in her rearview, and she realized she was being pulled over.

Wren wanted to kick herself for being distracted and waited for the officer to approach. He came up to the window and knocked.

Wren rolled it down, immediately apologizing. "I'm sorry, sir, was I speeding?"

He ducked down, shining his flashlight across his face, illuminating her brother Luke's wicked grin. "License and registration, miss."

Her eyes narrowed. "Are you kidding me?"

"I'm ISP, ma'am," he said, lowering his flashlight. "I never joke about speeding. You were going forty-five in a thirty-five."

Of course, her older brother had clocked her. "That's because I was getting ready for the changeover and speeding up."

"But you hadn't hit the sign yet. That's why they call it a speed trap."

Wren slammed her hand on the steering wheel. "This is ridiculous, Luke. I'm tired, and I wanna go home."

"Yeah, I heard all about it. You had a hot date tonight with Sam Griffin," Luke said.

"Who told you that?"

"Our brother's got a big mouth." Luke snapped the pen in his hand a couple times before pointing it at her through the open window. "Oh yeah, but you already knew that."

"I'm going to smother him in his sleep."

Luke shrugged. "He wasn't the only one. Other people mentioned that he was leaning over you in front of Kiss My Donut. We live in a small town and, just saying, rumors fly."

Wren went on the defensive, snapping, "Alright, so what is this, some kind of warning for me to stay away from Sam?"

"I don't care who you date anymore. You've been all over the country doing God knows what with God knows who. Besides, I got my own kid to worry about. I don't need to police your dating choices. Just your driving ones."

"Thank you for the support," she deadpanned.

"You're welcome, but I do need that license and registration."

Wren held up her middle finger. "I got your license and registration right here."

"Are you threatening an officer of the law?"

"Oh for the love of— You're really gonna give me a ticket?" she hollered, grabbing her information from the glove compartment and slapping the silver pouch in his hand. "Here. Does this make you happy?"

"Absolutely. Just because we're family doesn't mean I can let you get away with murder."

"It's a speeding ticket, and there's nobody around."

"I got quotas," he said, scratching that obnoxious pen against his pad.

"You know most brothers listen to their sisters. Call each other on the phone when they want to talk about something. They don't normally give out speeding tickets as a way to say hey."

"But we're not like normal siblings, are we? We're cool siblings. Besides, the guys at work think it's funny to give speeding tickets to other forms of law enforcement. When they find out I gave one to my own cop sister, I'm going to be the man for a month."

"It's asinine," she said.

"Big word. I'll have to look that one up." He patted the bottom of her open window. "Hang tight. I'll be right back."

Wren clenched her teeth. This was unbelievable, although she shouldn't be surprised that Luke would do something like this. Even though he was the oldest, he was always the one who liked to play practical jokes on the rest of them.

"Here is your ticket, ma'am," Luke said, handing her information and the ticket back to her through the open window. "Please slow down and be safe."

Wren took the ticket, glaring at her brother when he ducked down so she could see his grinning face. "Thank you so much for making my night."

"Well, you're welcome. I'm sorry that Casanova was a disappointment."

"I didn't say that!"

"If the highlight of your night was getting a speeding ticket, you didn't have to say it."

"I was being sarcastic!"

"Well, I'm glad I can be of service either way." Luke thumped the roof of her car with his hand. "I'll see you for lunch on Sunday."

"I can't wait, jackass," she said.

"Love you, sis."

"I hope you step on a Lego in bare feet!"

Chapter Twelve

Early the next morning, Sam found himself heading toward Holly Winters' house on Evergreen Circle. It had been a few months since he'd done a drop by, and he missed his friend. He'd been trying to give Holly and her boyfriend, Declan, space after Sam realized he'd been spending more time at Holly and Declan's than his own place. Well, Declan had helped him realize it when he asked Sam if they should just turn the guest room into his room.

Today the bigger man was going to have to deal with Sam's presence. He'd sent Holly a text to be sure she was up and available for company, and she'd sent back a thumbs-up.

Sam hoped she might be able to talk him through what happened with Wren last night. After she left, he'd cleaned up the kitchen and taken a shower, but once he climbed into bed, sleep eluded him. Sam couldn't stop thinking about how good she'd felt around his cock, the sight of her playing with her breasts, and the red circle on the pale skin of her neck his mouth left behind, branding her.

Fuck, how messed up was he? Thinking about marking her as his, like she was a damn cow. Nothing like it had ever crossed his mind before, but now, he couldn't stop thinking of doing it again. Maybe in a bed this time.

What confounded him was Wren taking off like her pants were on fire, even though he knew damn good and well she'd had as good a time as him. Unless . . .

Nope, there was no way she'd been faking it. He'd tasted her orgasm the first time and felt her body clamp down on his the second, so he knew she'd come not once, but twice.

Most women would stick around for round two with a skilled, considerate man, but not her. She'd shot him a good-night text, and that was it.

Sam might not know much about relationships, but even he recognized that as a bad sign.

He climbed out of his Jeep, his little duck collection reflected in the windshield, and locked it before making his way toward the front porch. Holly's home was a one-story with permanent Christmas lights placed along the trim and a giant animatronic Jack Skellington stationed in the middle of her lawn, wearing a Sandy Claws hat and suit. Other characters from *The Nightmare Before Christmas* were placed around the lawn, and Sam knew there were several scenes on the roof because he'd spotted them from a distance. Every house on Evergreen Circle signed a contract agreeing to put up elaborate displays during the holidays, which brought tourists from all over Idaho and even out of state to see them.

Sam stepped up onto the porch next to a bathtub with a giant sack inside, Santa's legs sticking out of the open top. Lock, Shock, and Barrel, Oogie Boogie's henchmen from the movie, were positioned around the tub with sinister grins on their faces.

The door swung open, and Holly leaned out, frowning at him. "Why are you standing out here like a creeper?"

"I was about to ring the bell. Were you watching me through the peephole?"

Holly swept her red hair back over her shoulder and rolled her dark eyes. "I got an alert that someone walked by the garage and came to greet you." Holly stepped out onto the porch and gave him a hard, tight hug. "I miss your drop-bys."

Sam squeezed her back. "I'm sure your boyfriend doesn't."

Holly rolled her eyes. "Declan still thinks you have a secret design on me."

"I've told him that you're too cheerful for me. What's it going to take to convince him?"

"Stop giving her long, lingering hugs?" Declan's voice echoed behind them. Sam swung around and saw the Ring camera on their doorframe lit up red, and he laughed, squatting down to get closer.

"Declan, are you spying on us? Jealousy is an ugly emotion."

Holly kicked his butt, and he almost went face-first into the wall. "Hey."

"Stop tormenting my man, and he'll stop thinking that you want to get in my pants."

"I'm not interested in her pants! Her head will do."

Declan had barely gotten out a "What the fuck—" before Sam realized what he said and clarified, "For her brain! Jeez!"

"Honey," Holly said sweetly, "will you just grab the burrito fixings and come home? It's cold out here, and I'm hungry."

"Uh-oh, what's the slang for cold and hungry? Cungry?" Sam asked.

Holly groaned, pushing past him into the house. "You are such a dummy." She stuck her face in front of the camera, speaking to Declan, "I love you, see you soon, bye!" Holly gave Sam a dark look, and he held up his hands innocently.

"What? I'm just saying, we could start our own language."

"Sure, and we can braid each other's hair and freeze our underwear, after you come inside the house."

"What if I'm not wearing underwear?"

Holly checked the camera and then glared at Sam. "You just can't help yourself, can you?"

"I knew he was gone. Don't want to make Declan any more insecure than he already is." Sam chuckled at her huffiness. "Thanks for letting me come hang out."

"Anytime." Holly held the door for him with a smile. "Want some coffee?"

"I'd love some." Sam shut the door after crossing the threshold, trailing behind Holly down the hall. "I have to say, while I love the décor outside, isn't *The Nightmare Before Christmas* more of a Halloween movie?"

"It's both," Holly grumbled.

"I don't know, Hol. Something about a black and orange snake sliding out of a package to eat a Christmas tree doesn't quite fit with the whole merry and bright theme the rest of the street is going for. How would Charlie Brown feel?"

"Like he dodged a bullet being created seventy years ago, because no one would watch his boring-ass cartoon now!" She stopped in his path and turned, hands on her hips. "Besides, when Santa goes missing and their presents try to eat them, it teaches people what the true meaning of Christmas is."

"Shooting down fake Santa?" Sam teased, following Holly into the kitchen.

Holly flipped him off over her shoulder without looking back at him. She wore snowflake pajama bottoms, a white T-shirt, and blue slippers on her feet that made slapping noises against the floor as she rounded the corner to the coffee maker.

"I do not need your lack of Christmas cheer this early in the morning."

Sam chuckled. "Maybe you should add a little Christmas cheer to my coffee?"

Holly grinned. "What time do you go to work?"

"This afternoon."

She squatted down, disappearing below the counter, and stood back up with a bottle in her hand. "I guess a wee bit wouldn't hurt."

"I love it when you get all Irish on me," Sam said, taking his cup of spiked coffee with relish.

"Hey, now, no flirting, or Declan will poison your burrito."

"You'd think he'd have figured out by now that I never stood a chance."

Holly shot him a warm smile over her steaming cup of joe, brown eyes twinkling. "Honestly, I love his grumbles. Who knew I'd be into the broody, possessive type?"

Sam took a sip of his coffee and shrugged. "They say opposites attract."

"Whoever they are might be onto something." Holly set her mug down on the counter. "I've got to grab the ring lights from the spare bedroom. Declan wanted to try this new recipe out this morning, so I hope you don't mind being a live, studio audience."

"Not at all." Sam watched her disappear down the hall and return with her arms full of four different ring lights. Holly had given up her YouTube channel last year in favor of starting a new channel with Declan where he teaches her to cook, and they argue the entire time. Although it was a complete leap from her Adventure Elf channel where she would perform outdoor sports in an elf costume, millions of people watched their videos, and they even had a cookbook in the works that would release in a few months. It was Holly's side hustle since she ran a year-round holiday shop called A Shop for All Seasons in town, so it was on Declan to market and promote their channel.

"Does Declan ever miss running the hardware store?" Sam asked, referring to his family's store that Declan sold to Anthony Russo and Pike Sutton to become their outdoor sports store.

"Not at all." Holly positioned the ring lights in a half circle around the kitchen counter, facing them toward the stove. "The store was his dad's life, but Declan loves to cook and be creative. He's such a loner that you wouldn't think he'd like being the center of attention, but Declan thrives on it. He's animated and funny—"

"Your grumpy, gruff, grumbling boyfriend?"

"Har har," Holly said, flicking him on the arm. "You don't get to see his good side because you are always messing with him." Holly grabbed her cup again, arching a brow at him. "But I have a feeling that you didn't come over to talk about Declan's virtues."

"Yeah, I'm gonna leave that one alone. Too easy."

Holly grabbed a dish towel and tossed it at him. "Spit it out, or I might poison you!"

"Alright, but no mocking me."

"Ohhhh, no promises. I have a feeling this is going to be good." Holly took a drink from her mug, leaning her hip against the counter. "Hit me with it."

Sam took a deep breath, his heart pounding. Talking about women wasn't natural territory for him, and he wasn't sure exactly how to begin. "I had an old friend over last night to catch up, and the minute we finished, she bounced out the door."

"Annnnd we didn't want her to?" Holly asked slowly.

"No, *we* didn't."

"Hmmm, interesting." Holly leaned across the counter. "Tell me more."

"I just . . . I'm not used to women not . . ." God, any way he said it, Sam was going to come off sounding like an arrogant jackass. "Enjoying my company."

"What you mean is that you aren't used to women bouncing before you do."

Sam's mouth thinned. "Yes."

"I can't be insightful if I don't know who she is."

"It doesn't matter who she is. She came over, we ate, reminisced, had sex, and when I asked her to stay, she left to take care of her dog."

"That sounds like a legitimate reason. Did she ghost you?"

"She sent a good-night text when she got home."

"Then what are you tripping out about? Have you tried contacting her today?" Holly asked.

"No, but it's early. We made plans for this evening."

"Sam, this is all normal dating behavior." She set her coffee aside, using her hands like she was lining up the series of events across the counter. "You hooked up, she had to go, but she texted you, and you made plans. What are you stressing out about?"

"I just . . . I wanted her to stay."

"Welcome to the world of We Don't Always Get What We Want."

"I know all about that world, which is why I moved back here," Sam snapped.

Holly balked and came around the counter, placing a hand on his arm. "I'm sorry. I didn't mean that the way it came out. I forgot about the shop you wanted to open."

"It's fine. I just . . . Most of the women I've been with would have been down to go again."

"It sounds like she had responsibilities and was behaving like a grown-ass adult."

Sam scowled at her. "So, you're saying that I am overreacting?"

"Without knowing her identity, my best guess is yes."

"Did you mean to rhyme just then?"

Holly grinned. "I did not, but it sounded good, right?"

He chuckled, relaxing for the first time since Wren walked out the door last night. "Yeah, it sounded great."

"Now, make sure you wait until three hours before your date to confirm. You don't want her to know you were feeling insecure." Holly patted his cheek. "Imagine the damage to your reputation."

"Oh, I think that ship has sailed. I was lucky we have history, or Wr—I mean, my friend wouldn't have given me the time of day."

"Oh, I almost caught you slipping." Holly rubbed her hands together. "And her name starts with R . . . Let me see . . . Renee."

"No."

"Rachel?" Holly asked.

"I'm going to the bathroom," Sam said, abandoning his coffee as she followed behind him.

"Ricki?"

"Not going to acknowledge that." Sam shut the door, muffling her last gleeful guess, and shook his head.

"Hey, Sam," she called through the door.

"Yeah?"

"I hope she's the right girl for you. Whether you believe it or not, you're an amazing guy who deserves someone special."

A lump seized in his throat, and he cleared the emotional ball with a cough. "Thanks, Hol. Now go away. I want to pee without you hovering and listening outside the door."

"Didn't you know that's my kink?" She cackled, but Sam heard her footsteps retreating. "Declan is pulling in the drive anyway."

Holly Winters might be a little wacky, but he was glad she was on his side.

Chapter Thirteen

W ren pulled out of the station that night, making her way to Main Street like she always did on the way home. Duke sat up behind her in the back seat, staring out the window with his tongue lolling out of his mouth. Christmas greenery stretched across the street and along the streetlamps, which sported strings of multicolored Christmas lights wrapped around them. A brightly lit sign that read *Happy Holidays* was the last piece of décor she saw before turning onto her street.

Wren parked in her driveway, noting the strange car in front of her house, and hoped that Pete hadn't come over with one of his idiotic roommates. She let Duke out of the back, and he followed her up the sidewalk as Wren thought about how she would get out of her hook-up plans with Sam. While last night was amazing, her goals didn't involve a situationship with her ex-boyfriend.

She should have just told him something came up when he texted her a few hours ago to confirm their date, but she'd been so taken aback by his message, she couldn't find it in her to cancel.

Counting down the hours. Can't wait to see you.

Now, Wren was stuck getting dressed and heading over there. Maybe this was a conversation for the two of them to have in person anyway. Although, after spending her downtime today remembering every detail of his naked, glorious body, being face-to-face with him wasn't the best idea for her willpower.

As she unlocked the front door, the Govee lights she'd had installed when she moved in flashed along the trim of the roof above her head in several different colors. It was all the Christmas she'd had time for, setting them up for every holiday season. The red and green gave her enough light to make out her shadow on the floor as Wren pushed open the door, letting Duke rush in first as she reached for the light switch.

Someone screamed just before she made contact with the switch, and as it illuminated the living room, Wren gasped in horror when she caught a brief glimpse of a naked woman straddling her brother while Duke stuck his nose in Pete's face!

"Fucking shit!" Pete hollered, dislodging the woman and crashing to the floor, his naked limbs thrashing. The woman was huddled on the corner of the couch, backing away from Duke's curious approach.

Wren ducked out the door with a curse and closed it, hollering through the wood, "What the hell, Pete? Don't you have your own place to take people?"

"I didn't think you would be home this early!" Pete yelled back.

"It doesn't matter! I told you that was a brand-new couch! If I don't want you getting Cheetos on it, I sure as shit don't want your bodily fluids on it either!"

The woman inside squealed again, and Pete said, "Can you please get Duke out of here? He's scaring her."

"Absolutely not! I'll be back in one hour, and at that time, I want my dog fed and in his crate and you and your guest gone!"

"Wren!"

She ignored her brother's shouting, her face flushed as she retreated to her car and climbed inside. Was there any way to erase the image of her brother getting reverse-cowgirled on her couch? Wren winced.

"So gross," she muttered.

Pulling out of her driveway and heading back toward town, Wren realized she was heading for Sam's, but he wasn't going to be home for another hour.

Using her hands-free, she sent a voice text to Sam. "Still working?"

His response was nearly immediate, and she pressed the button to play it. "I was just heading home. My last client canceled on me."

"Do you mind if I come by now?"

"Not at all. Everything okay?"

Wren shuddered, speaking slowly. "I walked in on my brother having sex on my couch, so no."

"Yikes! Which one?"

"Pete, not that it matters. I didn't have time to shower, and I'm still in my uniform."

"You could show up in a garbage bag, smelling like hot dog water, and I'd still want you."

Wren's stomach flipped like a flapjack, and despite her best intentions, smiled. "I can't figure out if that is sweet or disturbing."

"Go with sweet. I'll see you in a few."

Wren recognized that tonight she was using Sam to distract herself from walking in on her brother, but in all fairness, she did want to see him. Even though she knew it was a bad idea, the thought of hooking up with Sam again made her body hum with eagerness.

Besides, it was the last time. After tonight, she'd tell Sam that she couldn't have sex with him anymore because she wasn't looking for anything steady, even a friends-with-benefits situation.

Several messages had come through on the new profile where she'd included her objective of starting a family, and she'd gotten a call from the clinic in Sun Valley, letting her know that a man had reached out about sperm donation. While the ad might have seemed crazy at the time, it was obviously paying off.

Wren secured her weapon in the safe under the driver's seat and locked the door to the car, surprised by how quiet the neighborhood was on a Saturday night. She headed up the walkway and climbed the porch stairs, the yellow porch light shining down on her like a spotlight. She glanced over her shoulder, wondering if any of his neighbors had noticed her.

The door opened, and Wren barely had time to smile before Sam reached out and took her hand, pulling her inside.

"Hi," she said breathlessly.

"Hey yourself." He shut the door and backed her against it, his mouth claiming hers in a scorching kiss. Wren melted when his body plastered against hers, opening her lips to the onslaught of his tongue, and forgetting why exactly she shouldn't do this with Sam all day every day.

Sam broke the kiss, his lips trailing along her jaw. "I've been thinking about kissing you since you walked out my door last night."

God, why did his admission make every nerve in her body tingle with excitement?

He lifted her into his arms, and she wrapped hers around his shoulders, hanging on as he carried her over to the couch. The blinds were half-closed over the windows as he sat down, pulling her over his lap.

"How was your day?" he murmured, kissing his way down the column of her throat.

Wren tilted her head back, giving him better access. "It was a day. Yours?"

"Busy."

"Mmm, did that make the day go faster?"

"Didn't hurt," he said, cupping the back of her neck. "Do you mind if we save the rest of the small talk for after? I'm dying to be inside you."

Wren understood his urgency and reached between them for his belt, opening the buckle and slipping it through the loops. She wanted purchase and when she finally got his pants undone, Wren slipped her hand inside, wrapping her fingers around his hard, hot cock, and they sighed in unison.

Sam leaned his head back against the couch, eyes closed as Wren stroked him, sliding her hand up and down. Her pussy drummed with desire as she played with him, rubbing her thumb over his wet tip. Sam sucked in his breath and opened his eyes, watching her under heavy lids as she brought her thumb to her mouth and sucked.

"Mmm, delicious."

"Fuck me," Sam groaned, flipping her off his lap in a fluid movement and onto her back.

Wren gasped, gripping the fabric cushion of the couch as he hovered over her, shadows passing over his face when lights from a passing car slipped through the blinds. The intensity of his expression sent her pulse racing, and she released the couch to grip the top of his jeans, pushing them over his hips.

"You know, I was going to put this in my mouth," she murmured, her hand finding him again. "But somebody has control issues."

Sam chuckled and climbed off her, standing next to the couch. "I'm sorry I interrupted. Carry on."

Wren sat up and pushed his pants the rest of the way down his legs, past his knees, eagerly watching his cock flex with his motions. He'd put his hand behind his back, as if afraid he'd stop her again, and a rush of heat swept through her. Sliding her hands around to cup the cheeks of his butt, she brought him into her, then ran her hand along the head of his dick, exhilaration zinging through her when he shuddered under her mouth.

"I'm ready to show you all the new things I've learned," she breathed over him, glancing up at Sam teasingly. "Think you can handle it?"

Sam rocked his hips, his cock brushing her lips. "Try me."

Wren wrapped her hand around the base of his length and squeezed as she opened her lips and took him into her mouth, sucking him. The salty taste of his precum went to her head, and Wren forgot she was supposed to be showing him something new. Teasing him. Her hands were everywhere as she took him deep, a sloppy rhythm born out of the basic need to enjoy him.

"God, Birdy, your mouth is fucking magic." Sam thrust into her mouth, hitting the back of her throat, and she kept ahold of him to control the depth and speed. The two of them worked together, give and take, in and out, until Sam panted above her and his balls clenched in her hands, signaling he was losing control. Wren released him and dragged her tongue along the underside of him, teasing the pulsing vein.

Sam slipped his fingers into her hair and held her still. Wren glanced up at him in the dark, the feel of his intense gaze burning a hole in her soul.

"In case you have to leave when we're done here, I'm not ready for this to be over."

A wave of emotions tumbled through her, but before she could fully process the guilt, the longing, the fear . . . Sam lifted her off the couch and started stripping her, his hands stroking each patch of skin he exposed. Wren didn't care that her uniform lay in a ball on the floor or that his hands slipped around to cup her cheeks, his finger tracing her scar.

His warm breath heaved against her neck as he whispered, "You were gone, out of my life for nineteen years, yet the thought of you not walking this Earth terrifies me."

Her heart skittered at his admission, a warmth spreading through her at the raw emotion in his voice. She moved away from his mouth, enough so that she could take his face in her hands. "I'm here with you now, and I want to enjoy it."

Their mouths met, tongues and lips molding, tangling, and their hands all over each other's bodies. His calloused palms took the opportunity to travel up and around, slipping between their bodies to cover her breasts, fingering her puckering nipples. Wren jerked when he pinched her, squeezing her thighs together as her flesh pulsated between her legs. When he dropped to his knees and took her nipple into his mouth, sucking it with a savage tug, her eyes fluttered closed.

Sam switched to the other breast as his hand slid between her legs, rubbing between her lips. When he pushed two fingers inside, Wren bucked against the intrusion, sucking air like she couldn't catch her breath. As he gently bit and sucked her aching peak, she continued to ride his fingers, seeking satisfaction.

Sam released her nipple and met her gaze, a wicked grin on his face. "I think it's high time you showed me how you almost killed a man."

It took her a moment to remember telling him about riding another man's face, and Wren laughed. "Aren't you scared?"

"No." Sam smacked her ass with both hands, gripping her cheeks until her back bowed. "Are you? I think you're scared I'm going to wreck you for anyone else."

Wren gasped. "Fucking arrogant son of a— Oh, fuck!"

Her body shook when he found her clit, circling it, twisting it, pinching it in hard, fast strokes until she was panting above him.

"I'm going to lie down on that couch, and I want you to climb up and let me taste that sweet pussy," he growled, his teeth grazing the top of her breast.

How could he expect her to move when he was doing something so amazing?

"No? You're going to deny me?" Two fingers curled inside her, and her knees buckled. He caught her with his arm wrapped around her thighs, holding her in place as he played with her body. "That's not very nice, Birdy. Especially when I've got some new things to show you, too."

She held on for dear life as he stroked her, massaging that area inside that too many men forgot existed, and his fast circular ministrations left her riding his hand like a barrel racer heading toward the finish line. When his fingers twisted inside, her eyes rolled back, and she was done for, the hot rush of her orgasm surging over his hand, and she cried out his name, pushing herself forward to buck and shake until she finally came down, eyes opening slowly to find him watching her like he was ready to eat her up.

Have fucking mercy.

He slipped his fingers out of her and stood up, brushing her hair back from her face. "Still so fucking sensitive."

Wren laughed. "I'm not. You just knew what you were doing."

"Is that so?" Suddenly, he moved her aside and sat down on the couch at the same time he lifted her up, dragging her up his body until her pussy was hovering just below his mouth.

"Ride my face," he demanded, fingers gripping her hips as if antici-pating Wren climbing off him.

"Why? Are you hoping I'm gonna smother you?" she teased.

"If you did, what a way to go."

This time, Wren helped him adjust her over his face, and when his tongue found her open center, she arched her back. Most men would have been over foreplay after she got hers, but as he stroked her, licking her along her seam until he found her clit, her already sensitive and throbbing flesh quivered.

"Are you trying to go for a record?" she asked, her words ending on a moan as he sucked her clit into his mouth, flicking his tongue across it rapidly. Wren grabbed on to the only things she could, the back of the couch and his hair, as he licked her over the edge, and that second orgasm had her bucking so hard against his face, she nearly fell off the couch.

Sam caught her by her hips, dragging her down to straddle his heaving chest. "Whoa, there. What was that you were saying about a record?"

"Orgasms," she gasped. "Are you trying to beat my record?"

"What's your record?" he asked, stroking her thighs.

"Two," she said.

"Too easy," he said, sitting up until she slid down his body, settling in his lap. "It's in the bag."

"Earlier, when you were rubbing your wet pussy all over this cock, I wanted to slip it inside you so bad I almost burst."

Wren bit her lip, staring down into his intense expression, and for a split second, she almost said, *Do it. Fuck me raw.*

But if he asked her if she was on the pill, she couldn't lie to him. He'd probably think she was trying to trap him. But if she told him the truth, that would be even crazier.

"Hey, are you okay?" Sam asked, worry etched into the lines around his eyes.

"I'm amazing," she said, smiling at him as she wrapped her arms around his shoulders. "I do have one beef though."

"What's that?"

"You're doing way too much talking when we ought to be fucking."

"I can fix that," Sam said, picking her up with him and carrying her into the bedroom. He tossed her onto the mattress and pulled a condom from the side table, slipping it over his cock. Sam climbed up her body, her curves molding into him, familiar but different at the same time.

He slipped inside her easily, and she wrapped her legs around him, her arms holding on to his shoulders as he moved faster, faster, bucking against her, pushing deeper with every stroke, making her cry out with every press forward. Then he leaned up on his arms, staring down at her as he pistoned her with his cock. Although his face was leaner with more fine lines, Wren could still see that eighteen-year-old boy he used to be smiling down at her.

He changed his movements, and something about the way his hips swirled made her grasp for whatever she could, and that ended up being his arms, as she cried out, "Right there, right there, yes yes yes, fuck yes!"

Sam continued to circle his hips and thrust until she was flying again, soaring through the air in an out-of-body experience where she watched him continue to pump into her as he came, his mouth buried in her neck as his chest heaved against hers.

Wren took a deep breath, soft laughter escaping. She felt incredible, all the tension leached out of her by the amazing sex.

"They should bottle you up and prescribe you for tension," Wren murmured.

Sam lifted himself up and grinned. "Oh yeah?"

"Absolutely." She ran her hands over him, adding softly, "You certainly have learned a thing or two."

"Or maybe your body missed me." Before she could respond, he kissed her swiftly and hopped off the bed. "I'll be right back."

Sam headed into the bathroom while she lay there in his bed, thinking about how good it was with him. She rolled onto her side, her eyes so heavy she barely noted when he came back to the bed, snuggling against her back with his arm around her waist.

"I'm glad you're home."

Wren's eyes popped open at those sweet words, and panic formed in her chest. Their connection was too much, too fast, and she was afraid he thought that there was something more between them. How would she tell him that's not what she wanted?

Once Sam started snoring, Wren got dressed and slipped out, checking her phone. Pete had texted an apology full of excuses, but she was still pissed at her brother. She climbed into her car and took off for home, wondering if Sam would wake up before morning and realize she was gone.

Wren really hoped not, and when he did wake up, she prayed he would realize this was for the best.

Chapter Fourteen

Wren took the mile-long gravel road up the mountain to her father's retirement cabin. It was a two-thousand-square-foot cabin with a primary suite, a kitchen, dining room area, living room area, and loft. It was essentially his man cave. He'd sold the home all his children grew up in to his oldest son, Luke, when he got married, and then he'd bought this place. The old hunter's shack that had been the original home on the property sat off to the left with a little outhouse next door her dad had turned into a shop where he tinkered and worked on things all day.

Wren couldn't blame her dad for wanting solitude after so many years of listening to other people's bellyaching, but as he was pushing seventy, she thought about the safety issues of him being up here all by himself. Cell service was an issue, as was the road when it snowed, but her father said he'd just use his quad and plow down the road when he needed to. Wren's fear was that if an ambulance and paramedics had to get up the hill after a bad storm, he would be out of luck.

Robert Little didn't want to hear these things, though, and she didn't feel it was her place to say anything. Instead, Wren usually went to Luke, Pete, or Garrett with her concerns and let them say something.

Wren parked next to her brother Garrett's truck. He was the tech guy for the Mistletoe School District. Anything went down, he was the one they called.

"You ready, Duke?" Wren opened the door, and the big dog followed her across the seats, trailing beside her up the walkway.

On her way toward the front door, it flew open, and a strawberry blond toddler raced outside, screaming her name. "Wen!"

Her nephew, Lukas, launched himself off the top step and into her arms. Wren gave him a big hug, swinging his legs back and forth. Duke jumped around them, barking excitedly until Wren said, "Quiet."

"Hey, big guy! What are you doing?"

"Keeping his dad and mom on their toes," a sweet voice said from the doorway. Wren looked up and met Elizabeth Little's blue eyes. Elizabeth stood in the doorway, her pregnant belly leading the way. She was a year younger than Wren with honey blond hair and delicate features.

When her brother had decided to get married, he'd gone all in finding a great girl. She'd given him a picture-perfect replica of himself, with his mother's sweet disposition. They planned on at least two more after this pregnancy, and Elizabeth had quit her job to stay home and raise their kids. She seemed happy enough, but Wren thought her brother took Elizabeth for granted.

"He's just preparing you for when the new little one gets here and you have double the trouble," Wren teased.

"Hopefully, he makes an appearance sooner rather than later," Elizabeth said, arching. "My back is killing me."

Wren stared wistfully at her sister-in-law's belly, wishing she could use that excuse for why her back hurts.

Stop feeling sorry for yourself. It will happen soon enough.

She patted Lukas on the back and said, "Should we go inside and say hello to everybody?"

Wren carried Lukas inside with Elizabeth leading the way and Duke trailing behind. The first thing she saw was Luke, Pete, Garrett, and her father all sitting on the couch, watching football and stuffing their faces with various sandwiches and chips. The open room with the high ceiling was wall-to-wall cedar, with vinyl flooring nearly identical in color. Sports memorabilia hung on the wall between the windows, and a huge, curved TV took up nearly an entire wall. The kitchen island was covered in food, and the stairs that led up into the loft were blocked off with a baby gate to keep Lukas from climbing up and taking a tumble.

"Hey, who decided to start the party without us?" Wren called out, but none of the men turned her way.

Duke whined, and her dad finally looked over, holding his arms out. "There's my dog."

"My dog," she grumbled before she released Duke. He rushed into her dad's arms, the traitor. The two of them had fallen for each other the moment they met. Her dad hadn't replaced his last canine companion,

Ralph, because he said he was too old to own a dog. Wren knew that Robert missed having one, though.

"Alright, buddy, go to bed," Robert said, pointing to the giant fluffy dog bed in the corner. Duke trotted over, picking up the stuffed duck her dad had bought him, and curled up in the middle.

"We started eating because you were late," Pete said.

"I was not." She pointed at Luke, who finally looked away from the TV long enough to acknowledge her existence. "You said noon."

"But like Dad always says"—Garrett paused and lowered his voice, doing a near perfect imitation of their father—"Fifteen minutes is early, ten minutes is on time, and five minutes before, don't even bother showing up."

Robert Little reached out and smacked his middle child on the back of the head. "Smart-ass."

Wren rolled her eyes. "How could I forget?"

Although Luke had the darkest hair among them, all the Littles had a similar, light coloring. Her father's golden hair had turned nearly white, and he'd started shaving his mustache and goatee when Lukas told him that he looked like Santa Claus. Garrett was the only one with facial hair, and he had a reddish hue to his hair that Robert swore came from their mother's side of the family. None of them was particularly tall, but if they all stood up, Pete would have several inches on all of them.

It was clear as she settled in across from them on the couch that her presence was required to round out the family aspect of "family lunch" but that her father and brothers were perfectly content watching their sports program and ignoring her and her sister-in-law. Elizabeth was in the kitchen with Lukas, washing his hands, and while she felt bad bailing on her, Wren wished she was anywhere but here.

"So, Wren," Luke said, turning his attention her way with a mischievous grin on his face. "Been staying out of trouble since you got back to town?"

Resisting the urge to scowl at her oldest brother, Wren pasted a sugary sweet smile on her face. "Doing my best."

"How about your love life?" This came from Pete, who was obviously looking for a little revenge after she'd stomped on his hookup last night. "Anyone special since you got back to town?"

"I've had a couple dates, but no one special."

"Dates?" Pete asked, quirking his brow. "Is that what we're calling them?"

Wren scratched her forehead with her middle finger, earning identical grins from two of her three brothers. Garrett glanced between the three of them and shrugged, returning his attention to the TV. He'd always been the one to stay out of their sibling squabbles and keep to himself.

Wren turned her attention back to Pete and grinned. "What about you, Pete? Did your friend get home okay last night after that rough fall?"

"If the three of you are gonna yip-yap, take it outside," Robert snapped, directing his disapproving frown at his children.

While she settled back into the couch, zoning out on the program they were watching, her gaze flicked to the clock. Millie was going to text her in a few minutes, and if Wren sent back a banana emoji, Millie was going to call with a pretend emergency to get her out of there.

The show went to commercial, and Robert focused on her as he climbed to his feet with his empty paper plate in his hand. "You're not gonna eat anything?"

"I will, but I probably won't stay long. Millie needed my help this afternoon."

Her father harrumphed and tossed his plate in the trash as he headed out of the room toward the bathroom.

Wren got up and smacked Pete and Luke on the shoulders, then planted her hands on her hips. "What did you two say?"

"Ow, nothing!" Pete protested.

"He probably is just disappointed that you keep dipping out on family lunch," Luke said, invested in a detergent commercial.

"Please, the man barely acts like he wants me around when I'm here."

Luke shrugged. "Just because he's quietly enjoying Sunday football doesn't mean he doesn't want you here."

"Fine," Wren muttered, guilt weighing out over comfort. "I'll stick around until the game starts, and then I'm bouncing. And if the two of you say anything . . ."

Her dad walked into the room, so she had to settle on a gesture of sliding her finger across her throat and mouthing, *Dead.*

Neither one of her brothers seemed intimidated.

"Before the commercials are over," Robert said, taking his seat, "is there something going on I should know about?"

"What do you mean?" Wren asked, hating his pensive expression, as if he were already working out what he missed without her confession.

"Your brothers seem to be giving you a rash of shit. Something you want to share?"

"No, Dad. There's nothing going on with me." She ignored her brothers' expressions and picked up a potato chip, popping it into her mouth. "Nothing at all."

"I just don't know how we got here." Wren sat on her friend Millie Hammond's couch with a pint of ice cream in one hand and a spoon in the other, which she pointed at her friend. "Hooking up with no strings should be every man's wet dream, right?"

"Most guys would be happy," Millie agreed.

"Right? So, why is he all butt hurt?" Wren had gotten a text from Sam at her dad's place about her ducking out on him becoming a pattern, which it was, but that was what was expected from a casual hookup. Between Sam's pouting and her father's cool attitude toward her, she was ready to throw hands.

"He is supposed to be this big flirt with all these lady friends," Wren ranted, stabbing her ice cream with gusto, "but he acts like I'm the weirdo because I don't want to be boyfriend and girlfriend like we're kids again."

Millie sat across from her on the love seat with her feet tucked up under her. Her dark curly hair was thrown up into a bun on top of her head, and her glasses perched on the end of her nose pertly. They had been friends in high school, and when Wren left, they'd kept in touch over the years, meeting up for girls' trips and talking on the phone every chance they got. When they were finally back in Mistletoe together, they'd picked up their friendship as if they had never been separated.

"Oh, is it my turn to speak? Because you've been ranting for a full twenty minutes, and I wasn't sure."

"Ha ha, yes, please, speak," Wren said.

Millie shrugged. "Maybe he's changed?"

"In a week?" Wren protested around a mouthful of ice cream. "Come on!"

"Could be a game. Maybe he likes to chase girls until they fall for him, then dump them when he knows that he can catch them."

"Why would he play games, especially one like that?" Wren grumbled.

Millie threw her hands up in the air. "Who knows?"

"All I know is that something happened between us, and it was magical and electric." Wren knew thinking about being with Sam was a bad idea, especially when it made her want to give in and see him again. "It could be the start of a long run of the two of us getting our rocks off together, but he wants to ruin it by having feelings."

Millie laughed. "You sound like a total guy right now."

"Well, I wish he was acting like a total guy right now," Wren griped, devouring another bite of ice cream.

Millie watched her thoughtfully, tapping the end of her spoon against her full lips before she finally asked, "Would you rather have some jerk trying to mansplain things to you or a sensitive guy who wants to spend time with you?"

"I don't want either. I'm going to stick to my vibrator from now on because it doesn't talk back."

"Then just avoid him. He'll get over it and move on." Millie smiled sweetly. "It's not as if he doesn't have options."

"Thanks for that," Wren said sarcastically, looking around Millie's bright and cheery home, which was full of paintings of landscapes with rainbows and vibrant throw blankets and wall-to-wall bookshelves. Her house screamed librarian, which was what Millie was. She worked as the librarian at the middle school, and she loved it. She was even dating the school's science teacher, although she shared with Wren that she had the biggest crush on the PE teacher, Matt. Wren had teased her about a possible "why choose" romance brewing at the middle school, and Millie had rolled her eyes and informed her that that kind of thing didn't happen outside of books.

Millie pointed her spoon, wagging it like a finger at Wren. "I'm just saying that this town has very few studs, and Sam is one of them, but it sounds like he really likes you."

"I don't know if you're trying to pacify me or irritate me more."

"I guess it depends on how you look at life." Millie took a bite of her ice cream before adding, "If my dreamy ex-boyfriend was hurt that I snuck out on him, I'd be giddy about the prospect, but you run away to hide with your best friend and a couple pints of ice cream to avoid your feelings."

"And what are my true feelings?" Wren asked.

"Your mom and dad had a shit relationship, and it fucked you up."

Millie's blunt delivery stung like a slap, and Wren winced. "That is just one of many reasons why I know relationships don't work. Choosing to go see my mom showed me why they should be avoided at all costs."

"Please, the only reasons you went and saw your mom all those years ago was 'cause you happened to be going to college an hour from where she lived and your dad told you not to."

Wren smirked. "Are you saying I'm rebellious?"

Millie huffed. "I am saying that if somebody said you were too chicken to jump into a burning building, you would do it just to spite them."

"Depends on how many floors the burning building had and if the firemen had set up the blowup for jumpers down below." Wren caught Millie's wide-eyed stare and shrugged. "What? I'm not suicidal."

"Thank heaven for that," Millie muttered, setting her ice cream on the side table before turning Wren's way with a solemn expression on her face. "But seriously, with the amount of emotional baggage you've got between your mom walking out and your dad being overbearing, it's no wonder you're hesitant to get involved with anyone. And honestly, the way your dad was with you and Sam was not my favorite moment of his. I like your dad, but—"

"Millie," Wren broke in with a laugh. "You do not have to defend yourself for liking my dad. He has always been nice to you. I understand."

"No, I'm saying I thought what he did was pretty jerky." Millie reached out and squeezed Wren's hand. "If my dad did something like that, threatening my boyfriend with jail time, I would have lost it."

"Thank you," Wren said, squeezing Millie's hand back before releasing it. "But that's in the past, and I'm over it. Back to the matter at hand . . ." Wren sat forward with her elbow on her knee and her chin in her palm, mumbling, "What do I do about Sam?"

"It seems like you already took care of that situation by ghosting him. As long as you don't hit him up for a third round of fun, he should get the message."

Wren bit her lip, knowing Millie was right, but she couldn't help wanting him, thinking about him. Maybe she could explain everything to him, and he'd be down to keep things casual?

You are trying to get pregnant! You are going to be someone's mother, which means you do what is best for everyone and not just your loins.

"What are you thinking about so hard?" Millie asked, her tone laced with suspicion.

"Just that you're right. Letting things rest is what's best for everyone."

Chapter Fifteen

I t was close to ten on Monday night, and normally Inks stayed open until eleven, but Sam wasn't feeling it tonight. He had woken up in the middle of the night on Saturday to discover Wren was gone and hadn't left a note or message. He'd texted her yesterday morning and several times throughout the day with no response. He knew she probably had to work today, but that didn't explain the silence yesterday. Was she ghosting him because he'd spooked her?

He was finishing putting the instruments into the sterilizer and turning on the machine when the bell on the shop's front door rang. He went out to greet his visitor and saw Wren in a puffer jacket and jeans standing inside the door.

"Hi," she said.

"Hey," he said, noticing her normally slicked-back hair was hanging in loose waves around her shoulders. "Are you finally getting that tattoo you never wanted?"

Wren laughed. "No."

"I can't say I'm not surprised to see you. I figured after you didn't respond to my texts, I was getting the final brush-off."

"No, I just . . . I needed to think about what I needed to say." Wren glanced around the room nervously, her gaze focusing on everything but him. "This is a nice place."

"Yeah, it is."

"Alright, man, I'm headed out—" Mitch stopped talking when he spotted Wren, glancing at Sam as he finished shrugging into his jacket. "Hello."

"Hi."

"I've got this, Mitch."

His friend's eyes widened before his surprise melted into a grin. "Whatever you say, pal." Mitch gave a little wave. "Nice to see you, Officer Little."

"You, too."

Mitch paused in the doorway, pointing at Sam and mouthing, *You were holding out on me.* When Wren turned, Mitched ducked out the door, leaving them alone.

Silence stretched between them until Sam cleared his throat. "You didn't have to work today?"

"Oh, I did," she said, moving farther into the shop. "I just went home and had some dinner, then changed my clothes to come see you." Wren ran her finger over the back of his chair, adding, "I wasn't sure if you were here until close or not, and after I took off the other night and got busy yesterday, I wasn't sure you'd answer a text."

"Interesting," he said, leaning a hip against the counter. "I wasn't sure I was gonna see you again."

"It's kind of a small town, but I get it." Wren bit her lip, finally meeting his gaze. "I'm sure people have found ways to hide from awkward situations like this."

"Awkward, huh?" He snorted. "I thought you were going to say mind-blowing."

"It was, absolutely," she said hesitantly.

"Go on. I can practically hear the 'but' coming."

"But I just wanted to sleep in my own bed."

"Ah," he said, pushing off the counter and stalking toward her. "So it had nothing to do with avoiding me?" Sam stroked his hand over her cheek before burying it in the beautiful waves of her hair.

He forgot all about the hurt and frustration coiling inside him when she melted against his hold, the light casting a glow over her parted lips.

"Never wanting to feel my hands on your body again?" Her breath caught, and he took advantage, leaning over to brush his mouth with hers. "Never wanting me to kiss you until you have to come up for air?"

Wren arched to meet his lips, and he obliged her, covering her mouth with his. They grappled with each other's clothing with impatience, his hands sliding under her jacket and pushing it to the ground. Sam turned her, reaching for the door to lock it, and once he heard the click, he switched off the lights.

Wren giggled against his lips. "Making sure nobody walks in on us?"

"That's the plan," he said, stripping off his T-shirt before his mouth was back on hers. God, he loved her sweet, heady taste. Wren's fingers went to the belt of his jeans, sliding the leather out of the loops.

"I think it's about time I showed you something else, don't you?" She unbuttoned his jeans, pushing the rough fabric down his hips, taking his boxer briefs with them. He hopped from one foot to the other, kicking off his Hey Dudes and helping her divest him of his pants.

"What is that, exactly?"

She pushed him down onto the bench against the wall, standing over him with a grin as she tied her hair in a knot. She kneeled before him, pulling his pants, underwear, and socks all the way off until he was sitting naked in front of her.

Sam saw the flash of her wicked grin in the dim lighting just before she whispered, "How to make a man come in sixty seconds."

Sam scoffed. "Yeah, I don't know what tricks you think you have up your sleeve, but there is no way—" Sam grabbed on to the edge of the bench when her mouth covered him, and she drew him down in a long, slow suck. "Holy fuck!"

Her fingers were pressing behind his balls, closer to his ass than he'd let a woman go in a long time, and whatever she was doing with her fingers made his already tight balls jerk. Her mouth worked him in a steady, fast rhythm that didn't falter, each precise suck and lick bringing him closer to the precipice. He moaned, "Holy fuck, whatever you're doing, don't fucking— Wren!"

There was no way he was already on the verge of coming, but when he threw his head back, hitting the wall with his crown, he ignored the slice of pain as his cock jerked one final time, and he blew. Her mouth still wrapped tightly around the base, she milked him with those glorious lips, swallowing his essence, and he slumped against the wall for support. His body was boneless, and he had no idea how she did it, but if that was an apology for ghosting him, he humbly accepted.

As long as she did it again sometime.

Wren did one last swirl of her tongue around the head of his cock, making him shiver, and she grinned up at him. "What was that about there being no way?"

"I stand, or more accurately, sit corrected," Sam said, staring down at her flushed cheeks and glistening lips in wonder, "but are you going to tell me how you did it?"

"I hit your P-spot."

"My what?" Sam said.

"Your P-spot. It's your prostate, which can give a guy a super intense orgasm, just like a man can give a woman when he finds her G-spot."

"Well, kudos to you." His laugh was raspy, and he was still trying to catch his breath. "You are only the second woman to get that close to my ass without me freaking out."

Wren rubbed her hands over his thighs and squeezed. "Good for you, then?"

Sam traced her cheek with his fingers. "Amazing."

"Perfect," Wren said, climbing to her feet. "Then we're even."

Sam's brow furrowed. "What do you mean?"

"I felt a little bad that you've been doing most of the foreplay and I just sat back and enjoyed the fruits of your labors." She leaned over him, giving him a sweet, lingering kiss. "I thought I'd come over and show you how grateful I am. Make sure we were good." Wren smoothed her hands over her body before leaning over and picking up her coat. "This thing between us doesn't have to be anything more than two people having a moment."

Sure, because exes have moments all the time.

"I just mean that that wasn't what I came over for that first night," she said, obviously reading into his expression. "I thought we could talk and catch up, and then everything kind of happened."

Sam didn't like the way that sounded. "But you wanted it to happen, right?"

"Well, if I didn't, it wouldn't have happened, so, yes, I did."

That was a lackluster response to experiences he'd found mind-blowing. "Glad we're on the same page."

"I'm just not sure it should happen again," she said quickly.

And there it was. The rejection he'd expected before she'd given him the most incredible, intense blow job. He hadn't expected it to be a repayment, orgasm for orgasm.

"Are you angry with me?" she asked.

Not quite, but there were too many emotions rushing through him, Sam couldn't be sure. "Why would I be angry?"

"I don't know." Wren slipped into her coat, her tone too casual for his comfort. "Maybe you thought last night meant something else?"

"Well, what should I think of it? We had incredible sex twice, and then you disappeared. You show up here to make sure we're good, blow me, and then you're halfway out the door before I can get my pants on." Sam shook his head and leaned over to grab his pants off the floor. "I feel like you're trying to tell me something without actually telling me, and I'd rather you just cut to the chase."

"You want straight to the point?" she said sharply, her eyes narrowed. "I don't want a relationship. Ever."

Sam processed that for several beats. "Are we talking with me or—"

"I don't want to be with anyone. Someday, I might have kids. I just don't want a partner."

"I see," he said, realizing that he had been completely off the mark with Wren. She wanted to live her life on her terms, but what had been developing between them was nostalgic. Two people who had incredible chemistry getting their rocks off and nothing more.

Two weeks ago, he would have shrugged and moved on without so much as a twinge. But somehow, he'd found himself thinking that Wren coming back right when things were changing for him was a sign.

"Do you want to go get something to drink with me?" Her eyes were wide and luminous, and he wondered if she wasn't quite as resolved as she wanted to be.

Sam really did, but his brain was in overdrive, processing everything at half speed, and he needed time to think.

"Maybe another time?" he asked.

"Oh, well, sure. I'll see you later." She headed for the exit and glanced back at him, her gaze lingering. He realized he must look a sight, standing naked in the middle of the room with his pants in his hands. He felt vulnerable and exposed, and it took him back to every time he'd ended something with a woman. How many times had she been naked and sitting up in his bed, wearing just his sheet when he told her that he had a lot to do that day? Or when he snuck out and told her he'd call her?

He finally realized that they had every right to be pissed at him. He'd been a thoughtless prick.

"See you," Sam said, a million thoughts running through his head. It wasn't Wren's fault that he was disappointed and thought there might be more there. Maybe if he was serious about dating, he should try one

THE MISTLETOE MIX-UP   121

of the apps. If his brother and sister-in-law hadn't done that years ago, they might not have realized that they liked each other.

Only now that Wren had stepped back into his life, Sam knew no other woman was going to chase her from his thoughts. For nineteen years, he'd kept her at the back of his mind, but he'd awakened something inside him that wasn't going to just go away because she said it was over.

Especially when Sam didn't believe for a single moment she was done with him.

The minute Millie opened her door, Wren blurted, "That did not go well."

Millie stepped back, waving her to come in. "Are we talking ice cream or wine?"

"I might need something stronger," Wren said, walking into Millie's place and flopping face-first on the soft, green couch. She turned her head to the side so she wouldn't smother herself and added, "Got any vodka? Whiskey?"

"That bad, huh? Let me see what I have."

Millie disappeared into the adjoining dining room, leaving Wren to stew in her feels before returning a few moments later with a brown bottle. Millie popped the top and held it out to her.

Wren scrambled to sit up and took the whiskey bottle with a smile. "You're an angel."

"Let's hope you'll still think that in the morning. This stuff packs a punch." Millie took the bottle from her and downed a swig before handing it back. "So, what happened? You let him down easy?"

"I didn't exactly end things," Wren said hesitantly.

"You told him you didn't want anything serious, right?"

Wren nodded.

"And that you didn't want a boyfriend?" Millie started ticking things off on her finger as she recited the game plan Wren had told her. "You never want to get married. You want to have kids but without the complications of commitment." Millie watched her take another swig, one perfectly shaped eyebrow arched. "How does none of that end things if he's not down for a casual association?"

"I told him all that and gave him a spectacular BJ to soften the blow."

Millie held up her hand. "Hold up! You told him you two couldn't be anything to each other, and then you went down on him?"

"Yes?"

Millie gave her a come-here motion. "Give me the bottle."

Wren did as she said, and no sooner had the bottle left her hand, a throw pillow came flying at her head, smacking her sharply.

"Ow!"

"Talk about mixed signals! What were you thinking?" Millie scolded her, and Wren scowled back, rubbing her face.

"I was trying to even things up, since he'd done the same to me—"

"You know what? Never mind. I don't care why. How did he respond?"

"He seemed hurt and thrown, and I asked him to get a drink after all that, and he said he needed to think."

"Girl, that is not how you cut a guy off, but you might have just alienated him to the point that he'll never speak to you again."

Millie's words hit Wren like a fastball to the stomach, and Wren rubbed the ache with a frown. "I don't want that."

"No? What do you want then? Him to follow you around town, waiting outside your house, stalking you?" Millie gave her back the bottle, and Wren took an extra-large gulp, letting the liquor burn its way down her throat. "Listen, you got your rocks off, and the man isn't pushing you besides a few text messages. Sounds like you got off easy. Why is this bothering you so much?"

Wren blew into the top of the bottle, making the glass groan. "It was just nice. It was like, the most amazing sex ever, and I thought I could keep him on the back burner as something fun and enjoyable while I figured out what my next steps were."

Millie studied her for several minutes before offering, "I guess you have to talk to him about that, but what about your other issue?"

"Which would be?" Wren asked.

"You came back here to slow down and be a mom, and if you don't have a longtime partner or boyfriend, you have to find another way to make that happen."

"I know," Wren sighed, "but the clinic tried to follow up with the one guy who called, and he hasn't returned their phone calls."

"So, what if you pulled a Mindy Kaling?"

Wren frowned, setting the bottle down on the side table. The whiskey was already going to her head, and she blinked against the heaviness
of her eyelids. "What is a Mindy Kaling?"

"She has two children, and she doesn't talk about the father. People
assume that it's her ex, B. J. Novak, because he's involved with the kids,
but the two of them don't talk about it. They keep it under wraps, and
she's happy as a clam with two kids and no boyfriend, no husband,
single, and living her best life."

Wren scoffed. "But how many men do you know that would be
okay with a situation like that?"

"I don't know any," Millie admitted, poking Wren in the knee. "But
there's a lot of single moms doing their thing. You could just find a man
you're never going to see again and roll the dice?"

"And end up with an unfriendly reminder in my drawers for the rest
of my life?" Wren said, the prospect of ending up with an STD making
her squirm. "Thanks, but no thanks."

Millie sighed. "It sounds like if you don't want to keep searching
for someone random to inseminate you, you are going to have to pick
someone that you trust and respect who would be willing to do something like that for you."

The prospect of going into an arrangement with someone she knew
had its advantages. She'd know them well enough to ask about grand-
parents, find out their history when the kid started asking questions.

Only what if they changed their mind and started having opinions?

"Wren, breathe, you're going to pass out," Millie said, and Wren
realized she was sucking in air like she'd run a marathon.

"I don't think you want to do this."

Wren stiffened. "Yes, I do. I've wanted to be a mom for years—"

"I mean, raising a stranger's child. If you choose someone you
know, you'd have to tell him everything, of course. Most men don't
trust women to be on the pill unless they've been together a while, and
asking someone you know to just donate the sperm means giving up
the fun part for him."

Wren thought about Sam rolling the dice with her twice without a
condom and grimaced. "The fun parts? Jeez."

"I'm just saying, how are you going to get the stuff in you if you
don't have an expulsion method?"

Wren hooted when Millie used her hands to emulate the explosions. "Oh my God, stop! I could buy an at-home insemination kit!"

"I didn't know they used those?" Millie laughed, wiping at her eyes. "I thought I was going to have to prop you up and use a turkey baster."

This time, Wren hit Millie with the pillow. "I got the how part covered. It's the sample that's my issue."

"Tell me this: Would Sam be willing to donate to you?" Millie leaned her elbow on the back of the couch, cradling the side of her head as she watched Wren's expression. "He seems to be the one you're holding out for."

"I doubt it," Wren grumbled.

"Then I suggest you avoid the man at all costs and keep looking."

Wren groaned, grabbing one of Millie's throw pillows and pressing her face to it, screaming.

"Oh, come on, Mistletoe has other hotties. Check this out." Millie pulled out her phone and showed Wren the local men in her dating app. "See?"

"I remember him. He used to pick his nose," Wren said, grimacing.

"Well, he looks alright now," Millie said, continuing to scroll. "Plus, I heard they're doing a whole Mistletoe bachelor auction. You could always bid on your choice of bachelor and tell him your proposition then."

"Sure, I'll just pick him out of a brochure, then spend money to get him alone, tell him my woes, and he'll say yes." Wren rolled her eyes. "That's a great idea."

"Sarcasm is an ugly defense mechanism," Millie deadpanned. "Besides, it's a better idea than what you have right now, which is nothing."

"I have the profile I've already placed and a few leads," Wren protested.

"Leads that didn't pan out," Millie shot back.

Wren glared at her. "You know you are a bit of an assmouth when you've had too much whiskey late at night?"

"This is just my personality now," Millie said, blowing her a kiss. "Get used to it."

Wren laughed. "I really missed you."

"You're the one who wanted to go traipsing around the country, catching bad guys in big cities and getting shot in inappropriate places."

"Hey!" Wren was used to people cracking jokes about her injury, but it still stung sometimes. She'd done her job, and if she'd had all the information, it never would have happened. "It wasn't my fault. I was chasing the other guy and had no idea he had a buddy."

"Whatever," Millie said, grinning sheepishly. "I just think you like to tell that story to get guys to look at your butt."

"Girl, my butt is awesome," Wren said, hopping up from the couch and turning around. "I don't need an excuse to make them look.

"No, you don't," Millie said, smacking her butt. "But then again, why do you want them looking at it if they can't have you?"

"They can have me for a good time, just not for a long time."

Millie shook her head. "I would like to have somebody for more than just a good time."

"What about the science teacher?" Wren asked, flopping down next to her again. "I thought things were going well."

"He's fine." Wren's eyebrows hiked at the lackluster response, and when Millie saw her expression, she added with more enthusiasm, "He's nice, but I guess I figure, I've waited for so long. I don't wanna settle. I want somebody I'm excited to see every day."

"Then stop dating him and don't settle."

Millie made a face. "And the alternative is to sit at home alone, eating ice cream or drinking whiskey with my best friend?"

"You were doing that anyways while you're dating the science guy."

Millie brought her legs up on the couch and hugged her knees. "Because he is sick with a sinus infection and doing nose therapy."

Wren waggled her eyebrows. "Do you wanna know what nose therapy is? I could show you a video."

"No, you will not, because when I looked it up before, I almost threw up." Millie shook her head. "Normally, I would just call things off, but he is a nice guy, and having a date for all of the Christmas festivities at school makes it a little less awkward."

"Really?" Wren said skeptically. "'Cause it seems to me if you went to the school functions alone, you might be able to make the moves on a certain physical education teacher."

Millie rolled her eyes. "Matt is never going to look at me like that."

"And why not?"

"Because he's had three years to notice me and hasn't yet."

"You also act like he's your pal," Wren argued, pointing at her, "and don't put yourself out there."

"What else am I supposed to do?" Millie asked.

"Show him that you're interested and available?"

"And what about when I embarrass myself, and he rejects me hard-core, and I have to quit my job and move away?" Millie waved her hand in the air. "What advice would you give me then?"

"You know what I'm saying." Wren scooted closer and put her arm around her shoulder, adding, "If you never take a chance, how are you gonna know? Frankly, I would rather know that I did everything in my power to get what I wanted than sit on my laurels and lament about how I wish things could be different."

"So what you're saying is you're turning my advice around on me?"

"You caught that, did you?" Millie gave her a smacking kiss on the cheek. "You're welcome!"

Chapter Sixteen

The Wolf's Den was packed as usual on a Saturday night, and while Sam normally didn't hit any bar on its busiest night, it turned out he actually did need a drink after his encounter with Wren. Sam was drinking straight Jack and considering how he'd gotten to this moment. Two weeks ago, he was a strapping, virile man who had women eating out of the palm of his hands, and now he was a dating pariah. On top of everything else, he thought he might want a relationship with the one woman he knew who wanted to remain single for the rest of her life. The irony was not lost on him.

Sam had his phone out, scrolling through dating profiles, when he remembered the blonde in the black nightie. He went looking for her, and although it took a few minutes, he recognized her picture and clicked on it.

In search of sperm donor.

He choked in surprise, which turned into a full-blown coughing fit. When someone slapped him on the back, he turned and found Ricki taking the seat next to him. The gorgeous bartender from Brews and Chews had been a longtime friend and sometimes lover of his, but nowadays, they just stuck to being drinking buddies when they were in the dumps. Besides his brother and friends, Sam would consider Ricki his best friend. She was one of few women who'd never looked at him like she wanted to tie him up and keep him forever. On top of that, she never hesitated to tell him exactly what she thought.

Tonight, her long dark hair was loose with a single braid swinging next to her face and a teal feather hanging from the bottom.

"Are you okay?" she asked.

"Yeah, just read something surprising," he said, slipping his phone into his pocket. "How are you?"

"Fine. Now, tell me why you're avoiding Brews and Chews and hanging out here of all places." Ricki held up her hand to the bartender, who gave her a wink and a nod. "I thought you gave this place up years ago."

"That was before the entire crowd at my regular haunt decided to air my dirty laundry. Now I am on the lam."

"You're about to be a lamb to slaughter because I think the crowd has found you." She nodded, and he turned, spotting a few women who normally frequented Brews and Chews walking through the door. He ducked and rotated back to his drink, pulling his collar up to help hide his profile.

"Will you distract them while I sneak out the back door?"

"Not a chance," she said, dark eyes twinkling. "This is too funny for words. I have never seen you afraid of anything."

"Listen, I've had a really bad night. If you're not gonna be supportive, then maybe you should just leave," he said.

"This is me being supportive. I am supporting you getting the natural consequences of your actions."

"You are the most unsympathetic, ruthless woman I have ever met," he said.

"Sam," a woman's voice purred from behind him. He shot Ricki a desperate look before getting up from the stool and greeting the woman and her friends.

"Ladies." There were five of them, and while they were all vaguely familiar, the blonde in the back was one he'd hooked up with before. She looked about as happy to see him as he felt interacting with them, but Sam turned the charm on full blast. "Hello, how are you?"

"We're good," the brunette closest to him said. "We haven't seen you around."

"Yeah, I've been really busy at work and with personal stuff," he said, ignoring the "I bet" from Ricki. "So, what brings you ladies to the Den?"

"We've never been here before," said the second brunette, who looked similar enough to the ringleader to be her sister, "and we thought it would be a nice change."

Two men near the stage started arguing about their pool game, and one of them suggested that they go outside and finish it.

"Oh yeah, the crowd is a little more colorful here than at Brews and Chews."

"We're not afraid," the ringleader popped off, smiling at him. "We're always looking for a challenge."

The blonde hanging in the back of the group had been a friend of his, briefly, once upon a time, and although she ignored him, her other friends at least didn't act like he was a pariah.

"Well, I appreciate you ladies stopping by to say hi, but I'm actually hanging out with my friend Ricki tonight, so I'll see you around."

"Wait," one of the other women asked, grabbing his arm. "Is it true that you sometimes pretend to be a woman's fling so that her ex-boyfriend will be jealous and come running back?"

"I've never done that," he said, glancing at his drink longingly.

"Dang," she said, pouting, "I was really hoping that was true. My boyfriend broke up with me, and I was hoping that dating somebody like you would make him jealous."

"Someone like me?" he said.

"Yeah, like somebody totally unmarriable," the woman said.

Sam heard Ricki snort, and his eyes narrowed. "You're saying that I'm not relationship material."

"Isn't that the point of your reputation?" The blonde finally spoke up. Sam was pretty sure her name was Anna . . . or maybe Amber?

"I was never trying to acquire a reputation. I just wanted to live my life and be happy."

"Well, why don't you happily pretend to be my situationship for five hundred bucks," the woman said, opening her purse.

Sam stared at her, trying to gauge whether she was serious. After realizing that she was, he was beyond done. "Ladies, as much as I love the movies *Pretty Woman* and *The Wedding Date*, I do not want to be arrested for prostitution. So, I'm going to say good night and have a great time."

"Oh, I don't wanna sleep with you," she said, adding, "Yuck. No offense, but I like limited body counts in men."

"Oh no, she didn't," said Ricki, finally spinning around on her stool. She glared at the woman and pointed her finger. "I don't care if you are speaking to a man or a woman; you will not slut-shame one of my friends. Now, you need to take your little butt away from here, because we both know the reason your boyfriend doesn't love you is 'cause you're as vanilla as they come, and he wants himself some sprinkles!"

Her friends were a mix of snickers and horrified expressions as the woman turned tail and ran to the corner of the room, where they all proceeded to crowd around a table, shooting Sam and Ricki venomous glances. Sam sat down and spun around in his chair, picking up his glass of Jack with a grin.

"You know, as a bartender, it is not a good idea to make your clients angry."

"Oh, I've met that girl." Ricki picked up her glass, grinning over the rim. "She's a lousy tipper anyways."

"Well, thanks for finally stepping in there," Sam said dryly.

"You're welcome. I was going to come to your rescue all along." She knocked back the drink and set it on the counter. "I just wanted to see you squirm."

Sam stared down at his glass of liquor, considering how his life had spun out of control these last few weeks, and he asked, "Do you think people can change?"

The bartender handed Ricki another drink, and she slipped him a ten. "Thanks." The guy walked away smiling, and Ricki turned her attention back to Sam. "Are we speaking about anyone in the world, or are we speaking about specific people changing, because I am a firm believer that neither rapists nor pedophiles can change their spots."

"Speaking more along the lines of regular, handsome men who have been perpetually single their whole lives."

"Oh, so we're talking about you. Okay, alright, I got you. We're on the same page." Taking a drink from her glass, she seemed to mull his question over and finally said, "In that case, I think if someone wants to change, they can, but usually there is a catalyst that brings about that change." She leaned her cheek on the palm of her hand and gave him all her attention. "So, do you have a catalyst that you would like to share with the class?"

"Well, being torn apart on the radio didn't help."

"Yes, there was that, but was there something more? Something female that maybe made you think, 'I could change my ways. I could be a boyfriend, maybe even a husband'?"

"I don't remember saying I wanted to be a boyfriend or husband," he mumbled.

Ricki huffed. "Then what are we talking about?"

"Fine, I'm thinking about being a boyfriend or husband, but she doesn't want any of that."

"And who is this mysterious 'she'?" Ricki asked.

"I don't know if you remember me in high school—"

"Do I remember the kid who thought he was badass on that dinky street bike? Please." Ricki snorted.

"Well, the girl I dated my senior year is who I'm talking about."

"The sheriff's girl? The one who always fought the dress code and flirted her way out of trouble?" Ricki's eyes widened. "Is she that new cutie cop in town?"

"That's her."

"Wow, glad she did well for herself. Most of the time cops' kids go one of two ways," Ricki said thoughtfully. "They either follow in their daddy's footsteps, or they start breaking laws."

"Well, even when she was in high school, she wasn't breaking any laws."

"I bet she was just breaking Daddy's heart by dating you," Ricki teased.

"Something like that," Sam said, finishing off his drink and asking for another one. "Anyway, she's back, but she doesn't want anything with me."

"What do you mean she doesn't want anything with you?"

Sam tapped his fingers on the counter, listing all the ways. "She doesn't wanna date me. She doesn't wanna get married. She wants nothing from me except what she already got from me."

"Oh, and what did you get from you?" Ricki sang.

Sam shot her a dry look. "Grow up."

"Damn, she's really got you on the hook, huh?" Ricki studied him for the first time seriously, as if she couldn't believe they were really having this conversation. "And you're ready to get down on one knee and propose to this girl after she's been back in town for a minute?"

"No, I'm not saying that. We had dinner the other night, and I thought things were going well, but afterward she snuck out, and I woke up alone." Man, he sounded like a whiny sad sack, and Ricki was having none of it.

"Oh, so you got a little bit of the shoe on the other foot, and you're butt hurt about it?" Ricki asked.

"Can you please stop dragging me for my past behavior?" he grumbled, taking a gulp of his drink. "I know I've been a jerk, but I've been an honest jerk. I have never lied to a woman about what I wanted. If they thought that I would change my mind, that's on them."

Ricki held up her hands in surrender. "I'm just saying, it sounds like this girl is doing the same thing to you, and it bugs the crap out of you."

"Only because I want more with her." Sam stiffened in surprise at the admission, realizing that Wren had gotten completely under his skin in just a few days. Whether it was their history or the fact he was in a vulnerable place, he couldn't be sure, but dang, he was really exposing himself here.

"Well, I'm sure there were dozens of women who wanted more with you over the years. If you want her bad enough, you can play the long game and see if things change. Or, if you don't have the patience, you can set your sights on someone who wants the same things you do."

"I don't want anyone else," he mumbled.

Ricki smiled. "Sounds like you have your answer, then."

"What if she wants to see other people?" The thought of Wren with anyone else made him want to throw up and punch something at the same time.

"Who are you, and what have you done with my friend Sam?"

Sam glared at her.

"Alright, I'll stop teasing. It's like I've been telling you for years. If a woman is satisfied by what she's getting, she doesn't go looking for anything else. Even if you guys are just friends with benefits, as long as she is sated and elated, you're good."

"I am pretty good at what I do," Sam said, grinning salaciously.

"I remember," Ricki said, her eyes dancing with humor. "Now pull your britches up and stop acting like this sad sack of a man I don't even recognize."

"Yes, ma'am," he said.

Chapter Seventeen

Wren walked through the door of her father's cabin on Sunday at twenty-one minutes to noon with Duke on her heels and her nephew thrown over her shoulder. She dropped a squirming Lukas on the floor, but instead of staying on his feet, he flopped on the rug.

"Again!" he begged, reaching for her.

"Not until I've eaten something. I'm starving."

Lukas pouted by accepting her reasoning, running off to jump on his uncle Pete. Her dad gave her a nod, while her brothers barely glanced up from their plates of food. The TV blared with the voices of two sports announcers arguing over the projected outcome of the day's game.

It was like every Sunday was *Groundhog Day*, and she repeated the same experience, no matter what she did differently.

"I'm early this time, and you still couldn't wait," she called out.

Her father waved at her. "Help yourself to some food, Wren, and stop yammering. We're listening to this."

Wren rolled her eyes but grabbed a plate, filling it with food. Although it would have been nice to sit around a table like a family, that would also mean talking to everyone, which would lead to her brothers opening their big mouths about who she'd been seeing, if they hadn't already. Not that her dad would care at this point. She was grown and had no plans to settle down, least of all with Sam Griffin.

When Wren noticed her sister-in-law hovering next to her, she looked up at Elizabeth and asked, "Did you get to eat?"

"Oh yeah, the guys let me go first, but I haven't been very hungry lately." Elizabeth rubbed her swollen belly, appearing tired and elated at the same time. "Once you get into that final trimester, your uterus kind of smashes your stomach and curbs your appetite."

"Something to look forward to." Wren laughed.

"Oh," Elizabeth said, leaning against the counter and lowering her voice to a whisper. "Are you thinking about having kids?"

Wren wasn't offended by how surprised Elizabeth sounded. She knew that most of her family probably didn't think she'd ever get married and have kids, especially because she'd never talked about anyone special.

They'd be right about the first part.

"I have been thinking about it a lot recently," Wren said.

"Really?" Elizabeth's face lit up. "That would be great! Lukas and this little one would love some cousins to play with!" Elizabeth grabbed a chip from the bag, popping it into her mouth. When she finished chewing, she asked, "Are you seeing anyone?"

"I don't know if 'seeing' is the right term, but I have a few ideas in mind."

Elizabeth nodded. "It's good to keep your options open and everything. You want to settle down with someone who is going to be a good husband and father."

"I understand what you're saying, but I think I'm going the untraditional route."

Elizabeth's brow furrowed. "What do you mean by that?"

Wren shrugged. "I honestly am thinking it would be better if it was just me, nobody else in the picture."

"Then how would you . . ." Elizabeth's eyes widened. "You're talking about insemination?"

Wren wasn't sure if that was horror mixed into her sister-in-law's surprised tone, but there was nothing she could do if people didn't understand. Or worse, judged her for it.

"Yes," Wren said, glancing briefly at the men in the living room to see if they were listening, but their attention was still glued to the TV. "I just think it would be what's right for me. I never really saw myself getting married, but I always saw myself as a mom."

"What are you talking about in there?" Luke asked, drawing both women's attention. Wren almost said, *Nothing*, but Elizabeth beat her to it.

"Your sister is just telling me that she's thinking about having a baby."

Four male heads whipped around and stared at both women as if they'd grown horns.

"Have a baby?" Luke asked.

Pete scratched his head. "Like you wanna be pregnant?"

Wren scowled at them. "Why is this such a crazy concept to all of you?"

"Because you're not married," her father said gruffly, his bushy brows drawn low over his eyes.

"It is the new world, Dad," Wren said flippantly. "Women do not have to be married in order to have children."

"This conversation does not concern me. I'm gonna keep watching football before it gets ugly," Garrett said, giving a little salute.

Wren's temper flared at their dismissal of her. How could they be so ignorant? Wren put her plate down before slamming her hands on her hips. "There are plenty of women raising not just one child, but multiple children, on their own, and they do amazing."

"Who are these women and children?" her dad asked.

"Lots of actresses are raising their children alone—"

"Let me stop you right there," Luke said, his face scrunched in disgust.

"Luke," Elizabeth said warningly. Out of the corner of her eye, Wren saw her sister-in-law shake her head and mouth, *No*.

"Actresses have money," her dad said, getting up from the couch. "Which they use to pay nannies, and their children do not always turn out as normal as you may think. Things can be faked. Most children turn out best with a mother and a father in the picture."

Pete chose that moment to pipe in. "Are you saying that we didn't turn out alright?"

"Hey," Robert barked, "was I talking to you?"

"Sorry, carry on."

Luke shook his head. "I'm gonna piggyback on what Pete said and tell you that we're all doing alright."

Robert scoffed. "You guys are doing alright, huh?"

"Yeah, what's wrong with my life?" Luke asked.

"You're thinking about going back to school for finance, for one thing," Robert said, surprising Wren. No one, least of all Luke, had mentioned him wanting to get out of law enforcement.

"I want to make more money for my family," Luke growled.

"Accumulating thousands in student loan debt just to change your career path in your forties is going to get you more money?" Robert shot back, and Luke stepped forward, his fists clenched at his side.

"Financial people make mucho dinero," Pete mumbled, but when their father glared at him, he pretended like he hadn't said anything.

"You're going to quit a job with a pension and retirement, all while you have a wife and kids to support?" Robert said, his voice growing louder with each word.

"I'm not going to quit until I've finished school and found a new job, but I'm trying to do better for my family. I'll make twice as much and be home more." Luke glared at his dad. "Why did Wren's announcement suddenly become all of our issues?"

"Since Pete's living with a bunch of roommates and crashing on his sister's couch like a fucking freeloader," Robert snapped.

"I pay my rent," Pete said, heading over to the food. "It's just expensive, and I don't wanna buy a house until I've got somebody to share it with."

"Apparently, you do have somebody to share it with," Robert said disdainfully. "Frick and Frack. Then there's Garrett, who seems to be doing alright for himself, except he looks like he should be driving a tractor on a farm.

Garrett looked down at his T-shirt tucked into his Carhartt pants. "What's wrong with that?"

Their father didn't answer, but his attention swung to Wren, who laughed bitterly.

"Oh, you're coming for me next? Where is my criticism?" she asked.

Her father was on a tear now, and Wren had a feeling he was ready to steamroll over all of them.

"For one thing, you took off, bounced all around the country, and didn't come back until you got shot. You're not married. You've barely been in your job for six weeks, and now you're talking about getting pregnant?" Robert shook his head. "If I didn't know better, I'd think that bullet hit your brain instead of your ass!"

His barrel chest heaved as he ranted, but Wren was about done listening to his macho, chauvinistic bullshit.

Before she could blow her top, Pete got up and danced over to Wren, slipping his arm around her shoulder.

"We were going to have it be a surprise, but Dad's offered to buy everyone a Christmas tree out at the Winters' farm. After lunch, we're going to cut down trees as a family like we used to."

"Surprise!" Luke grumbled.

"Sounds like a blast," Wren said.

Chapter Eighteen

It was Sunday, and since the tattoo shop was closed, Sam liked to help at the Winters' Family Christmas Tree Farm, especially the first week after Thanksgiving when it was the busiest. Sam lifted a big Douglas fir into the back of the Andersons' truck and tied it down with straps. They passed him a ten as a thank-you, and he told them to have a nice day before he headed back toward the tent. He noticed several trucks pull up, and he watched in horror as Wren and all her family got out of several vehicles, identical glowers on their faces except for the small child, who was grinning from ear to ear. Wren's big dog sat by her side, watching her. The kid took hold of Wren's hand and dragged her toward the tent.

Sam ducked into a row of trees, and Wren didn't notice him, but her dad did. Sam gave the older man a small wave, and he responded with a slight incline of his head. They hadn't spoken much since Sam had returned to town, and without Wren as a note of contention between them, Robert's hostility had dissolved to mild tolerance.

Sam went back into the tent where Clark and some of the other guys were flocking trees. Clark looked up as Sam approached, watching him steadily. "Who pissed in your Cheerios?"

"No one," Sam said.

"You look upset," Nick Winters said, sliding a flocked tree through the net.

Sam didn't like that his emotions seemed to be written all over his face lately. "Not really. I'm just tired. Had a late one at the Den with Ricki last night."

"Oh yeah? Are you guys back together?" Clark asked.

"We were never together. We've been friends with a few perks."

Clark nodded. "It's good to have friends."

Sam noticed Wren and her family walk by the front of the tent and head farther down the row of trees. Although he didn't want to have a big group talk with her family, Sam wanted to at least let her know he was here for whatever she needed.

Sam patted Clark's shoulder. "Good talk."

He headed out of the tent, making a right in the direction the Littles had gone. Sam walked down several of the rows, pretending to be inspecting the trees, when he spotted them again. Wren had lost her little companion and was walking in silence with her dad and her dog. As they slowed to a stop in front of a cluster of trees, something changed, and suddenly, it wasn't so silent. There were rumblings between them that started in low and then started to grow.

Sam snorted. He needed to stop watching *How the Grinch Stole Christmas* with Jace.

"You have absolutely no say in how I live my life now. I'm a grown woman."

"It's not control. It's called parenting."

"You tried 'parenting' me nineteen years ago, and that didn't work out so well, did it?"

Sam heard the pain in Wren's voice, and he clenched his fists, flashing back to that last day he'd shown up at her house and her father answered the door. The shorter man had stepped into Sam, making him stumble back off the porch.

I'm going to tell you this once. If you can't stay away from my daughter, you should leave town before I call the Mistletoe PD.

You're going to call the cops on me? Sam had asked, completely thrown. Wren's dad had never been warm and fuzzy, but this aggressive hostility was new.

If you don't leave her alone? You bet your ass.

Sam closed his eyes, pushing the past back where it belonged. Robert Little's voice deepened to a guttural growl. "Only because you didn't learn anything."

"What was I supposed to learn, Dad? Not to fall in love? Well, congratulations, that's exactly what I learned, and that is why I never want to get married. I saw what falling in love did to you after Mom left, and I don't want to go through that."

Sam took a step back, guilt needling him as he listened to Wren pour out her heart to her dad. This conversation wasn't meant for him, but it was as if his feet were rooted to the ground.

"I didn't tell you not to fall in love. I just didn't want you to throw your life away on a boy with a motorcycle who wasn't gonna go anywhere."

While his pride stung, Sam figured he deserved it. If he was going to listen in on the private conversations of others, he should expect to hear unpleasant opinions on his character.

"But he did end up going somewhere," Wren said softly.

Her father scoffed. "What, back to Mistletoe to work in a tattoo shop?"

"First, he went to Oregon, and he spent years honing his craft. Sam's been saving for years to buy his own shop, and now he's really close to doing that. Just because his goals don't align with yours—"

"Why are you defending him to me now?" her father asked. "Is there something going on between you?"

"No, but your railing against Sam is just part of my issue! I am talking about your opinion on my choices and how they are not the be-all and end-all." Wren took a deep shuddering breath, a sound of frustration and concession. "I left and went to college. I finished my degree. I am doing exactly what you wanted, which is putting myself first. I am thirty-five years old, and I want to be a mom."

"You have children with a life partner," Robert argued gruffly. "You don't just have children because you want to. There is a time and a place—"

"I hate to break it to you, Dad, but people have children every day who don't have life partners. Who don't have their crap together, or it's not the perfect time for them. Just because you don't agree with my choices doesn't mean they aren't valid."

Sam wanted to cheer her on for standing up for herself.

"How are you going to do this? You're really going to get pregnant by a Popsicle? You wouldn't even know if the guy had weird quirks that could show up later in the kid."

Sam froze, the reality of what they were discussing sinking in. Wren wanted to have kids by insemination?

"Those won't affect me. Anything medical, they test for."

Robert sighed. "Do what you want. You always have, and there's nothing I can do about it. However, you'd be better off picking a man you at least know than going off and having a stranger's child."

Her dad stormed right for Sam, and when they spotted each other, Sam stepped out from behind the tree, trying not to look suspicious. "I was just picking out a tree for one of our elderly customers."

Her dad pointed at Sam. "This guy would be better than anything you got cooked up right now. At least we know who his family is."

Sam took another step into the aisle until he could see Wren. She shuffled her feet from side to side, giving him an embarrassed look. "I guess I don't have a partner to find a tree with, huh?"

"I can help you find a tree," Sam said, guilt eating him up inside. Not only had he eavesdropped, but then he'd allowed himself to be ammunition in her dad's argument.

"Thanks," she said, holding the tree saw in her hand, "but you don't have to. I'm sure it's really busy up there."

"I don't mind if you want the company."

"What about the other customers?" she asked.

"Other . . . Oh—" Sam grinned sheepishly. "They can wait."

"Then why not?" she said, sounding tired and defeated.

They walked along the rows of trees in silence for several minutes, neither of them willing to break the ice. Finally, Sam couldn't stand the tension anymore and said, "So, I know I'm supposed to pretend like I didn't hear anything—"

"But you did," she finished for him.

"Sorry about that," he said, running a hand through his hair. "I was going to try to catch you alone to talk to you about what happened yesterday, but then I heard you arguing with your dad, and I didn't want to get in the middle of it. Only I couldn't get out of there without somebody noticing me, and I decided it was better if I didn't move."

"It's fine, Sam. If anyone was going to overhear us airing our dirty laundry, I'm glad it was you. At least you can relate to some of it."

"Yeah, it took me back for a minute. Your dad can sure be . . ."

"Overbearing? Unreasonable? Obnoxious?"

"There are probably a few more adjectives I could come up with, but I'll keep them to myself." Sam went back and forth in his head on whether to broach the topic and ended up diving in with, "Not that it was any of my business, but did I hear that you want to have a baby?"

"Yes, I do," she said defensively. "I don't feel like I need to be married or in a relationship to do that, but apparently the rest of my family doesn't agree."

"Why do you care what they think?" he asked, shoving his free hand into his jacket pocket. "It's what's best for you."

"Yes, but I also believe that a child needs a village, which is something you lose if your family doesn't support you. I just wish they could understand this hole inside of me. It's like a driving force of need."

"Sometimes you can build a new family if your real family isn't being there for you the way that you need them to be." Sam thought about the Winters and all the friends he'd met since moving back. "If that is the case, you find people who will step up and have your back no matter what."

"I guess before I completely cut my family off, I should first figure out how I'm going to do this. I don't want to have a one-night stand with someone I don't know and end up with an STD reminding me of my mistake the rest of my life." She sighed, tugging on a strand of her hair nervously. "I posted an ad on a dating site, but so far the few potential responses I've gotten haven't panned out."

Sam blinked at her in surprise. "Your profile picture wouldn't be you in a black nightie with your back turned?"

Wren's face flushed. "You found that."

"I did." Another thought occurred to him, but he was afraid to ask. "When we had sex, you said that I didn't have to wear a condom. I realize that I should have asked, but are you on the pill?"

Wren's gaze dropped to the toe of her boot. "No."

"So, when we had unprotected sex, was that you trying to use me to have a kid?"

"No!" She audibly swallowed, her voice low and shaky. "When you were asking me, your hands were doing spectacular things, and I got carried away. I wanted to feel you and figured one time wouldn't hurt."

"Then the next night you came back for seconds?" he asked, sifting through his thoughts to figure out how this development made him feel. If any other woman had omitted important information like whether they were on the pill, he'd be losing his shit right now, but with Wren? Getting her accidentally pregnant didn't send him into a blind panic, and that made him wonder if he'd officially entered a mid-life crisis where his biological clock was ticking, or if he just wanted to make Wren happy because he had such strong feelings for her.

"I love being with you, Sam," she said, reaching for him. "That was something I hadn't banked on when I came back. Wanting you."

Her honesty hit him right in the stomach, sending a painful burst of butterflies beating their wings inside his rib cage. As much as he loved hearing that she wanted him, Sam didn't see being her fuck buddy as a sustainable position.

"And the traditional route of meeting someone, falling in love, getting married, and then having kids is out of the question?" She shot him a dark look, and he held his hands up. "I'm just asking."

Wren sighed heavily, stopping next to a bushy tree with her shoulders slumped forward. "I watched my parents argue over every decision for six years. Every birthday or sport or school activity could put them at each other's throats. They were miserable together, so I understand my mom leaving. What has torn me up is my mother couldn't be bothered to take any of her kids with her. She left all of us and never bothered to make a phone call or send a birthday card. When I went to see her after I graduated, I thought there would be a moment where we fell into each other's arms and cried. Instead, she had told me what a relief it had been to not have to be a wife and mother anymore." Sam watched her eyes shimmer as she stared into the branches, lost in the painful memory. "As I sat across from her on those cream couches, with the art on the walls and the perfectly posed pictures of her with her boyfriend on the mantel above the fireplace, something broke inside of me. I realized that her relationship with my dad poisoned her relationship with us." Wren met his gaze through the green branches, her jaw locked with tension. "I don't ever want to resent my child because her father and I couldn't work it out."

"You're not your mother, Birdy," Sam said, taking a step closer to wipe a tear from her cheek. "You already know what she did was wrong. That your parents both made mistakes. While I think your dad is wrong in so many instances, he is the one who stuck around. Not being wanted by your mother has nothing to do with you or your dad; it has everything to do with her."

"How can you say that? People don't just have four kids and wake up one day done with their lives. They don't suddenly decide to stop being a parent." Her voice softened as his arms gingerly went around her, bringing her against him. Her dog let out a low growl, and Sam hesitated.

She didn't fight or try to push away. Instead, she softly said, "Down," and rested her cheek against his chest. She wrapped her arms around his waist, mumbling against his shirtfront, "It has to be something more than that."

"I can't answer that. I'm going to go out on a limb, though, and tell you that her decision is why you're so strong. So sure of yourself and what you think is best for you. All qualities that are incredibly admirable."

Wren looked up at him with her chin on his chest, smile trembling. "You think so, huh?"

"Obviously. Women who speak their minds and are independent are superhot." Sam was keeping it light and flirty, when what he wanted to say was that she was incredible. That she was special.

"See, now I feel like you're buttering me up for something."

"No, I respect the fact that you don't want anything more between us, and I'm being a supportive friend." Sam pulled back, meeting her eye. "I'm willing to stay within your boundaries if I still get to spend time with you. Whatever you need."

"So, you are willing to just be in a situationship with me and not ask for anything more if that's what I want?"

"That's what I'm saying, yeah."

Wren smiled brilliantly, backing out of his embrace. "I'll keep that in mind. Come, Duke. We still need to find a tree."

Sam stood back, watching her and the big dog walk away.

"You do that," he said, grinning as he trailed behind the pair. It wasn't much, but it was something.

Chapter Nineteen

S am had no idea how he'd ended up shadowing a group of drunk men on a Tuesday night, listening to them butcher an alternative classic. When he'd agreed to meet up for a guys' night, he hadn't expected it to be a roundtable talk on how Clark's friend Anthony could get his girl back. After listening to some of their suggestions, he wondered how any of them had ended up married or with girlfriends.

"Follow me!" Anthony called, like a general commanding an army. "To victory!"

Whoever decided traipsing four miles across town to serenade Anthony's girl was a fucking idiot. There were at least five inches of snow on the ground, and the temperature had dropped since they started walking. Sam pulled his winter coat closer to keep the warmth in as he watched Pike Sutton skip along with the others, laughing loudly. Although he liked the guy, he could be annoying.

The group slowed down, and suddenly, Pike fell into step with Sam. Anthony, Nick, and Clark were practicing the song ahead of them while Declan typed on his phone. Maybe giving Holly a heads-up they were on their way?

"I'm surprised you're coming along on this little adventure," Pike said.

Sam shrugged. "I've got nothing better to do tonight." It was true. Although he'd helped Wren pick out a tree and they'd agreed to talk, besides a handful of texts, their communication had been sporadic.

"Really? I'd think you'd be out with whichever woman caught your eye this week."

The balls on this guy.

"Why do you act like I'm some lady-killer when you've got a reputation yourself?" Sam asked, his voice gruff with irritation.

Pike's eyes widened in obvious surprise, and he spluttered, "What? I'm not judging you."

"Sure feels like it." Sam shoved his hands into his pockets to hide his fists, which were white-knuckle clenched. "Every time you open your mouth, you've got something smart to say, usually directed at me."

"Sam, honestly, I was just messing with you."

"Yeah, well, I'm over it. Not all of us are made for a happy ending, you know."

Sam realized how vulnerable he sounded when Pike said, "I didn't think you wanted one. I thought romance made you hurl, as you've so eloquently put it."

"We always scorn that which eludes us," Sam said, wishing whatever emotional diarrhea was erupting from his mouth would stop. He didn't talk about his feelings, especially not to Pike Sutton.

"Are you telling me the great Sam Griffin is looking for love?"

The ginger dork sounded way too amused for Sam's comfort. Still, he found himself being partially honest with his traveling companion.

"Even if I was, I'm the bad guy. Women don't look at me for a long-term commitment. I'm the guy they use for a good time."

Pike gave him a long, assessing look. "If you weren't that guy, and you were trying to get back into a woman's good graces, what would you do?"

The question hit a little too close to home, and Sam swung Pike's way, frowning. "Are you asking me for relationship advice now?"

"No, I was just making friendly conversation," Pike said casually, although Sam didn't believe it. "Since we're on a quest to help our friend woo his girl." Pike ran a hand over his red beard, a sheepish expression on his face. "Like you, I'm not exactly the guy women want to settle down with."

Sam smirked, thinking about all the stories that had gone around Mistletoe about Pike and his blunders with women. "Maybe don't tell them they snore like a trucker, and you'll get a little further with them."

Pike sucked in a breath. "Who told you that?"

"Sally, after the two of you broke up." Sam saw the other man's expression darken, and he held up a hand. "She wanted a rebound, and I wasn't in the mood to oblige, but apparently, spilling her guts about what went wrong between you was the next best thing." Sam wasn't going to get into the fact that she'd been one of the women to slander him on air because of his rejection, but if Sally was the one Pike was pining for, hopefully this revelation would steer him away. The woman was bad news.

Pike grimaced, tilting his face up to the sky as they followed the rest of the group through the back end of Flint Street. "Yeah, well, my tendency to tell women exactly what's on my mind without sugarcoating it seems to be a pattern I need to break."

Sam almost felt sorry for the guy, but learning how to talk to women was something every man had to do on his own. "You can be honest with women about the important shit, like feelings and whatnot, but if they ask you how they look in an outfit, use finesse when answering." Sam clapped him on the shoulder. "And if you fuck up, I'm a firm believer that being earnest and vulnerable with any woman is the way to get back into her good graces. Especially if you care about her." This reminded him of Wren, and he almost pulled out his phone and texted her, but he didn't want to seem needy.

"For a guy who isn't relationship material, you make a lot of sense," Pike said.

"Maybe that whole saying 'Those who can't do, teach' has a point." Man, Sam really hoped that wasn't true. Although he was being patient and giving Wren space, Sam held out hope that she would realize they were good together.

They'd been walking for over a half hour, and Sam wished he hadn't had one last shot with these idiots so he could have driven them to Delilah's. He pulled out his phone, and forgetting all about playing it cool, he texted Wren.

What do you call a group of drunk men walking across town to serenade a woman?

A few moments ticked by, and his notification went off. He opened her reply.

A misdemeanor?

Sam smiled, appreciating her humor. Not yet, but that might change once they all start singing.

Why are they singing?

Something about proving their love through song? I'm just along for the ride.

That poor girl.

Sam laughed, typing, What are you doing?

Standing around with a bunch of women I don't know trying to mingle, when I really just want to go home and snuggle my dog.

Sam stopped walking for a second, the hairs on the back of his neck standing on end.

"What's the matter?" Pike asked.

"Nothing," Sam mumbled, his attention glued to his phone. Ignoring Pike's curious looks, he responded, Are you at Delilah Gill's book club?

The bubbles popped up and then her message. Yes, but how did you know about it?

Nick's wife told us about it when she picked up Ricki from Brews and Chews.

She's the bartender, right? They got here about thirty minutes ago.

There was no way to beat them there since we are all walking. You've probably got another fifteen minutes before we arrive.

Arrive where?

Wait, are you coming to book club? To sing? Why? No!

Yes, we are coming to book club, but don't worry. If it makes you feel better, I won't let on that I like you.

They popped out of one neighborhood, and Anthony waved them on. Sam sure hoped that the guy knew where he was going and wasn't dragging them around in circles.

His notification beeped, and he opened Wren's message. You like me, huh?

As if he hadn't been clear on that.

I do.

Rows of cars were parked on either side of the street, and Anthony called back, "It's just ahead."

Sam's phone beeped again, and the message was clear.

You shouldn't. I'm bad news.

Funny. I was beginning to think you were too bland to be bad. The lawful job. The early bedtime.

You're criticizing me for being an adult?

An adult who doesn't know how to cut loose and have a good time.

Oh, I'll show you such a good time, Griffin, you'll be ruined for other women.

Promise or threat, because I'm down for either.

They were nearing the end of the road, where Anthony waved them onto the lawn of a blue duplex.

"Alright, we need to practice so we can get this right," Anthony said, hopping from foot to foot. "On my count— And a one, two, three."

All the men started singing "Hey There Delilah" by the Plain White T's, even Sam, although he was drowned out by Pike's voice. After what seemed like hours of singing, the front door opened, and several women poured out. Sam recognized Delilah, since she was Holly's best friend, at the front of the group, but the brunette behind her was new.

When Sam spotted a familiar blonde step out on the porch, he grinned at her slack-jawed expression.

"What are you doing here?" Delilah asked, her face burnished in the porch light.

"We have come courtin'," Pike called, bowing with flourish.

Sam rolled his eyes and grabbed the other man by the back of the jacket, discreetly lifting him out of the ridiculous pose. "No, we've not."

Delilah disappeared back inside for a moment, only to return to the porch with her jacket. "Again, why are you all gathered on my lawn?"

"I'm getting to that," Anthony said, clearing his throat. "Nick?"

Nick held his phone up, and the first notes of "Hey There Delilah" sounded, and suddenly Anthony was singing at the top of his lungs. All his friends started humming along, but Sam hesitated; with Wren watching him, he felt like a giant dweeb. Declan interrupted his vocals and leaned over toward Sam, his voice low and commanding. "If I have to be here singing this crap, so do you."

Sam coughed, smothering a laugh. Although Sam liked to mess with the big guy, he actually liked Holly's grumpy, antisocial boyfriend.

"Oh, it's what you do to me!" Anthony belted, slightly offbeat and slurring his s's, but as Sam vocalized with the rest of them, they didn't sound half bad.

More women filed onto the porch, while others moved the curtains back and were watching from the window. Wren shook her head, and Sam couldn't take his eyes off her as she leaned on the banister, her blond hair tied back in a ponytail.

Anthony threw his hands out to his side, nearly smacking Nick, who stepped back closer to Sam. Anthony didn't notice as he sang, "And you're to blame!"

The men chorused, "Oooooooh," and Sam crossed his eyes, making Wren laugh. The neighbors were gathered in their yards, investigating the strange noises. Some of them laughing. Others turned and went back inside, obviously over the group's drunken antics.

The song ended, and Delilah didn't move as Anthony took a few steps toward her.

"Aren't carolers supposed to sing Christmas songs?" Delilah asked.

"Not when they're trying to win back their girl."

The women on the porch released a collective "aw," even Wren. He could tell by the way her mouth opened.

Anthony stopped. "I didn't know you were having a party."

"It's a book club."

Sam watched him climb the steps, swaying slightly, and thought someone should be behind him in case he lost his balance. But the guy finally made it, giving Delilah a goofy smile. "What book are you reading?"

Sam nearly groaned aloud. *Get on with it!*

"Stay focused, man! I am freezing my balls off!" Declan said as if he'd heard Sam's frustration.

"Right, sorry." He cleared his throat. "Delilah Gill. I like you and want to take you on a date. 'Cause I like you."

Sam couldn't hear her response, and although he was part of the collective, all he wanted to do was talk to Wren.

"I like the hell out of you," Anthony said, raising his voice, "and I will shout it to the world any time you doubt me."

Holly made an exasperated noise. "Would you kiss him already?"

"I swear, if you don't, I will!" another woman called from inside the house.

"Will you date me, Delilah?" Anthony asked.

Delilah laughed. "You are very drunk."

"That is a statement of fact but not what I'm looking for."

"And you'll get an answer when you're sober."

"Boo," the men on her front yard hollered, including Sam. After all that romantic effort, walking four miles in the cold at night, piss drunk, that was all they got?

"Sloshed or not, that was pretty epic," the unfamiliar brunette said, leaning against the railing on the other side of Delilah. "Although the redhead was pitchy."

Pike glowered at her. "Witch, I have the voice of an angel."

"A fallen angel."

Suddenly, Pike bent over and gathered up a handful of snow, letting it fly. It missed the strange brunette and hit Holly on the side of her face. Delilah's mouth dropped open as Holly dived off the porch.

"You're a dead man, Pike!"

"I wasn't aiming at you!" he protested, hiding behind one man after another. When he ended up behind Declan and Sam, his voice hit a high note as she gained on him. "Declan, control your woman!"

"I don't know, man. I kinda wanna see what she does when she gets you."

Wives and girlfriends joined in the fray, while the bystanders whooped and cheered. Snow exploded against the side of the house and the window, and women dived back inside, slamming the door closed. Sam started walking toward the porch, bending over to pick up a handful of snow. Wren shook her head and shouted, "We're going to get the cops called on us if we don't simmer down." She made a quiet motion with her hands, and Sam tossed a snowball at her, hitting her in the chest.

"Officer Little, is that you?" Sam called. "I didn't think you knew what fun was."

"Smug son of a bitch," she muttered, launching herself off the porch at him. Her high ponytail swung like a lasso as she bent over to get a handful of snow. "You've been asking for this for weeks."

"Well come on, hot stuff! Catch me if you can!"

Wren chased Sam around the yard, throwing snowballs at him. He chucked them back at her just as fast, laughing and slipping in the snow.

"Come on, Birdy, is that the best you got?" Sam teased, accidentally planting one in her face. Wren stopped in her tracks, wiping her eyes, and when he saw the fury there, he took off running.

If he hadn't lost his footing at the edge of the lawn, there was no way she'd have been able to tackle him. Wren rode him to the ground, and he landed on his stomach with her weight on his back, knocking the wind out of him.

Sam groaned loudly, his arms trapped under his body. "You've killed me."

"Serves you right, tossing snowballs at an officer of the law."

Sam rolled, dislodging her from his back. When he could look up at her, Sam grabbed her arms and pulled her back down on top of him, grinning. They were far enough away from the others that they couldn't hear him.

"What was that about ruining me for other women?" he said softly, his hands smoothing her back, under her jacket.

"Not here," she whispered.

Sam stilled. "Because you don't want anyone to know?"

Wren grinned, leaning down until her mouth grazed his ear. "Because what I want to do to you doesn't require an audience."

"Can I at least get a hint?" he asked, arching his hips against her, his cock already locked and loaded from just the feel of her. "Or should I tell you what I want?"

"Sam, it doesn't matter what you want, because I won."

A sharp sting to his face, and he realized while he'd been distracted, she'd picked up a handful of snow and pushed it into his face.

"I got you!" she crowed, trying to get up off him, but once he cleared some of the snow off his face, Sam lifted her up and got to his feet.

He pulled her against him, laughing. "And I got you."

"What do you mean?" she asked.

"I mean, if you're looking for someone to donate, I've got you. I'll be your person." Sam had no idea where the words came from, but he didn't regret them. If this made Wren happy, he was more than willing to follow through.

It took her several seconds, and her eyes brightened, shimmering with unshed tears. "You don't have to do that."

"I know I don't, but you said you needed someone, right?" Sam shrugged, releasing her body but taking her hand. "Why not me? We've known each other a long time. I want to think we can make this work. I'm willing to sign whatever you want and stay in the background."

"Why would you do that? Give up rights to a child? Won't you regret it?"

Sam had offhandedly imagined being a dad, but it wasn't something he had to do, a driving force in his life.

"No, because I'll know they are in good hands." Sam ran his free hand over his hair, wishing he'd practiced this and that they weren't discussing it on the front lawn of someone else's house with a snowball fight going on ten feet away. "You need to do this with somebody you trust, and I hope that person is me."

Wren squeezed his hand hard, bringing it to her chest. "I don't know what to say."

"Just tell me when and where, and I'll be there," he said, feeling like a king as she looked up at him warmly, his chest tightening at her wide, affectionate smile.

"If there was ever a time I wanted to kiss you, this would be it," Wren said softly, her mouth brushing over his knuckles.

"People will talk," Sam murmured, her lips on his skin leaving tingles of joy behind.

Wren pulled him around the corner of the alleyway, behind the neighbor's house, and pushed him against the wall.

"Let 'em," she said, pressing into his body as she lifted herself up. He met her mouth, heat rushing through him as their lips fused, her delicate perfume enticing him, and he slipped his hands down over her back to the globes of her ass. Sam lifted her against him, shifting their positions until he was pressing her back into the wall.

"I want to fuck you so bad right now," Sam said, his mouth finding the pulse on her neck and sucking it.

"Me, too," she whispered, fingers threaded in his hair. Sam rolled his hips against the juncture between her thighs, grinding against her pussy until she was panting. He knew there were people a yard away, that one of the neighbors could come out and see them, but Sam didn't care.

"Do you remember the time we fucked in the church parking lot?" He released her right ass cheek to reach up and pull the V of her neckline lower, exposing the top of her breast. Sam ran his tongue over her, sucking her flesh into his mouth.

"Yes," she whimpered.

"You were so hot, so ready. So fucking bad." Sam exposed her nipple and dipped his head, sucking the pebbled peak into his mouth, flicking it with his tongue until she was arching into his mouth. He released it with a quiet pop, his hand coming down to cover her, his finger rubbing her through her jeans. "Be bad with me again, Birdy."

His fingers continued to move against her pussy, the heat of it scorching his skin. "Do you want to be bad with me?"

Wren bit her lip.

Finally, she released a breathy moan. "Yes."

Sam didn't give her a chance to change her mind, making swift work of the button on her jeans and pushing them down. While he discarded her clothes, their mouths and bodies fused against the backside of a house in the dark, all he could think about was being inside her. Bare skin to skin. He'd never done that with another woman besides Wren. He'd never even been tempted to try it with another woman, the thought of being tied to them by an accidental pregnancy terrifying.

With Wren, all he wanted was to be with her.

When he freed his cock from the confines of his jeans and took his length in hand, rubbing the tip against her wet pussy lips, he closed his eyes. He wanted to bury himself inside her again and let his come fill her, over and over.

The heat between them chased away the cold as he pressed forward, sinking into her slick channel, the walls squeezing him, and he gripped her hips in his hands, listening to her breath hitch.

"God, you feel incredible. Better than I remember." Sam slid back and shoved back in, this time all the way to the hilt, and Wren gasped, arms wrapped around his shoulders. As he pumped into her, he kissed along her collarbone, finding the column of her throat and gently sucking the skin where her pulse pounded. He kept his mouth close to her skin, whispering as he thrust, "Your pussy is so fucking wet for me. Is it because you know there's nothing between us? Does it make you hot, knowing I'm inside you without a condom? That when I come, you're going to feel it?"

Sam used her hips to speed up their motions, forgetting about the noise of their flapping flesh as he pounded her. Wren tremored against him, and he knew that she was close.

"Does it make you wanna come, thinking about how I'm going to give you everything you want, Birdy?"

Wren spasmed in his arms, burying her mouth in his shoulder as she trembled with the force of her orgasm, and her muscles clamping down on his dick took him over the edge with her.

They stayed there, for several minutes, heaving and connected.

Sam heard Clark calling his name, and Wren lifted her head from his shoulder, staring down at him.

"Come over Thursday? I'm off Friday, so we can . . . take our time."

Sam grinned. "I'll be there."

Chapter Twenty

"We have a report about stolen property at 314 Evergreen Circle."

Wren picked up her radio, answering, "Officer Little. I'm a few blocks from there. I'll take it."

"Thank you, Little."

Wren flipped her cruiser around. She'd been heading back toward the station when the call came in. It was a little after six in the evening, and Sam was supposed to be coming by tonight when he finished with his last client. Since their intense encounter behind Delilah Gill's house, Wren couldn't get being with him out of her head.

When he'd agreed to help her get pregnant, Wren was so moved that she couldn't help kissing him. The rest of it had happened like a snowball rolling downhill, unstoppable.

And the things he'd said . . .

Wren gripped the wheel, wiggling in her seat. She should have kept things professional. She'd ordered the home insemination kit with the plan to use it, but after Tuesday, it all seemed moot. They'd had sex without a condom, broken that boundary down with a hammer, and now, she didn't want to go back. She wanted to have sex with Sam again and again.

How would that affect their deal? Blurred lines meant muddy expectations, and Wren didn't want Sam to think she'd changed her mind about doing this alone.

Wren parked down the street from Evergreen when she saw the long line of cars waiting to get in and see the displays. Duke barked from the back of the SUV, and Wren told him "Quiet" before exiting the vehicle. She passed by the line of cars on the shoulder and then crossed the street. There were people three deep on the sidewalk, checking out the lights displays. Every house on the street was shining bright, with elaborate scenes of Grinches stealing Christmas and Peanuts dancing around a Christmas tree. People oohed and aahed around her as she approached a house with scenes from *Elf* taking over the front yard, garage, and house. Mrs. Delany met her on the walkway, her silver hair in a shoulder-length bob.

"Someone stole my giant ornament," Mrs. Delany said grimly. "It was right there"—the older woman pointed to an indentation in the snow—"two hours ago, and when I came outside to watch the visitors, I saw it was missing."

Wren saw footprints in the snow leading down to the sidewalk. She could grab Duke and track the guy for a bit, but it probably happened hours ago. Besides, the circle was filling up with people checking out the lights displays, and seeing an officer and police dog tracking would bring cause for speculation.

"Have you seen anyone suspicious hanging around?" Wren asked, tapping her pen on her pad softly. "Maybe somebody wearing a hoodie?"

"I didn't, but my Ring camera caught something." She pulled out her phone, scrolling through until she found what she was looking for. "Here it is. My daughter set this up for me to make sure people didn't steal my packages."

Wren took the phone and pushed play, watching the video of someone in a dark hoodie and pants picking up the ornament and running away with it. They looked slight, maybe a teen.

"Can you send this to the station email?"

"Absolutely, but why would anyone take my ornament?" Mrs. Delany asked.

"I'm not sure, but I would guess you're not the first house they've hit. I'll ask around at the station and get back to you."

"Well, I hope you catch them, whoever they are. It's not right for anyone to steal things, but especially not before Christmas."

Wren agreed with her. A giant ornament wasn't exactly an easy resell. Maybe whoever took it was getting off on the thrill, like the guy who was obsessed with stealing troll dolls when she lived in Texas. When they caught him, they found thousands of dollars' worth of dolls in his room and learned he like to use the hair on himself during happy-fun-time.

Hopefully, they'd find the ornament with a less gross ending.

"Thank you for meeting with me, Mrs. Delany," Wren said, holding her hand out to the older woman. "Hopefully, I'll have more for you soon."

"I appreciate you coming by so quickly, Officer Little."

Wren headed back down the driveway to the sidewalk, following along with the crowd as they circled the neighborhood. It was nice to see so many families out and about. She spotted a woman stopped in front of one of the houses, holding a baby bundled in a snowsuit. Wren paused, imagining herself in the woman's shoes. Showing her baby all the world has to offer.

A man suddenly appeared behind the woman, wrapping his arms around her waist and pointing to something on the roof. They made an adorable threesome.

That could be you and someone else if you were open to possibilities.

Wren wound her way out of Evergreen Circle and jogged back up the road to the cruiser. When she climbed inside, Duke made a high-pitched whine, and Wren nodded. "I know, buddy. We just need to go home, huh? Too much going on in town tonight."

She headed back to the station to clock out and then home. Her stomach twisted into knots the closer she got to the house, thinking about the night ahead. Wren pulled into the driveway and let Duke out the back, still contemplating how tonight was going to go. She should set up the kit, just in case.

Wren unloaded everything on the bathroom counter, including the sample cup. Was she supposed to have porn here for him? They'd slept together, so should she be the stimulation? Wear something sexy?

Oh God, this is crazy.

She changed her nightgown three times, staring at herself in the mirror. She finally settled on a black one when the doorbell rang. Duke barked twice, and she pointed to his kennel.

"Duke, bed."

The dog went inside without a fuss and lay down on his bed, watching her as she locked the door to his crate. The bell rang again, and Wren raced to answer it, fluffing her hair along the way.

When she opened the door, it wasn't Sam on the front stoop but her brother Pete.

He covered his eyes, screaming, "Oh my God, what are you wearing?"

Wren grabbed her coat off the hook and covered up, glaring at her brother as she buttoned the coat to her neck. "What are you doing here?"

"It's my roommate's birthday, and they're having a party. I have to get up early, so I figured I'd crash here."

"You should have called," she said.

"I tried texting, but you didn't answer." Pete's eyes widened. "Are you having company over? Is that what the getup is all about?"

"It's none of your business, Pete!" she snapped.

"Ugh." Pete threw an arm over his eyes and groaned, "You banging anyone is just gross."

"Oh, shut up and be a grown-up for once! I walked in on you having sex on my couch, and I didn't lose my shit."

Pete spluttered to a sitting position. "Yes, you did! You abandoned your dog and ran out the door!"

"I was allowing you and your friend time to collect yourselves," she said, grinning when his face flushed maroon.

"I've never pranced around you in my good underwear."

"First, I wasn't prancing." She tapped on one finger, counting her arguments. "Second, you have good underwear? And third, I was expecting someone else, not you!" Wren tossed a throw pillow at him and added, "Now, get a grip and stop being dramatic."

"I can't when we're talking about my little sister getting her freak on."

Wren pointed toward the door with a huff. "I'm not going to be doing much of anything if you don't get the hell out of here."

"Where am I going to go?" Pete asked, climbing to his feet.

"Can't you go spend the night with Luke or Garrett or even Dad?"

"I'm not driving up the mountain in the dark. Luke and his rug rat and his hormonal wife make me nuts, and Garrett is well . . . Garrett."

Wren pushed Pete back toward the closed door. "Well, it sounds like Garrett is your best option, so how about you get out of here and give me some privacy?"

Pete leaned into her pushing hands. "You'd really throw your favorite brother out into the cold?"

Someone knocked on the door, and she glared at him. "Yes, absolutely I would, hundred percent."

"Fine. Let's get a look at this guy and see what's special about him." Pete threw open the door, revealing Sam standing on the stoop, his brow furrowing.

"Hi, Pete."

"Sam." Pete glanced over his shoulder at Wren. "I should have known." Pete faced Sam once more, arms folded over his chest. "Did you know that my sister will not let me spend the night here, even though I am in dire need, because she would rather do the devil's tango with you? The humanity, right?"

Sam cleared his throat. "Should I come back later?"

"Later is definitely better," Pete said at the same time as Wren blurted, "Absolutely not!"

Wren and Pete glared at each other.

"If you do not get out of my house in the next five seconds, I am going to get my Taser and take videos of you peeing yourself and post them on TikTok!"

Pete made a face before sniffing derisively. "Well, I can tell when I'm not wanted."

"You are loved and wanted, just not here tonight!" she called after him.

"Whatever, have fun!" He flipped her the bird, and Sam turned around, saw the gesture, and gave her a sheepish grin.

"I didn't mean to kick him out of his bed."

"His bed is at home with his two roommates. He has a couch here, but as I told him, he should have called." Wren gave Sam a nervous smile. "Hi."

"Hey." He stepped inside, and she shut the door, taking in his button-down shirt and jeans.

"You look like we're headed out instead of staying in."

"Yeah, I was a little nervous, so I may have overdressed, and I wasn't sure if this is the kind of thing you bring flowers to, but"—Sam pulled out a single red rose and held it out to her—"here you go."

"Thank you very much," she said, taking it with a small smile. "I may have a single rose vase that was my grandma's. Come with me."

Sam followed her into the kitchen and stood in the doorway as she searched the cupboards, finally finding what she was looking for. She filled the skinny vase with water and slipped the rose inside. There was a packet on the counter, and Wren picked it up, handing it over to him. "It's a boilerplate agreement. If you could just read through and sign."

Sam didn't bother reading the packet but flipped to the last page and signed.

"You don't want to read through it? To make sure I didn't promise myself your kidney?"

Sam shook his head. "I trust you."

They stared at each other over the rose as if trying to figure out how to start.

"How should we . . ." He trailed off.

And she finished, "Proceed?"

"Yeah, proceed."

"I'm not sure," she said, rubbing her hands over the jacket. "I'm so nervous. I wasn't sure if you needed porn or something more stimulating to get things going."

Sam cocked his head, confused. "Porn? It's not like we haven't done this before."

"It's different because this is official, right? You agreed to provide sperm, and there's all this pressure to perform. I have the kit set up on the bathroom counter for privacy—"

"Whoa, show me this kit?"

Wren saw his mouth twitch like he was trying not to laugh.

"Yes, it's an insemination kit." She took him to the bathroom and opened the door, revealing a towel on the counter along with the box's contents, including a sample cup.

Sam whistled. "That's intimidating."

"I know."

He stared at the bathroom counter for a long time before he turned her way, leaning against the doorframe. "Look, I don't want to cross a boundary, even though I feel like we already have, but can I be honest?"

"Sure," she said.

"Do we really need this? Can't we just . . . be us?" Sam reached out and took her hand in his. "We've had sex before, most recently two days ago, sans condom. We both enjoyed it, so why not cut out the middleman?" Sam glanced at the counter. "Or cup, as the case may be."

Wren blinked at him, emotions warring inside her. While the reference to them as an "us" made her heart beat faster and brought out the warm fuzzies in the pit of her stomach, she was mildly irritated that he didn't want to keep this professional.

Then again, he had a point. They'd already had unprotected sex multiple times, and sex with Sam was amazing.

"Did I say something wrong?" Sam asked, threading his fingers with hers.

"No, it's just . . . I can't believe Millie was right. You don't want to miss out on the fun."

"What?" he spluttered. "You talked to Millie about us?"

"No, I mean, we talked about insemination, and she said that whoever I chose would want to do it live instead of just into a cup because doing it was the fun part."

"I can't argue there," he said with a grin, pulling her into him as he backed her down the hallway. "Being inside you, tasting you? Definitely a blast." Sam nodded over her head. "Is this the way to your bedroom?"

"Yes," she murmured, letting him guide her.

"I can't wait to have you in a bed. We never seem to make it that far, do we?"

Wren shivered at his words. "So, we're just going to go about this the normal way?"

Sam chuckled, his breath rushing across the skin of her neck. "If you can call it that."

"In that case, I'm kind of prepared." Wren backed out of Sam's embrace once they stepped over the threshold of her room, and she unbuttoned her coat, letting it fall to the ground. Wren watched Sam's face as he took in the lacy number she'd donned that hugged her body, showing off her curves.

By his intense expression, she wouldn't be wearing it long.

"Damn, Birdy, you look fucking delicious."

Wren laughed. "Thanks. Unfortunately, you were not the first to see this tonight. I answered the door, thinking it was you, and it wasn't."

"Oh, damn." Sam reverently ran his hands over her arms, then wrapped his arms around her waist. "I would say something to make you feel better about flashing your brother, but everything that comes to mind would probably make you feel worse."

"I'm a little scared of what you think would be worse."

"At least you're hot?"

Wren smacked him in the arm with a squeal. "You're so gross!"

"I tried to tell you." Sam pulled her into his body, dipping his head to hover his mouth over hers. "Still want me?"

This wasn't supposed to be about wanting, but something about the way he said it melted every bone in her body, and Wren turned to mush in his arms. "Yes."

Sam kissed her tenderly, his fingers trailing their way up her back to her shoulders. "I keep thinking about Tuesday. I haven't been able to think about anything else for days."

Wren huffed softly. "Why? Because you got your bad girl back?"

He paused, fingering the straps of her lingerie. "I couldn't stop thinking about how fucking turned on I am when I'm making you happy."

His words lit through her like striking a match, and she caught fire, meeting his mouth in a slow-burn kiss. What was happening between them shouldn't involve emotions or need, but Sam's hands on the straps of her nightie, dragging them down over her arms, made her breasts tighten in anticipation. He exposed her flesh, pushing the lacy scrap of fabric to her waist, and bent over to blaze a series of kisses down the column of her throat and along her collarbone, dropping to his knees in front of her.

Sam stared at her, his hands covering her breasts, and she closed her eyes, concentrating on his touch. He ran his hands over her skin, fingers playing with her nipple, and she arched her back, heat pooling in her core. "You're so perfect, Birdy. Every part of you."

His mouth covered her left nipple, sucking it into his mouth and running his tongue over the tight bud in slow strokes.

Wren held on to his shoulders as he turned his ministration to the other breast, squeezing her left one in his hand, massaging it gently. Then he squeezed her sharply, and she gasped, the intensity of the contrast overwhelming. Her back muscles spasmed, and her knees trembled as he sucked her nipple hard and deep. Wren tangled her hands in his hair, holding on while trying to stay upright.

"So sensitive and responsive," Sam murmured, traveling down her stomach to where the lingerie gathered. He slipped the lace over her hips, exposing every inch of her, and with every piece of flesh he exposed, his mouth found contact. She stepped out of the nightie, staring down at him and his golden head as his tongue delved into her belly button. His eyes rolled up, staring into hers as his hand reached between their bodies, finding her with his fingers.

Wren leaned against the doorjamb, letting him lift one of her legs over his shoulder, eyes closing as bliss washed over her. His mouth and fingers worked her like she was an instrument, hell bent on making music with her body. She moaned as his tongue swept up her seam to her clit, and his fingers spread her labia, giving him better access. He flicked his tongue against her in rapid motions, giving her no quarter, and she gripped the doorjamb.

"Oh God," she whispered at the sudden fullness from multiple digits curling inside her, touching her spot in heavenly strokes that left her panting. Her fingernails dug into the wood as she bowed, the pressure inside her building until she was climbing to great heights, soaring into the air, weightless.

Suddenly, she was screaming with release, shaking with the force of her orgasm, and through the haze of pleasure, she heard Duke barking. Sam's laughter. It was too good.

She collapsed back against the hard wood of the doorframe, his tongue still softly soothing her raw pussy.

Sam stood slowly, kissing his way up her body until his mouth reached her ear.

"Did you know a woman is more likely to become pregnant if she orgasms?"

"What?" she whispered.

Sam lifted her into his arms and smiled down at her. "I said, did you know that a woman is more likely to become pregnant if she orgasms?"

"No. How do you know that?"

"I did a little research," he said, almost shyly. He lowered her onto her bed, hovering over her. Wren had changed the sheets earlier and straightened up the room, but he wasn't looking anywhere but at her.

"That is sweet, but why?" she asked.

"Because this is your dream, and I wanna make you happy. I was just excited that something I already do is gonna help the process."

Wren laughed softly, a sweetness spreading through her that he was here for her. That he'd looked up ways to help her get pregnant because she wanted it. While she was sure that he would enjoy the process, she was still blown away that he was here. Now. For this.

For her.

Despite the years apart and the misunderstandings, he still had her back.

"Ready?" he asked as he hovered over her.

Wren nodded. "Ready."

Chapter Twenty-one

Sam released a shaky breath, his cock flexing with the need to be inside her. To feel her heat. Hovering at the entrance of her body, Sam stared down at her, memorizing the softness in her gaze, the sweet curves of her face. Her stomach pressed against his and he imagined it round and full between them when she was carrying the child. His child. His balls tightened at the thought, and he thrust in, shallow and slow. Her lush lips parted as he slipped inside her. Her brown eyes earnestly stared back into his, and he wondered if she had a baby, would they have her eyes?

He had to keep reminding himself that this was all part of the plan, that he was here to give her a baby, and when they succeeded, this would stop. No more kissing Wren against buildings or licking her sweet pussy in doorways. Once he fulfilled his part, he'd go back to being her—what? Friend? Acquaintance?

"Hey," she whispered, her hand cupping his cheek. "Where did you go?"

Sam realized he was fully inside her, unmoving, hovering over her on his arms.

"I was just imagining the future."

"Don't," Wren said, running a finger over his lower lip. "Stay here with me."

Wren slipped her hands up behind his head and pulled him down to her, her tongue sweeping across his mouth, and he opened for her. Their kiss deepened, and he let her set the tone. Slow and steady.

Sam pulled out slightly and slipped back in, short, even strokes in and out. Wren broke their kiss with a gasp, holding on to the back of his neck to keep their faces close.

"Sam . . ." she whispered, hands moving to his shoulders. She held on, watching his face as she lifted her hips to meet his thrusts. "I can't believe you're here. Inside me. God, you feel so good. When I think about you coming inside me, it takes everything in me not to touch myself."

Suddenly he couldn't control himself, her words echoing his own racing thoughts. Since he'd exploded inside her the other day, all he could think about was doing it again. His body longed to move faster, but he wanted this to last. Thoughts of her warmth and her tight body surrounding him, squeezing him, were too much, and he picked up the pace, tension building like a volcano inside him when she wrapped her legs around his waist, holding him to her.

"Yes, God, faster. Harder. I want you so deep inside me— Oh!"

Sam had no trouble giving her exactly what she wanted, grabbing her ass and slamming into her. His balls tightened when she screamed his name, and he closed his eyes, shouting hers as he came with a violent shudder, his cock flexing inside her. He'd be embarrassed of how fast he came except this was the goal. This was the point, and oh, it felt good. It felt right.

When he finally stopped shaking, he kissed her sweetly, tenderly, and slipped to the side. He mourned the loss of her pussy warming his cock, but when he reached for her, dragging her against him so her ass was cradled in his lap, she let him wrap his arm around her waist and hold her to him.

"It's also good for you to stay lying on your back for a half hour," he murmured against the side of her neck.

"Hmmm, I'm good right here," she said, wiggling against him. He tightened his hold on her, and she placed her hand on his arm, her fingers drifting over the skin of his forearm. "For a second there, I thought you weren't going to go through with it."

Sam stayed silent for several minutes before he finally said, "Did you know that you're the only woman I've ever had sex with sans condom?"

Her hand stopped stroking him, her voice hesitant. "No, I didn't."

"When we did it before, I was young and thought the pill was foolproof. Besides, I was so in love with you, being inside you was the best thing in the world next to riding my motorcycle." His hand drifted over her stomach, his palm flattening against it. "I didn't hesitate, wrapped up in wanting you. It was fiery and intense.

"Tonight was different. I thought about you getting everything you wanted. I imagined what you'd look like with a child growing inside you, and I was so turned on, I nearly lost it right there."

Wren turned toward him, a wide grin on her face. "Do you have a breeding fetish?"

"What the heck is that?"

"That's when you are excited by getting women pregnant."

Sam scowled into her amused expression. "No, I do not have that. If I did, I'd have kids scattered all over the place."

"Maybe you just discovered it because the opportunity arose," she said, waggling her eyebrows.

Sam pressed her face against his chest, growling, "You be quiet and stop projecting your weirdness onto me."

"It's a real thing," Wren mumbled.

"I don't care, I don't have it."

"Alright, you aren't turned on by getting women pregnant. Just me," she teased, but Sam didn't argue because she wasn't wrong. His breeding kink—or whatever one would call it—was limited to Wren Little.

She kissed his chest, snuggling into him. "While I appreciate your enthusiastic help, thank you for signing the papers."

"You are welcome," he said, stalling a moment before adding, "I did want to ask you something."

"Yes," she said, her voice sounding groggy.

"When you get pregnant, are we going to still continue this until one of us is no longer interested? Or is it over when you find out?"

Wren didn't answer right away, and Sam wanted to kick himself for bringing it up, worried he'd scare her away.

Then she finally said, "I'm not sure. Maybe we just take it day by day?"

Sam kissed her forehead. "Sure, we'll do that."

He started to pull back and climb off the bed, but she held on to him. "Where are you going?"

"I didn't know if I should take off."

"Do you want to leave?" she asked.

"Not a chance."

Wren smiled, pulling him back onto the bed with her. "Then stay."

Sam curled his naked body into hers, listening as her breathing evened out and she fell asleep.

Unfortunately, sleep eluded him, and he extracted himself from her and got up, using the bathroom first. When he came out, he slipped on his boxer briefs from off the ground, and Wren's dog whined at him.

"Do you have to pee, too?" he asked the dog as if he expected to get an answer.

The dog pawed at the gate, and Sam squatted down, mumbling, "Just don't eat me if I let you out of here."

The dog calmly trotted out, heading for the back door. Sam checked and noted that it was fenced in, so he let the dog out. He went to the cupboard and grabbed a glass, filling it with ice water from the refrigerator door.

With a cup of water in one hand, he picked up the contract he'd signed and sat down with it, reading through as he took several long drinks. Nothing he wouldn't expect to logically see in an insemination contract, except the section where if the child becomes ill, he was required to get tested for organ matching.

I can't claim my child, but if something happens and they need a kidney, I have to give it up?

If the kid was sick, he would give up anything to make them healthy again. There wasn't even a question there.

Why was he even thinking about these things now, before the kid was born?

The dog scratched at the door, and Sam opened it, sitting back down at the table to read the rest of the contract. The dog came over to him and put his head in Sam's lap.

"Hey, buddy. You're a friendly one, aren't you?" Sam twisted his collar around so he could read his tag. "Duke. That's a good name." He rubbed his ears, listening to the dog moan in happiness as he finished reading the contract.

"What am I gonna do, Duke? I think I love your mistress, but she doesn't want a man in her life."

The dog whimpered, and Sam took it as a note of sympathy.

"Thanks. I appreciate you not wanting to rip off my balls for being in your house."

"Sam?" Wren called from the back bedroom.

Sam got up and put the contract back. "Yeah?"

"What are you doing?" she asked.

"Duke was whining, so I let him out." Sam looked down at the dog. "We better get back in there."

Duke trotted along beside him, heading straight for his kennel when they got back to the bedroom.

"Was I out long?" she asked.

"Only ten minutes or so."

She yawned. "Come back to bed."

Sam did what she asked, crawling under the covers and tucking her into his body.

"Wren?" he asked.

"Hmmm."

"Just so we're clear, if I donate a kidney, then I get to meet the kid."

Wren glanced up at him, confused. "What?"

"Your contact says if the kid gets sick, I have to get tested to see if I'm a match. I'm just telling you that if I donate a major organ, I get to meet him or her."

Wren pulled back, staring at his face. "You read the contract?"

"I did."

"And that's your only beef?" she asked.

"All I ask."

Wren shrugged. "Okay."

"Okay?"

"I'll amend the contract and get a copy sent to you."

"Or you can bring it by during our next session," he said, kissing her forehead. "If this is going to work, we are going to have to do this every day, maybe even multiple times."

Wren smirked. "Whatever you say, boss."

Chapter Twenty-two

Wren walked down the rows of trees inside the community center with Duke at her side, studying each beautifully decorated spruce and fir with a smile. The Festival of Trees was one of the biggest charity events of the season, and the organizers had asked a couple of officers to rotate throughout the day to keep an eye on things. Not that there was usually any trouble at this event, but after Wren's conversation with the chief in regard to the Christmas Bandit, it was decided that they could never be too careful, especially with the amount of money that exchanged hands during the event. Although she'd rather be out patrolling the streets, it was fun to at least see some of the Mistletoe holiday events. Wren thought about her Christmas tree sitting in a bucket with bare limbs in her living room. If she ever got the chance to get over to A Shop for All Seasons before it closed, maybe she would grab a few special ornaments to start off her collection. Wren had very few that had survived her childhood, and although she imagined many handmade ornaments in her future, it would be years before that came to pass.

Wren was still coming down from the high of being with Sam and couldn't believe that this was all happening. He had stayed over last night, too, and they'd made love twice more throughout the night with no talk about what was best for insemination or anything like that. They'd just spent time together, snuggling and watching TV. It had been wonderful.

Wren kept thinking about Sam's question, about whether what they were doing would stop once she got pregnant. If this was just an arrangement, then everything else should end once it had been fulfilled, right? So why was it hard to think of Sam not being a part of her life now that they had reconnected? It wasn't just that he was incredible in bed, which he was, but that he was kind and supportive. Funny and infuriating. He made her smile, and when he wasn't around, she missed him.

You were the one who said that you didn't want a relationship. Are you changing your mind already?

Wren was so confused by what she wanted and didn't want. She'd never been around anyone like Sam, who made her feel comfortable and at peace. Her first instinct was to tell him they'd continue until one of them wanted to stop, but would that get complicated if she became pregnant? Would watching her make decisions in regard to the future for her and the baby be painful for him?

The last thing Wren wanted to do was hurt Sam. He'd given her everything, including a reason to smile again.

"Hey, Wren!" Millie said, coming over to join her in front of the trees. "You were zoning out. How's it going?"

"Oh, it's going," she said, waving her hand to indicate the rows of evergreens. "Just checking out all the trees."

"They are really pretty," Millie said, reaching out to finger a glass piano ornament on the music store's tree. "Unfortunately, I know I would never be able to keep the tree and ornaments in one piece at my house with my two cats who live to destroy everything I love."

"Sounds like two creatures that need to be taught some manners," Wren said.

Millie snorted. "Cats are rude dudes with attitudes, but I love my babies."

"I know you do," Wren said, smiling at her friend. She turned her attention back to the trees, scanning some of the glittering, glass ornaments that caught her eye. "They are pretty to look at, but I don't know if I'd want a theme for my own tree."

"Did you get a tree this year?" Millie asked. Usually, Wren pulled out a Charlie Brown Christmas Tree statue and sent Millie a pic with her gifts around it.

"My dad bought me one, but it's just sitting in my living room, staring at me with distain, wondering why I haven't decorated it yet."

"Why haven't you?"

"Because that involves going and buying ornaments and tinsel."

Millie laughed. "You make it sound like a trip to the dentist."

"I don't know why I'm not excited about decorating a tree. It's almost overwhelming, because eventually, I will include other ornaments that remind me of people I love. It feels like a waste to go purchase a bunch of balls so that my tree gets decorated, when I know I'm eventually going to replace them."

"This sounds like the tree is a metaphor for something bigger going on in your life," Millie said suspiciously.

"Maybe it is," Wren murmured, turning the corner with Duke and Millie. She stopped in front of the A Shop For All Seasons' tree. "I should bid on this one. It is pretty and has a variety of ornaments. There will be at least a couple I like."

"Don't be silly. You can get ornaments you want online without buying a whole tree." Millie slipped her arm through Wren's and added, "By the way, how are things going tracking down the Christmas Bandit?"

"Not great. He struck again yesterday when I was off. A blowup Frosty went missing from a home on the south side of town."

"That is crazy. I wonder what he's doing with it all?"

"Probably selling it online for drugs or money," Wren said.

"Would he get a lot for it?" Millie asked.

"I'm not sure. 'Tis the season to overspend."

"Hmmm," Millie said before laughing. "Nah. Even if I wanted to, I am not hard-core enough to be a criminal mastermind." Millie lowered her voice and leaned in close. "By the way, how is Operation Get the Splooge going?"

"Ugh, that's gross, don't call it that."

"Sorry, I was just curious."

"As it happens, there has been a new development."

"Go on," Millie said.

"Sam agreed to inseminate me."

Millie stopped suddenly. "No way? Did you make him go through the whole home kit thing?"

"No, he thought that was a bit complicated."

"It is, but then what? Did you find a clinic for him to donate semen to?"

"Not exactly," she said, concentrating deeply on an ornament of a man skiing. Although Millie had been behind Operation Find a Guy and Pick, Wren never thought she was being serious. Heck, Wren had never imagined that she, herself, could be serious until she'd been presented with the two things she wanted most: Sam and a baby.

"Are you saying that you are barebacking it with Sam in the hopes of getting pregnant?" When Wren looked away, her cheeks burning, Millie said, "Oh, Wren."

"Why do you say it like that?" Wren asked defensively. "Sam agreed to it. I didn't force or blackmail him. He even signed papers giving up his parental rights."

"And that's not gonna be weird? Having his baby and walking around town pretending like he's just kind of there?" Millie shook her head. "I know I said look at Mindy Kaling living her best life and pick a sperm, but I didn't think you'd actually do it!"

"I know it's a little controversial, but I think this is gonna be what's best."

"For who?"

Wren wasn't sure how to answer that, especially when she'd already been dwelling way too much on how much she loved having Sam around.

"I guess we'll see."

"When did all this get started?" Millie asked.

"Well, we did it once Tuesday, and then we did it several times Thursday and last night. If he comes over tonight, too . . ."

"I get the picture." Millie gave her a suspicious look. "Are you enjoying this?"

"Depends on what you mean. Sam is a very considerate man in the bedroom, which helps, because according to experts, it's important for the mother to orgasm to increase the chances of conception."

"Oh God." Millie shook her head. "This is the weirdest thing I have ever heard outside of a Hollywood gossip magazine."

"Oh, come on, it's not weird to enjoy sleeping with someone."

"You're doing a little more than sleeping."

"Can we move on?" Wren asked.

"Sure, but I'm just wondering, if you've got his tadpoles, should I just call him Prince Frog?"

"Don't be a jerk," she said.

"Truth?" Millie asked.

"As if I could stop you."

"I think you are going to put yourself in an uncomfortable position when you realize that you are in love with him."

"I am not in love with Sam."

"You were in love with Sam nineteen years ago, and that is the reason why you have never moved on. Now you're going to get pregnant with his child, and he is going to think you want nothing more to do with him."

"I was in love with him, past tense. Then I grew up and realized I don't want a relationship because I saw what it did to my parents. That is why I never got serious with anyone else, not because I was carrying a torch for him."

"Bullshit," Millie said, lowering her voice when a few people passed by the end of the aisle. "The true reason is, he has always held your heart, and this is your way of keeping him close subconsciously. You think that if you do this pregnancy with him, eventually you two are just going to fall back into a relationship, and you won't have to admit that you want to be with him."

"I'm walking away from you," Wren said, skipping over the Parks and Rec tree and stopping in front of the tattoo parlor's tree. The ornaments were various and abstract. Some of them were painted glass balls, with the pastel colors of a sunset, while others were darker. Wren fingered a skull with red eyes, wondering who had chosen this tattoo and where they'd put it.

They were all signed with the initials of the tattoo artist who created them, and Wren found herself looking for all the ones that read S. G.

"Hey," someone shouted, the voice echoing throughout the metal building. "Someone stole my wreaths out of the back of my truck!"

Wren took off without saying goodbye to Millie, Duke running next to her. Wren reached the front entrance where a middle-aged man was angrily pointing outside.

"What happened?" Wren asked, telling Duke to sit.

"I was loading up the stuff that I bought into the back of my truck. I turned around to talk to a friend on the phone, and suddenly, I see this guy hanging over the edge of my truck bed helping himself to two of my wreaths. When I yelled at him, he took off running toward the woods with one on each arm!"

"Could you give me a description of the man?" she asked, pulling out her notepad and pen.

"I don't know. Teenager maybe? I didn't get a good look at his face, but he was skinny. He had his hood pulled up, but I could tell by his hands he was white. He didn't take off that long ago; can't you just go get him?"

Wren nodded, heading in the direction he indicated. It was after five in the evening, so it was already dark outside. Pulling her flashlight from her utility belt, she scanned the trees and made her way several steps in.

"Duke, heel." The last thing she needed was her dog to take off searching for a suspect in the dark and end up facing off with an angry bear.

"Hey, Wren!" She turned toward the sound of her name and saw Sam standing outside one of the community center's side doors with a couple of women. They glanced her way briefly, but then their focus returned to Sam, gazing at him in adoration, and Wren frowned.

"Oh, hi," she said, searching the tree line for movement. It was better than watching Sam's fan club fawn all over him.

Sam jogged over, stopping next to her. "What are you looking for?"

"Did you see a man run by in a hoodie?" she asked, noticing the women were following him. *Great.*

"No, but we only just walked out. I was helping them load their tree in the back of their truck—"

"Sam," a petite brunette called out, linking her arm with his. "I was trying to ask you about that tattoo on your arm with the ladybug and the leaf. The watercolors are gorgeous. If I did something similar, where would it look best on me?"

Wren's eyes narrowed at the other woman's grip on him, and it was on the tip of her tongue to tell the woman to get her mitts off Sam. Duke seemed to sense her unease, and to her surprise, he approached Sam and the brunette without being released by verbal command, and Wren watched in horror as he pushed his way between them, nearly knocking the woman over.

"Duke, come," Wren said, laughter bubbling under her breath. "Sorry, he's working right now, and you're in his space."

"We should go back inside and let the officer do her job," the woman said, reaching for Sam again.

"I'm sure he can make it without you hanging on him," Wren snapped, stiffening when she realized that she sounded like a jealous girlfriend.

Jealousy! Where had that come from? She didn't have time for jealousy.

"I— I gotta go," Wren said, ignoring Sam's smug, smiling face, and she took off for a closer look at the woods, cursing herself under her breath. Why was she behaving so stupidly? Just because some woman had attached herself to Sam like a leech didn't mean he was interested, and even if he was, Wren didn't own him. He could do whatever he wanted.

On her way deeper into the trees, Wren shined her flashlight, but all she saw was a red velvet bow on the ground. She picked it up and kept looking around, waiting for her flashlight to illuminate more missing pieces.

Duke whined, taking a few steps toward the darkness, and Wren shook her head. "Heel, Duke. Even if he's in there, I don't need you chasing him down when I can't keep up." Tucking her flashlight back into her belt, she ordered, "Let's go."

Sam was waiting for her on the side of the building, but he was alone.

"He didn't catch your Christmas Bandit?" Sam asked, pointing at Duke.

"I didn't want to let him loose when it's too dark for me to follow safely. Especially not for a couple fifty-dollar wreaths." Wren shook her head. "Why anyone would want to steal a couple wreaths is weird."

"Maybe they're decorating their house in order to win the best display?" Sam offered.

"Well, an extra-large ornament did go missing from another person's house." Wren smiled, forgetting for a moment she'd been irritated with him. "Could be he's making a wreath toss?"

Sam chuckled. "Who'd have thought Mistletoe would end up with our very own Grinch?"

"No idea. All I know is that he's skinny and young. Now the back of a truck." Wren shook her head.

Sam pushed off the wall, falling into step next to her. "So how are you going to catch him?"

"I don't know. Figure out why he's doing it and set a trap?"

"That could work." Sam stopped next to her, nodding. "What was that thing Duke did, pushing his way next to me?"

"Uh, I have no idea. I think it's all the food you've been sneaking him. I guess he's claimed you."

"So, not a command from you to keep Ilsa Potter away from me?"

"Who is Ilsa Potter?" Wren grumbled, knowing dang well she was the pushy brunette.

"Never mind, I must have imagined it," he muttered. "Are you still off at six?"

"Barring an emergency, yes. Why?" she asked.

"I thought maybe we could go get some food. Listen to some music and hang out."

"I don't know. I'm kind of tired. Plus, I have to figure out what I'm doing with my Christmas tree."

Sam chuckled. "You mean, the one you set up in the corner of your living room in the Home Depot bucket?"

"Yes, smart-ass," Wren said, because Sam was the one who'd helped pick it out. "I just don't know what to do with it. I don't have any ornaments and don't feel like running around town looking, even when I do have time. I could order them online, but most of them wouldn't make it by Christmas anyway."

"What if we made ornaments?" he asked.

"What?"

"Yeah, why not? I've got all kinds of stuff that we used to make ornaments for the tattoo parlor's tree. I can pick up some food, and you can come over to my place, and we'll make ornaments for your tree."

"That's sweet, but I have Duke."

"Bring him. I'll put a big blanket down, and he can chill while we create."

Wren pursed her lips. "You're serious about this?"

"Course I am. Now, what do you say? Do you wanna do some crafting with me?"

Wren forgot all about the girl hanging on him and Millie's opinion of their arrangement, because making ornaments with Sam sounded like fun to her.

"I'm in."

Chapter Twenty-three

W hat made you guys decide to make your own ornaments instead of just buying some really pretty ones that had to do with tattoos and art?"

Sam sat at the table with Wren, holding a glass ball in his hand as he swirled paint on the inside of it, coating it in white, red, green, and pink. The kitchen table was covered in black trash bags, protecting the surface from paint and glue. As promised, he'd laid a thick blanket on the floor for Duke, who was curled up on his side, snoring.

"I guess when you're artistic," Sam said, turning the ball in his hands until it was fully coated, "it's hard to not want some control over how you're viewed by the world."

"Do you get along with the people you work with?" Wren asked, dabbing glue on a red pom-pom.

"I do, but I also have a hard time trusting people after what happened in Oregon, so we're not close. Especially since I want to go out on my own eventually. They're the only tattoo parlor in town, so I'll have to look at opening in Fairfield or somewhere else. I don't wanna burn any bridges, especially since my current boss has been good to me."

"That makes sense. Is the owner anywhere near wanting to retire?"

"No, she's been here for fifteen years, and she wants to stick around for probably another twenty before she calls it."

"That sucks," she said.

"It is what it is." Sam sat up straighter, checking out her side of the table. "What are you making over there?"

Wren covered up her workspace, shaking her head. "This is a surprise. You don't get to be nosy."

Sam chuckled. "Alright, fine, I'll just focus on my stuff."

He poured the excess paint from inside the ornament onto a canvas and tilted it several different ways, watching the paint spread out over the surface. He set his ornament down to dry with the open end up, then he picked up a paintbrush and used it to cover the rest of the canvas.

"What are you gonna do with that?"

"That's for me to know and you to find out," he said.

"Oh, so that's how we're gonna play this?"

Sam arched a brow, staring at her. "You started it, not wanting to show me what you're making."

"I'm embarrassed because you are an artist and I am not." She held up her Popsicle stick reindeer with buggy eyes and a puffy red nose. "Obviously."

Sam tilted his head to the side and laughed. "I don't know. I mean, it's got a little something."

"Yeah, it's got something alright. It's got 'a fifth grader made this' vibes."

"You have talent in other places, Wren," he said, smirking. "You can't be the best at everything."

"Well, I think that sucks," she said with a sigh. She pointed her Rudolph ornament at him. "So are you gonna tell me what you're making?"

"I'm making a ball ornament with swirls on the inside, and I am going to paint a design on the outside."

"What kind of design?" she asked.

"I want it to be a surprise."

She huffed, picking up one of the clear glass balls and setting it in front of her. "I'm surprised that you guys bought Popsicle sticks and stuff to make reindeer and snowmen."

"Oh no, I got that special just for you," he said.

Wren scowled. "What do you mean?"

"I stopped by the market and grabbed a few of those kid ornament-making kits for you."

Wren threw a white pom at him. "You think you're a funny guy, huh?"

"I am a funny guy," he said.

"Just ask your fan club," Wren grumbled.

Sam slapped his hands against the surface of the table with a whoop, startling Wren and waking up Duke. "I knew it."

"You knew what?"

"Seeing Ilsa talking to me bothered you."

Wren snorted. "Please, she was doing more than talking to you."

"How do you mean?" he asked.

Wren sighed. "Seeing you with another girl hanging all over you bothered me."

"I don't know how to take that, since we really were just talking, and more to the point, you aren't interested in anything from me, right? So what's with the note of jealousy I'm hearing?"

"That's why I debated even saying anything," Wren said, avoiding his gaze. "I was just pointing out that if I acted a little weird earlier, that's why."

"Because you were bothered that girls were quote, unquote hanging on me?"

"Maybe a little more than bothered, since my Taser hand was twitching."

Sam chuckled. "Well, if it makes you feel any better, I am not doing anything with anyone else in town."

"That does make me feel a little better," she said softly, pouring two shades of green and baby pink into the glass ball, then swirling the paint inside.

Sam didn't understand how she could admit to being jealous and yet act as though him promising to be monogamous wasn't a big deal.

"What about you?" he asked, fighting his aggravation. "Are you going to be seeing anyone else from town?"

"No, I hadn't planned on it." She dumped the excess paint on a palette, casually adding, "I'm concentrating on one thing here. I don't need to complicate my life by having a harem of fuckboys waiting in the wings."

Sam's jaw clenched. "You are so funny I forgot to laugh."

Wren looked up from her project, watching him thoughtfully. "It really does bother you."

"What, the term 'fuckboy'? Yeah, it does because you've used it to describe me."

"I'm sorry, but to be fair, that was before I got to know you again."

"Well, to set the record straight, I'm not a boy. Second of all, I have a brain. I have talent. I have ambitions, and I don't want to be reduced to a tool that someone uses to scratch an itch."

"Sam," she said, getting up and rounding the table, settling onto his lap. "You're not a tool."

"Thanks," he grumbled.

She kissed him soundly before she got up and whispered in his ear, "However, your tool is fantastic."

Sam laughed, smacking her ass, and she squealed, rubbing her posterior all the way back to her seat. Sam picked up the paintbrush again, smiling as he made little strokes, concentrating on his task. He could feel her eyes on him, watching, and he caught her gaze.

"What?" he asked.

"Nothing. You're just adorable. Even with your tongue sticking out of the corner of your mouth."

Sam hadn't realized he'd been doing that and tucked his tongue back into his mouth.

"I wonder if our kid will do that when he or she is concentrating," she mused.

Sam's heart skipped a beat, imagining a little boy with blond hair biting his tongue as he helped his mom do something. Would she think of him?

"Sam," she whispered, catching his attention. "I know you offered to do this for me, but if this is too much, we can stop now. I'm sure we haven't succeeded yet."

"Why are you sure that we haven't succeeded?" he asked.

"I don't know. I thought this was something that usually took most people some time."

"Well, we're not like most people," Sam said, tired of his heart seizing every time he thought she was going to bail on him. "I'm not backing out of this. I told you I would do it. I signed a contract, and I'm going to see it through."

Wren cleared her throat. "Thank you very much. I appreciate your friendship."

"You're welcome, although I'd rather you didn't thank me," he said gruffly.

"Sorry."

Sam put his brush down and studied his handiwork. "Do you want to see what I was doing with my ornaments?"

"Yes, I do."

He turned the ball around and in beautiful calligraphy, it read *Baby's First Christmas*.

"Even though I can't be in the kid's life, he'll have something in it from me," Sam said, setting the ornament in the egg carton he'd grabbed to let it dry, pain twisting inside him like rope being tightened with every turn.

"Sam, it's lovely."

"Thanks," he said, his chest squeezing so tight he was afraid he might pass out. He got up from the table before he made a fool of himself.

"Where are you going?" she asked.

"I'm getting some air." Sam grabbed his coat from the hook by the front door. "I'll be right back."

"Okay."

Sam didn't like the hurt he heard in that one word, but damn it, could Wren really not see how this was killing him? Not even the kid part, but the fact that it hadn't taken much for him to fall in love with her again, although this time was different. She wasn't the same wild child she'd been, and he respected the calm, collected woman who could walk into an unstable situation and put everyone at ease. The way her mood could shift from sassy to playful, keeping him on his toes. The way her touch could leave him weak, desiring her with an intensity that made him want to keep her in his arms forever.

Wren couldn't see any of that, though. She thought that he was just being a good friend, that offering her a part of him without any strings attached was just him being supportive. Part of him had hoped that by being there for her, she'd realize her love for him, too, but that hadn't happened.

The door opened behind him, and Wren stepped out, her jacket zipped under her chin.

"Hey, what are you doing out here?" he asked.

"I feel like you need this," Wren said, wrapping her arms around his waist and pulling him in close.

Sam's arms returned the embrace, his lips pressed against her hair. "Thanks."

"Sam?"

"Yeah?"

"Maybe you'd like to come over and help me decorate the tree, since you don't have one?"

She had no idea how painful that sweet invitation was to hear. Wren wanted him to be part of something special, but couldn't see the significance. Trees were for couples. For families to decorate as they changed and grew.

Yet just like everything else she'd ever asked, Sam couldn't say no. "Sounds like fun."

Chapter Twenty-four

This time, Wren didn't sneak out on Sam in the morning. Instead, she kissed him goodbye before she left, whispering, "I'll call you later."

"Where are you off to in such a hurry?" he mumbled sleepily.

"I have to get home and get ready for lunch with my family." Plus, Duke usually got breakfast around this time, but Sam's eyes were closed, so she didn't bother explaining the rest.

"Well, have fun. I'll miss you."

Wren's heart squeezed at his barely audible whisper. Even though she knew Sam was half asleep, she thought he might actually mean it.

And if he did mean it, how did she feel about that?

So many things had shifted between them, especially last night. They'd gone from reconnecting sexually to becoming friends. Then last night she'd been so moved by his gift that she couldn't resist touching him. It was strange because up until she had returned to Mistletoe, she knew exactly who she was and what she wanted, but this place seemed to change her every day. It was like the warmth of the people and tight-knit community of the town made being alone almost impossible. There was so much to share with someone, and the person she'd been reaching out to the most was Sam.

After they'd gone to her place and fed Duke last night, they'd decorated the tree, then curled up on the couch under a blanket to admire it. She'd been overwhelmed with the idea that they'd created this beautiful tree together and that they could be creating a baby, but then the heaviest thought of all hit her like a ton of bricks.

What they had together felt like a real relationship, maybe even one that wouldn't turn to stone after a few years. Or was that just her wishful thinking? They had been apart for so long, imagining that they could be together. But maybe because Wren was nostalgic, she was seeing things that weren't real. The only time she'd ever been in love was when she was a teenager, and it had torn her apart to let him go. When she'd found out that she hadn't needed to, that they could've spent the last nineteen years together, it ate her up inside. What would their life look like? Would he have followed her to Arizona while she went to school? Would Sam have opened a tattoo shop there? Would she have left the police force in Arizona and moved on, or would they have stayed there because of his dream? Maybe he would have followed her to her next job in Houston and loved it there. Would her father have forgiven them both or gone through with his threat?

If Wren had told Sam that she'd taken a pregnancy test all those years ago, would it have ended the same way, with a false positive and her period starting a few days after he left? Even when it had turned out to be nothing, if she'd told him, would he have stayed no matter what?

She thought about that moment all the time. Deep in her heart, Wren knew Sam would have taken on all her father's wrath if she'd given him hope. Especially if he'd known the reason her father lost his head that day.

Even now, with his paper signed and his parental rights terminated, she couldn't imagine Sam not being there for her or the baby.

Suddenly, shame overwhelmed her, so intense that tears pricked her eyes. How had she been so selfish, so cruel? Despite what was said about him in town, Sam had always been good to her. He was kind. He was strong. He was honest and trustworthy. He was a catch, and she'd done the same thing every other woman in town had.

Wren had made him think he was less than.

That sick feeling became more intense when she pulled into her driveway and saw that it wasn't Pete's truck parked in his usual spot, but her father's. He was sitting on the top step, waiting for her when she got out of her car and waved at him.

"Aren't I seeing you in a few hours?" she asked, climbing the steps where he was sitting.

"Yes, but," he said, getting to his feet with a groan, "I thought we might want to talk away from the family."

"Oh, that sounds ominous." Wren wiped at her eyes as she passed him, realizing that she had tear streaks on her face.

"Have you been crying?" he asked.

"Yes, but nobody made me cry. I was just crying."

"People don't just cry."

He followed her into the house, and Wren hung up her jacket while he greeted Duke.

"Hey, bud."

"Women cry all the time, and people blame hormones. You can blame our overactive imaginations. Heck, you can even blame female hysteria, because apparently, it's still on the books as a ticketable offense." The last was said with an air of irritability, and Robert Little gave her a quizzical look.

"Are you okay?" her dad asked, sitting down on her couch. Duke immediately put his head in Robert's lap, sitting by his side.

No, because I've made a mess of my life, and I don't know how to fix it.

"I really don't know, Dad."

He seemed to be waiting for her to elaborate, and when she didn't, he said, "I guess we could start with an easier question. Where were you coming from this morning?"

"Sam's place," she said, waiting for the snarcasm to start.

He didn't acknowledge her answer, waving his hand toward her Christmas tree. "I see you got your tree up."

"Yeah, and I even decorated it."

He walked over to the ornaments she and Sam had made last night. They'd come over after their moment on his porch and fed Duke before getting to work on the tree. She'd even found the tree base so they could get it out of the bucket. After they'd snuggled a while on her couch, they'd headed back to his place and made love.

"Who helped you make all these?" he asked, fingering an orange ball with a sunset painted on the front.

"Why do you think I didn't make them all myself?"

Her dad smiled at her as he walked back to the couch and sat. "I love you, sweetheart, but you're not exactly the artistic type. I still have a drawing you gave me when you were sixteen that looks like a cross-eyed four-year-old did it."

"That's mean and inaccurate," Wren said dryly. "Sam helped me do them. He came over here last night after making the ornaments, and we decorated. Then we went back to his place."

"So that started up again?" he said, his tone resigned.

And there it was. The snarcasm. "Nothing 'started up,' and even if it had, I don't wanna get into it with you."

Her dad's expression turned thunderous. "What does that mean?"

Wren threw her hands up. "I don't know. You've never liked Sam, and I've kind of made things overcomplicated. So, if I was going to get it off my chest, I'd rather talk to someone who won't tell me to just 'dump him.'"

"Isn't complicated enough? What does 'overcomplicated' mean?" For a moment, she thought he was trying not to laugh. His amusement rubbed her wrong, and suddenly, she was furious.

"You're making fun of me, but I have spent so much time thinking about you and Mom—"

"Honey—"

"No, let me finish please," Wren said, pacing the floor. "When Mom left and you were so sad, I was angry. I assumed it was something us kids had done that drove her away, and then I thought it was you. That she was so angry at you, she refused to come back. Then I went to meet her, and I realized that it was her. She didn't want to be a wife and mother, but I couldn't see that at the time. I thought that maybe if she had left you sooner, she would've been happy and she would've loved us still." Wren sighed, her shoulders slumping with the release of her frustration. "It took me a long time to realize that she did what society said she was supposed to by getting married and having kids, and she was miserable. And instead of trying to find the joy in the life she had and continuing a relationship with her children, she left. But you didn't."

"No, I didn't," he said, shooting her a wry smile. "Although I'm sure there are times in your childhood when you wished that I had."

"No. As mad as I was at you at times, I never wanted you out of my life." Wren hesitated, unsure if she wanted an honest answer to her next question. "Would you have called in charges if I hadn't given Sam up?"

Her dad sighed, running his hands over his face. "I wanted to. You have no idea what it's like to try and do everything you can to keep your kids safe and happy and on the right track. Then you find a pregnancy test in your kid's bathroom, and it can only belong to your seventeen-year-old daughter."

"I was technically sixteen."

"Yeah, you don't need to remind me of that," he said dryly. "I was a mess. I was running on anger and terror, and all I could think about was your future. I saw that eighteen-year-old as a man on a motorcycle with no prospects. I pictured you staying in Mistletoe, moving into some dump apartment because that's all you guys could afford. I saw you repeating your mother's life and being miserable because we got married too young and the passion faded. When real life settled in, we were not prepared for it, and that's why we fell apart. I didn't want that for you, and I thought that if I could scare him away, it would save you."

"But what if there had been a baby and I chose to keep it?"

"I would've helped make sure you could still continue your education. The last thing I want to do is fail you, and sometimes that comes through as me trying to control you, but that's just because I've been there. I know what it's like to make mistakes, and I didn't want that for any of you."

"Dad," Wren said, sitting next to him. "You didn't fail anyone, but you have to let us make our own decisions. You can give us an opinion, but treating us like we're still kids and calling us stupid doesn't work. I've decided that having a child on my own at thirty-five, with a good job and a house, is what I want to do. That's my decision, and you need to respect it and be the best grandfather you can."

"Is that really what you're going to do? Are you going to go to one of those clinics and pick a man out of a book?"

She laughed. "Did you see that on television?"

"Is that not how it's done?" he asked innocently.

"There are other ways. They have at-home kits now, so if you have somebody who's willing to donate, you can take care of it yourself."

He put his hands on his forehead, massaging it. "Are you interviewing potential fathers for my unborn grandchild here in Mistletoe?"

She laughed. "No, although it was topic of conversation between me and Millie one night over a pint of ice cream."

"God help me."

Wren patted her dad's shoulder. "I have a friend who offered to help. Now I'm worried that I may have made things weird between us."

"Does this friend drive a motorcycle and bring back PTSD to your father?" he grumbled.

Wren laughed. "Most definitely."

Her father grunted. "Well, maybe some artistic ability will rub off on the kid."

"Dad!" She laughed. "It hasn't happened yet, and now that all this other stuff has come up, I'm not sure if it will."

"Do you want to talk about other stuff with me?" he asked.

"I'd like to get through a conversation without you telling me what an idiot I am first."

"Sweetheart, I am so used to boys. I grew up with boys. My mother didn't have any girls. My dad was hard on me. It's just the way I was raised. Sometimes I'm a little tactless and forget you need something different from me, but I wanted you to be tough."

"I know, and I'm grateful because if you hadn't raised me the same as my brothers, I wouldn't have been able to live this incredible life that I have. I wouldn't be as strong and self-assured as I am, but right now, I just need you to listen and be my dad and tell me if I'm crazy."

"Lay it on me, and I promise to tell you if you're crazy," he said.

"When I first got back to town, I was angry at Sam because he left me all those years ago, and I was angry with you for a long time because of everything you'd done to make him leave. Then he and I had a moment—"

Her father held up his hand. "I don't need details."

"And we talked, and he told me about a letter he left in a tree trunk." Her dad looked away, confirming her suspicions.

"You took my letter, didn't you?" she said softly, fury spreading through her body like a fever, her skin pricking with heat.

He glanced at the ground, avoiding her gaze. His voice came out soft and gruff with more emotion than she'd seen from him in years. "I was afraid you were planning on running off with him, so yes, I took your letter. After a while, it seemed like you'd moved on, and it didn't make sense to give it to you, especially after you got accepted to college in Arizona."

"But you kept vital information from me," she snapped, her voice thick and trembling.

"You're right. I shouldn't have kept it from you."

"No, you don't understand how much I loved him. Giving him up broke something inside me, and I never healed from it, not until I came back here and saw him again." Wren's tears spilled over, and she dashed at them angrily. "When he told me about the letter, that was the moment I believed that he hadn't abandoned me. I didn't even need to see the letter to know that he had written it, because deep down, I knew he wouldn't lie to me. I think a part of me had created this wall because I felt so betrayed by him not fighting for me. But now I know that even after I told him to leave back then, and I gave him so much crap when I got back, he didn't give up. He brought something to life inside me I hadn't even realized was dead. When you told me that my desire to have a child on my own was crazy, he supported me and does these amazing things, like help me decorate my Christmas tree." Wren took a deep, bracing breath in an attempt to rein in her emotions, and she admitted, "I don't think I ever stopped loving him, and the thought that I might have had another life with him, a life you stole, is unforgivable."

Wren got up from the step, and her father leaped to his feet, grasping her hand. "Please, Wren. I know I was wrong, and that I should have told you a long time ago. I don't always make the right calls. I know I can't change what I did, but I will do everything in my power to make it up to you, to earn your forgiveness."

She stared down at his big hand wrapped around hers and shook her head. "Why do you care? You spend most of the time ignoring my existence, so why do you care if I forgive you or not?"

"Because you're my daughter, and I love you. I might struggle with showing my softer side, but you kids are my world. I would do anything to protect you, to make sure that you have an amazing life. Maybe that made me a little controlling—" Wren cleared her throat, and he conceded, "or a lot. But please know, I wasn't being malicious. I thought I was doing what's best for you."

Wren wasn't quite ready to fully let him off the hook, but she could at least see how he thought that he was protecting her. He didn't want her to become a dissatisfied housewife, stuck in a loveless marriage.

Her dad didn't want her to relive his life.

Wren squeezed his hand gently, her expression solemn. "It's going to take time, but I'll try to forgive you."

"Thank you," her dad said, pulling her in for a hard hug. The smell of cedar and smoke wrapped around her like a familiar cloak, and she laid her cheek against his chest, having forgotten how good a hug from her dad could feel.

When he finally released her, he asked, "Can I ask why you're going along with this arrangement if you love Sam Griffin? Why don't you just be with him, and if a child comes from it, deal with it together."

"I'm afraid if I tell him, it's all going to blow up in my face."

"Wren," her dad said, covering her hands with his, "it doesn't matter that after thirteen years together, your mom walked out and found a whole new life. The good times we had together included love, sorrow, and growth. They were amazing, and I don't regret them, not for a single second. Especially because they gave me you kids."

"Even Pete? Have you seen him eat chips?" Wren asked, making a face. "It's disgusting."

"Yes, even Pete with his chips and Garrett with his pit stains."

Wren laughed and gagged at the same time. "Gross! Who taught him to do laundry?"

"Apparently me, and I failed miserably."

When they sobered, Wren squeezed his hands. "Thanks for talking to me, Dad."

"I'm here for you. Even when you might not like what I have to say, I'm here."

Chapter Twenty-five

Sam and Clark were sitting in Clark's living room, drinking a couple of beers together. Merry was with her committee, talking about the Mistletoe Winter Games and the last few little wrap-ups for the Mistletoe Christmas season while Jace was at a sleepover. The two brothers hadn't had a lot of time together lately, so Sam was enjoying the one-on-one hangout.

"How are things going with getting your shop? Is there any chance your boss wants to retire in the next year?" Clark asked.

"She's only forty-five, dude. She wants to keep going for years to come, so if I'm gonna set up shop, I'm gonna have to find a place outside of town." Sam sighed. "Honestly, I'm wondering if it's worth the headache. Besides, both her and her husband are good to me. I make my own schedule. I just give her rent for my station, and the rest is up to me, so it's like being my own boss."

"Sounds like you have the benefits of your own business without the headache. Why don't you stay there and continue to do what you love but save money for other things? If you have to leave Mistletoe in order to start a new shop, it kind of defeats the purpose of moving back, doesn't it? I thought the point of being here was to be close to your nephew and watch him grow up."

"I guess it's hard to let go of something that's been your dream since you were a kid."

"Do you really want to make schedules and pay for repairs and deal with disgruntled employees?"

Sam squeezed his eyes shut. "That actually sounds like a massive headache."

"It is. I might not own the tree farm, but I still have to deal with people calling out sick and getting the schedule covered. Then there are the constant calls when there are issues—"

"I get the picture."

"What about settling down or having a family?" Clark asked.

Sam's chest tightened at the thought of Wren and having a child with her. Of the two of them building a life. But he wasn't sure if she would ever realize they should be together or if it was a pipe dream to stick around, support her, and always be in the background until she hopefully got over her fear.

"I've thought about that a lot lately, especially with Wren coming back to town, but there are a lot of factors to it," Sam said.

"I thought you guys were hanging out a lot, and things were progressing?"

"They are, just . . . not in the way you think." This was an awkward conversation to have with his little brother, but here goes. "I offered to help Wren have a baby."

"Wait, dial that back for me again. What?"

"Wren wants to be a mom and was looking into insemination. I offered to be her Huckleberry."

Clark's jaw dropped. "Like . . . you father her child, but you're not in the picture?"

"Yeah. It's the way she wants it."

"Are you—have you lost your mind?" Clark stood up, dragging his hands through his hair. "You are going to sign away the rights to your child and live in the same town as them? After having a relationship with Wren? Don't you know how people talk? They will speculate all kinds of things, mostly about your character for abandoning your kid—"

"Whoa, buddy, calm down," Sam said, holding his hands up. "Wren and I are friends. I'm just doing this because I want her to be happy."

"Because you love her, but how does she feel about you? No one who truly cared about you would ask this."

Sam's temper pricked. "She didn't ask, I offered."

"Regardless, she should have said no." Clark ran his hand through his hair. "This is not something people do—"

"Hey, news flash, little bro, I am almost forty years old, and if I decided to walk into a sperm donation clinic and give them my entire nut sack, that wouldn't be an issue. I want to give Wren a piece of myself, like a kidney, and you're flipping out?"

"Except this isn't a kidney!" Clark argued, clapping his hands with each word. "It is a living, breathing kid!"

"Look, I appreciate your concern, but what happens between us is not up to you. I shouldn't have discussed it with you."

Clark shook his head. "I'm sorry, okay? I just don't want to see you get hurt or put into a terrible situation where you regret your decision and have no recourse."

"I know you're worried, but I'm not. You never know how things are going to turn out. Maybe playing the long game will make her realize that I'm the man of her dreams and she can't wait for me to be her boyfriend."

"You know, this whole situation is kind of ironic."

"And you're going to tell me how that is?" Sam said, the tension in his shoulders dissolving as Clark picked up his beer and settled back into the couch.

"Well, for starters, you're the guy who could have had any woman he wanted, but when you're finally ready for a relationship, the one woman you want isn't."

"Yes, several people in my life have had a good laugh at that fact," Sam grumbled. "My most pressing concern is how to convince her that she belongs with me."

"I don't know, man," Clark said, his expression sympathetic. "When I was still on the fence about Merry, I did a lot of stupid things and almost lost her. It was only because of your great advice and meddling that I was able to repair the damage I had done."

Sam smirked. "Was that a thank-you for your older brother's genius relationship help?"

"Yes, that was a thank-you. I figured admitting that I wouldn't be with Merry right now if you hadn't meddled was thank-you enough, but if you need to hear the words, I appreciate you."

"I'm glad to hear it," Sam said, finishing his beer and getting off the couch. "So, your advice is to be honest and not give up. Is that correct?"

"What's wrong with that?" Clark asked.

"Just seems like a pretty simplistic strategy for convincing the potential love of someone's life to let their guard down and be together."

The door opened, and Merry came in and removed her jacket, shivering loudly. "Brr, it's cold outside."

"Tell us something we don't know," Sam shot back.

"Whoa, what's wrong with you?" Merry asked, crossing the room to lean over the back of the couch and stare down at him.

"He's having trouble with the woman he loves," Clark offered.

"Gotcha." Merry came around and sat down on the other side of Clark. "How can we help?"

"You want to help me with my relationship woes?" Sam asked.

"Why not?" Merry asked, her hazel eyes boring into his. "You're my brother-in-law, and I want you to be happy."

"Alright, I'll take it." He leaned forward with his elbows on his knees. "What advice would you give to somebody who wanted to date a woman who wasn't ready for a relationship?"

"Find somebody who is ready for a relationship?" she deadpanned.

Sam scoffed and shot Clark a knowing look before Merry reached out to him, laughing.

"I'm sorry, I was just kidding. What is it about this person that tickles your fancy?"

"This person is like a once-in-a-lifetime, never-gonna-give-you-up kind of thing."

"First of all, it's too late for you to Rickroll me," Merry said, reaching across to poke him. "Your nephew already does that to me all the time."

"It was unintentional, I promise," Sam said, leaning back against the couch. "I know she's the one, even after I lost her almost two decades ago, I never found anyone else. It never felt right. She came back into my life, and I realized it's because she was it. No one could take her place."

"Then I would just tell her how I felt," Merry said.

"Boom," Clark hooted. "I told you; honesty is the key!"

"Wait a second," Merry said, leaning forward to study Sam's face. "Are we talking about Officer Little?"

"No," Sam said sharply.

"We are," Clark said, grinning.

"Absolutely not." Sam glared at his little brother, silently telling him to *shut the fuck up*.

Merry's gaze shifted back and forth between them, trying to figure out who was lying. "And . . . you're in love?"

Sam groaned but didn't confirm or deny the allegations.

"Wow," Merry said.

"I know." Clark nodded. "I couldn't believe it, either."

"Does she feel the same way?" Merry asked.

"He isn't sure, but they're sleeping together."

"Dude," Sam said, throwing his hands up, "your wife doesn't have to know everything!"

"Well, I think that's great. Maybe she'll stop trying to give every-body tickets for jaywalking if she's happy and in love." Merry made a face. "It's such a stupid law."

"I think she'll continue to give tickets for jaywalking because it's breaking the law," said Sam, earning a dark glare from Merry.

"I stand by my opinion."

"I appreciate that, and I want to thank you for all the pep talks. Both of you," Sam said, getting up from the couch. "I guess now that you're home, I should see myself out."

"You don't have to go," Merry said, snuggling into Clark's side.

"No, I probably should bounce. I need to mull over all this good advice and plan my next move."

"Drive safe, then, and remember," Merry said, pointing at him, "you are the prize."

"Whatever the hell that means."

"She means that while you think Wren is the best thing in the world, you deserve someone who feels the same way about you," Clark said, his expression pensive.

Sam placed his hands over his chest, above his heart. "That was so sweet. I'm going to make that my next tattoo." Sam turned, starting to push his jeans down. "What do you think? Should I put it on the left ass cheek or—" Clark chucked a throw pillow at him, hitting him square in the backside and making him stumble.

"Stop trying to show my wife your ass! You know she has a sensitive stomach."

Sam chuckled, pulling his pants to rights. "Seriously, I love you both."

"We love you, too," they chorused.

Sam lost his smile and shivered. "That was very Stepford. The horror."

He ducked out the door as the next pillow narrowly missed his head. As he crossed the front porch, heading to his Jeep, Sam sent Wren a text.

Leaving Clark's. Feel like company?

Sam slipped his phone into the cupholder and climbed in, thinking about Merry's and Clark's advice. Honesty.

So simple and sound, it just might work.

Chapter Twenty-six

Wren was finishing up her patrol, taking the long way by the high school. The day had been full of domestic disputes and shoplifting calls. She'd arrested two teen girls for stealing lipstick from the supermarket, and when she was putting them in a holding cell, one of them swung her purse, hitting Wren in the head. It was as if there was a full moon coming up, and it was sending everyone into a tizzy of off-the-chart behaviors.

At least tonight she was looking forward to a nice, relaxing bath after she got home. Sam was hanging with his brother, and although he didn't say he'd be out late, Wren figured they were probably going to take their time catching up. He and Clark hadn't hung out since the guys had crashed book club, which was over a week ago.

Wren couldn't believe that Sam had been at her place every night, but even more perplexing was why she hadn't made him go home after the deed was done.

The simple answer was, she wanted Sam with her. When they slept and he cradled her against his body, she'd never felt safer. She'd even started leaving him breakfast in the microwave with little notes. *Have a great day. Can't wait to see you later.*

It was as if she'd become a completely different person, a happier version of herself, and that was in large part due to how Sam made her feel.

Wren was curving along the backside of the high school when she saw something strange. It was a hooded figure pushing a wheelbarrow overflowing with what looked like ropes or snakes, who kept passing below the school lights.

"That's not weird at all."

She veered her cruiser slightly to the right, and her high beams caught the figure and what he was pushing.

It was a wheelbarrow full of Christmas lights.

"I got you now," she said, flipping on her siren. Wren took off around the school and into the parking lot, gunning the engine to gain some ground on the thief. Duke bared his teeth from the back a split second before she saw the figure headed for the woods behind the Ag building.

"Not this time!" Wren parked the SUV and jumped out, releasing Duke from the back.

"Seek!" Wren said, racing after the dog.

"Stop, police officer!" she called, identifying herself. Wren could see him stumbling as he pushed the wheelbarrow over the rough terrain. Duke leaped through the air and knocked him to the ground. The wheelbarrow tilted and dumped its contents. The man struggled with Duke, but Wren was still too far away to do anything.

His hood had come off, but it was too dark to make out his facial features. Wren did see him reach for a large branch, holding it over his head.

"You hit my dog, and you're getting tased." The guy dropped the branch, and she called Duke off. He ran back to her, his tongue lolling out of his mouth happily.

The guy started to scramble upright, and Wren hollered, "Take one step, and you're going to know what being struck by lightning feels like."

He froze, glancing back to see the Taser in her hand.

"Get on the ground."

He did so without hesitation, and Wren kneeled to put the cuffs on him.

Duke stood next to the guy's head, and any time he twitched, Duke would let out a deep snarl.

"You have the right to remain silent," she said, snapping the cuffs in place before she put the Taser away. Wren lifted him to his feet, reciting his Miranda rights as she led him back to the car.

Duke panted beside them, and when they broke through the trees at the edge of the woods, Wren pulled out her flashlight and shined it in the perp's face. The kid winced, probably no more than fourteen, and fury rushed through her like a lightning bolt.

"What the hell were you thinking, taking off like that? You could have been hurt."

The little snot had the audacity to smirk at her. "Worked at the Festival of Trees. Figured I could outrun you again."

Wren shook her head, continuing their march toward the cruiser. "Catching charges for stealing a bunch of Christmas decorations is pretty random. What were you doing with them anyway?"

"People pay a buttload for that stuff, and I needed money," the kid said.

"Ever heard of a job?"

"Nooo," the kid drawled sarcastically. "What's that?"

Wren pressed the button on her radio and contacted dispatch, ignoring his question. "Hi, this is Officer Wren Little. I just chased a suspect on the high school property who was pushing a wheelbarrow full of Christmas lights. I've got the suspect in custody. Heading back to the station with him and the evidence."

"You caught the Grinch, Little?" Becker, her brother Luke's buddy, tsked. "Did you set a trap like the Scooby gang, or did you suddenly gain wings on your shoes?"

"I bet she used crazy glue and a net. She looks like the type to have a secret crafting dungeon," one of the other guys quipped.

Wren released the radio, muttering under her breath, "Jackass."

"I don't know," the kid said, dragging his feet. "I kind of like them."

"Shut up," she said through gritted teeth.

She could still hear their laughter and teasing, choosing to tune them out rather than engage. Being the new officer on the force, and a woman, some of them had taken to giving her a ration of shit. Wren wasn't sure if they wanted her to quit or if this was their awful way of welcoming her to the squad. Either way, she was getting tired of their antics.

Not that she didn't expect it in a male-dominated field, but the razzing seemed to be more prominent here than in the bigger cities. As she headed back to the cruiser with Duke by her side, she thought for the hundredth time since coming back that maybe she was done being a police officer. The politics and boys' club were bad enough, but after being shot, she had been thinking of hanging up her holster. The only issue was figuring out what to do next. With her degree, she could look into teaching maybe a self-defense class or a criminology course through an online high school, but it felt a bit like giving up.

The peanut gallery was still talking, but she ignored the chatter as she returned to where the wheelbarrow was tipped over, ordering Duke to watch the suspect while she righted it. Wren wasn't sure where this latest stash had come from, but if the kid didn't want to answer questions, once they put out a bulletin of what had been found and what was still missing, people could come look.

Wren picked up all the items and shoved them back into the top of the wheelbarrow, nodding her head at the kid. "Let's go."

The kid stumbled forward with Duke hot on his heels, and Wren pushed the full wheelbarrow along the bumpy terrain until sweat poured down her neck. She glanced down at Duke, who happily walked beside her, and grumbled, "You are so lucky you don't have opposable thumbs."

Once she hit asphalt, the final walk back to where the cruiser was parked didn't make her arm muscles scream in protest. As she drew closer, Wren saw a figure standing by her car, and Duke barked twice, dancing in place. She dropped the wheelbarrow handles and removed her flashlight, her other hand on her gun.

"Who are you?" she hollered. "Show me your hands!"

"Birdy?"

Sam's voice was strained and hoarse, but Wren took her hand off her gun, sucking in a deep, relieved breath.

"You scared me," she said, taking the kid's arm, heading for the back seat. "I got this guy with a wheelbarrow full of lights." The minute she got the kid inside, Sam rounded the car, eating up the ground as he barreled toward her, and for a second, she thought he was going to tackle her. Wren took a step back, bracing for impact, but instead he jerked her into his arms and squeezed her tight.

"I thought something happened to you," he murmured, his mouth buried in her shoulder.

"No, nothing happened to me," she said, putting her flashlight away so she could rub his back. Sam was trembling against her, and she realized how it must have looked for him to drive by and see her cruiser abandoned, door open, and neither her nor Duke in sight.

He's so sweet.

"I got the Christmas lights."

"Thank God you weren't hurt. I was driving by on my way back from Clark and Merry's, and I saw the SUV. All I could think was what if it was your car, so I looked inside for anything identifiable, and I saw your computer. I panicked and was about to start screaming for you when you came back."

"Yeah, no need for all that. This is what I do."

Sam held her tighter. "I don't want you chasing people into the dark alone." He pulled away, his worried eyes boring into hers. "What if he had been armed or if he had had a friend waiting?"

"Oh, yeah, I've had that happen. That's actually how I got shot in the ass." When she noticed how pale he was, Wren sobered. "Sam, I get you were worried, but this is my job."

"But you want to be a mom, right? What happens if you are raising our child alone and something happens to you? Once you have someone else to think about, you can't make decisions that put your life in jeopardy. You have to come home every night."

Our child. Those two words overwhelmed Wren, making her warm and weak at the same time. He wasn't telling her to be careful because he was some macho man who didn't think his girl could handle it. He was worried about her being around for years to come. He was asking her to be cautious and take care because she was living for other people, too.

Like Sam?

Wren squeezed him tight, breathing in his cologne, and the comforting scent washed over her. "I promise, I'll be more careful, and I won't do any more foot chases alone."

Sam released a rough, shaky breath. "Thank you."

Now that her heart rate and adrenaline had come down, she could feel Sam's body shaking against hers and realized how truly scared he'd been. Wren didn't remember being scared when her dad went to work, but then again, her older brothers kept her shielded from anything on TV that might have made her worry. Besides, she'd been under the impression her dad was invincible, even when she was grown up.

Rubbing her hands over his back, she soothed him. "It's okay."

Suddenly Sam was kissing her hair, her cheeks, her face, her lips, murmuring, "I just found you again. I'm not ready to say goodbye."

She realized she wasn't, either. The thought of Sam not being a part of her life left an empty place inside, a spot he'd claimed nearly twenty years ago, and only he could fill it. He was her support system. Her best friend. Her everything.

She loved him.

A lump lodged in her throat as those three words sank in. This was everything she'd fought against, had tried to avoid, but he'd gotten to her anyway.

"No one is saying goodbye to anyone," she whispered, finding his mouth and kissing him slow and deep.

We're just getting started.

Sam broke the kiss, resting his forehead against hers. "Do you wanna meet up for dinner after you clock out and change?"

Wren smiled, looking up into his eyes, her body radiating with joy. She loved him.

And Wren was almost positive he loved her, too.

Now, how was she going to tell him?

"There's nowhere else I'd rather be."

Chapter Twenty-seven

You should think of this as an upgrade, Sam," Victoria Winters said proudly as she placed the Santa hat on his head. "Last time we asked you to cover the float at the Parade of Lights, you were an elf."

Sam scowled at her from under the hat. He'd come to the parade looking for Wren and had only stopped by the Winters' float to say hi. That was when Victoria had caught Sam, begging him to be Santa with Holly.

"Technically, Santa is an elf, too," Sam grumbled.

Victoria patted his cheek. "But he's the head elf, and he gets to drink whiskey in a warm sleigh while riding around on a parade float, waving at kiddos. So stop your bitching and get in the sleigh."

The last sentence was a firm command as if he were a naughty child throwing a tantrum. His mouth dropped, and he turned to look at his brother, who was laughing uproariously.

"Did you hear what she just said to me?"

"Yeah, I did," Clark said, pointing to the sleigh. "So you better do what she says before she comes back with a wooden spoon."

Sam climbed up into the sleigh, adjusting the beard and mustache over his face as he took a seat. "I'm doing this because I want to help, not because I'm scared of her."

Clark gave him a thumbs-up. "Whatever you say, bro."

Holly stepped up onto the end of the float, waving at them. She was dressed in a Mrs. Claus costume, her chest and butt three times their normal sizes under the red dress. Her white wig covered up her natural red hair.

When she slid in next to him, Sam leveled her with a dark scowl and asked, "Is there a reason why your boyfriend isn't in here with you, dressed up in this ridiculous costume?"

"His shoulders are too broad for the suit," she said, pushing her fake spectacles up the bridge of her nose. "Besides, this is too much holiday cheer for him. He likes to sit on the sidelines and drink spiked hot chocolate with my brother."

"I wanted to sit on the sidelines and drink hot chocolate with your brother," Sam protested.

"Now you get to spend two hours with me, waving and smiling at the crowds like a celebrity, because you kind of are, Santa." When he didn't return her smile, she poked him in the arm. "Oh, stop being a grinch. You know I'm your favorite Winters."

"That may be true, but that does not mean I want to be sitting in a sleigh, wearing this itchy suit, only to change into another, equally uncomfortable suit so I can perform like a trained animal for your bachelor auction."

"Oh my gosh, will you stop your whining? I have been dealing with a hormonal sister for weeks, a boyfriend who is Scrooge incarnate during the holidays, and the only thing that keeps him remotely cheery is when I dress up in this little negligée that lights up like a Christmas tree—"

"Why the fuck are you telling me this?" he asked, covering his ears with his hands, but she grabbed them, dragging them down his body.

"Because I want you to understand that I am not the one to put up with your attitude!"

"Well, you should be nicer to your sister," he said, fixing his black gloves. "She is making a whole human being and doesn't need your first-world problems."

"I am very nice to my sister, but that does not give her the right to snap and boss me around every time we're together."

San glanced up at the starry sky, looking for any sign that a lightning bolt was going to strike him down. He loved Holly, but tonight her dramatics were a bit over the top.

"Why aren't you telling her that instead of me?" Sam asked.

"Because she is so sensitive that anything you say to her makes her cry. If you tell her there was a tornado in Michigan, cry. The Broncos are going to the Superbowl, cry like a fountain. Look, there is a soup commercial. Inconsolable." Holly threw her gloved hands up, wiping them in the air. "I wash my hands of it, and I am telling you right now, if I act like that when I'm pregnant, you better slap me back to reality."

"Any chance I could smack you now?" Sam asked, feeling infinitely better when she smirked.

"There is the Sam Griffin I know and love."

Sam's gaze swept over Holly, his friend and confidant. They were ten years apart in age, and while a lot of people in town had thought that they were going to get together once upon a time, Sam had only ever thought of her as a friend. Since she'd started dating Declan last year, the two of them hadn't been spending quite as much time together, but it didn't feel right to keep something so big as falling in love from Holly.

Still, he couldn't kick off a conversation with her and make it all about him. So he asked, "Speaking of our long-standing friendship, what's new? Been a while."

"I know, it's weird. There was once a time when you were constantly hanging out at my house, eating my food, annoying my boyfriend. Is Declan's annoyance why you stopped coming by?"

"Only because I grew to like and respect your boyfriend, and I knew he was sick of me always being at your house and eating your food. So, I took two steps back and gave you both some space."

"I appreciate that, but you do know that we are friends and we will always be friends, right?"

"Yes, we will always be friends. What is your point?"

"My point is, if you have anything you want to tell me, I'm here to listen," she said, wiggling her Mrs. Claus spectacles up and down on the bridge of her nose.

Sam stared at her for several beats before her knowing gaze registered, and he cursed under his breath.

"Shit, one of them told you?"

"Told me what?" she asked innocently.

"Who told you about Wren?"

"Oh 'Wren,' not Officer Little, huh?" Her full lips curved into a smirk. "Actually, everyone told me. Ricki. Merry." Holly tsked. "You should know you can't keep a secret in this town."

"You would think if two people were still trying to figure out how to define their relationship, the people in their lives wouldn't draw attention to it until they decided how to label it."

"How can we do that when we're so excited for you?" Holly said, nudging him with her shoulder.

"You are?" he asked.

"Of course we are. I mean, she's a little straightlaced for who I figured you'd end up with, but she's pretty and she's funny and she seems nice." Holly made a face. "Her obsession with eradicating jaywalking is a bit unsettling."

Sam groaned. "Not you, too! It's called a crosswalk!"

"No matter, all that is important is that my friend Sam has found love."

"Except there is one small issue," Sam said, grimacing.

"What's that?" Holly asked. The floats started to move, but as they were closer to the back, they didn't budge.

"She's not interested in having a relationship with me," Sam admitted.

"Really?" Holly asked, her forehead knitting in obvious confusion. "Then why did I see your car at her house on my way home yesterday?"

"We had dinner."

"Oh, so you're gonna tell me that you did not stay the night?" Holly asked, her tone taunting as if she already knew the answer.

"I don't feel that I need to tell you."

"Busted," she said.

Sam shook his head. "Look, I've gotten all the advice I can take on my love life, so please, can we just leave this alone for now? Concentrate on smiling and waving to the kids and when we're finished, go about our busy lives?"

"No, because you know when Declan and I were doing our thing, you were right smack in the middle of it. Yet you have kept me in the dark about this whole shindig, so I'm going to spend the next hour pumping out all the information you have held back from me."

"If you've talked to everyone, then you know what's going on," he said.

"I want to hear from you that Officer Wren Little is the one for you. Only then can I be at peace."

Sam snorted. "Fine, but not because of the cockamamie crap that just exploded from your mouth. Wren was the one for me nineteen years ago, and that hasn't changed."

"Oh, that's so sweet," Holly's voice squeaked, hurting Sam's ears.

"Okay, that's enough of that."

"No, seriously, I never thought I'd see the day when you would fall in love. I thought that you were going to end up being a lifelong bachelor even into your senior citizen years, hanging around with all the girls, being like, 'Hey, you know I used to drive a motorcycle and have a six-pack?'"

Sam glared at her. "Have you always been such a brat, or am I just now noticing?"

"I just rarely ever use my brat on you," she said.

"Oh, I see."

Their float finally took off at a snail's pace, and as they passed by the crowds, Sam waved to the kids calling out to Santa. He recognized a familiar face in the crowd and beamed as he watched Wren in full uniform say hi to people.

"Wren," he called out. She looked around, finally angling her chin up to where she could see him, and he blew her a kiss.

Wren made a face indicating her disgust and confusion at his creepy behavior.

Sam realized that he had never told her he was going to be Santa, because he'd gotten thrown into the position ten minutes before the parade started. He couldn't take off his beard and show her who he was, so instead Sam made his hands into the best bird he could and started flapping his hands like wings.

Wren turned around and walked through the crowd.

Holly laughed uproariously. "That was the funniest thing I've seen in a while. She had no idea who you were. She just thought you were some random creeper making gestures at her. You're lucky she didn't climb up here and arrest you."

"I'm glad you find this so amusing," Sam grumbled.

"Only because I've never seen you so besotted."

"How 'bout less talkie, more wavie?" Sam said.

"Whatever you say, Santa."

Chapter Twenty-eight

Even though it was twenty degrees outside, being stuck in that Santa suit for two hours left Sam overheated, which didn't help when he had to switch right over to a tux for the bachelor auction. He stood backstage, waiting for his name to be called, loosening his collar and taking off his jacket for the fiftieth time, trying to get some airflow with sixty bodies huddled in a cramped space. It felt like a sauna of cologne and breath mints, and he wanted to get the hell out of there.

Sam hadn't spotted Wren yet, but when he'd seen her after the crowd dispersed at the parade, she'd said she would be there. Sam wasn't expecting anyone else to bid on him, given everything that had happened, but he didn't wanna take a chance of going home with anyone else.

"Next up, Sam Griffin!" Merry called from the stage, and Sam walked through the curtain, carrying his tux jacket over his shoulder. Merry smiled at him before addressing the crowd. "This talented artist enjoys sunny weather, boating, and a bottle of good whiskey on a cold night. Ladies, not only do you get to enjoy Sam's charming company, but you win a tattoo appointment of three hours and up to two hundred dollars. We will start the bidding at thirty dollars; do I hear thirty?" Sam smiled into the audience, even though he was blinded by a spotlight and couldn't tell who was who, but a paddle went into the air.

"Thirty!"

"I'll give you forty!"

"Whoa, easy ladies, the night is young. Will anyone go to fifty?"

"Fifty!"

"Sixty!"

It was like rapid-fire succession one after another, up and up it went until someone shouted, "Three hundred and sixty dollars!"

Sam's throat seized up. It didn't sound like Wren. Sam held his breath, waiting for Merry to count down to 'sold' when he heard his girl.

"Four hundred dollars!"

Sam grinned, spinning in a circle as his heart pounded in anticipation.

"I have four hundred once . . . twice . . . sold! To Wren Little for the bargain price of four hundred dollars."

Sam heard some rumblings in the crowd, probably commenting that he wasn't worth it, but their opinions didn't matter.

Still, maybe there was a way to pacify the women of Mistletoe with some good clean revenge?

"You can pay up and pick up at the table by the stage."

Sam held his hand out for Merry's mic, shooting her a sheepish grin. "May I address the audience?"

Merry hesitated for several beats before she handed over the mic.

Sam brought the mic to his mouth and said, "Ladies, I know I haven't always been the most sensitive guy. Although I pride myself on being honest, I wasn't always tactful and conscientious of your feelings."

There were a few angry boos and catcalls, but Sam kept going. "A lot of you called in to Jilly G a couple weeks ago and vented your frustrations with my character. I wanted to let you know that I heard you, and I want to apologize. More than that, I want to give the ladies of Mistletoe the opportunity to enact their revenge. Next Saturday, I will be at the Mistletoe Winter Games in the pie-throwing area. If you wish to throw a pie in my face, please come on by from noon to two, and I will take it like a man."

Sam handed back the mic to Merry, who clapped along with the screaming audience. "Sounds like we're gonna have a lot of fun next weekend at the winter games. Next up, we have the witty and wicked . . ."

Sam headed down the stairs, searching the crowd for Wren. He spotted her at the payment table, counting out hundred-dollar bills. Sam walked up next to her, grinning mischievously. "You do know that the prize is a tattoo under two hundred dollars, right?"

"I do know that," she said, slipping her hand into his. "That's why we're headed to the shop now, so I can collect my prize."

Sam's jaw dropped. "You're actually going to get a tattoo?"

"I guess you'll have to come with me to find out." Wren tugged on his hand, and he let her lead him out the double doors. Sam was surprised she didn't drop his hand as they walked by the women of Mistletoe, who watched her curiously. He wondered what had changed, and although he'd expected her to bid on him, why the sudden interest in a tattoo?

When they reached her car, she unlocked it, tossing him the keys. "Do you mind driving? Heels are a killer."

Sam caught the keys in the air and unlocked the door. "No problem. Where is Duke tonight?"

"At home. He doesn't look as hot as you in a tux."

Her playful demeanor made him smile. "You seem different tonight."

"In what way?" she asked, getting into the car and shutting the door.

"I don't know," he said, putting the keys in the ignition. "Happier, maybe. You seem pumped up."

"I'm just excited to see where the night takes us," she murmured, placing her hand on his knee.

Sam started the car, and as they drove to the tattoo parlor, he covered her hand with his, lacing their fingers together. He had no idea what was going on in her head, but just the small gesture of holding hands in public gave him hope that maybe she was coming around.

He parked along the back of the tattoo shop and came around to the passenger side to help her out of the car. The long black dress she wore had thick straps, the neckline dipping into a deep V in the front, the material shimmering as she walked.

"You're so beautiful," he said.

"Thank you. I feel beautiful." She tweaked his bowtie playfully. "You look good, too, but you always do."

"You didn't think so earlier when I was in my Santa suit," Sam grumbled.

"That was you?" She laughed. "How did you get roped into that?"

"Victoria threatened me."

"With what?"

"I don't know, but her tone was scary."

Wren laughed again. "Poor baby."

"I'm not kidding, it was a rough night. I had to listen to Holly gripe and moan about her life and then bombard me with questions about mine. It was a nightmare."

"But you did it," Wren said, smiling.

"Of course I did. They were backed into a corner, and they needed a Santa."

"Yes, but they asked you to do it. They knew you would come through for them, and even though Victoria threatened you, I'm sure she really didn't have to, because you're a good man."

"Thank you." Sam flipped on the lights inside the parlor, rubbing his hands together. "So, are you really going to get a tattoo, or did you just bring me here to seduce me?"

"It's actually a little of both," she murmured, and Sam's heart slammed in his chest rapidly as Wren held out her arm. With her fingers, she traced something across her skin, and it took him a moment to realize it was a heart. "I want something like this." She traced a second interconnecting heart onto her arm. "On this first heart, I want the date that you and I met nineteen years ago. Do you remember it?"

"Of course I do," he said softly.

"Good. On this one," she said, pointing at the imaginary heart on her forearm, "I want the date we reconnected, and then, hopefully very soon, we can add another heart. Smaller than the other two, with the date we find out I'm pregnant."

Sam stared at her, processing what she'd just explained to him. A lump formed in his throat, and he swallowed, trying to speak. "So, you want two hearts, one with the date we met nineteen years ago and the other with the date we reconnected?"

"Yes. Maybe you have something I could look at? I'm not quite sure how I want the hearts."

Sam pulled her in close and kissed her, cutting off her words, his fingers sliding into her hair, keeping her immobile as he poured all his love from his mouth to hers.

When they finally broke apart, they were both panting, although Wren released a breathless laugh. "Wow. I never knew you'd get so excited over giving someone a tattoo."

"It's not about the tattoo," he said firmly, brushing back her hair. "Are you sure about you and me? I know you said that you didn't want anything except a child, no complications, no relationships, and I don't want you to regret this."

"The only thing I regret is that I didn't figure out what I really wanted before all of this started." Wren brought his hand up to her mouth and kissed his palm. "I've done a lot of soul-searching the last few weeks, and I realized it wasn't that I didn't want a relationship, it was that I didn't want one with anyone but you. It just took me a little longer to figure it out." Wren held Sam's hand to her cheek, gazing up at him as she continued, "You have always had my back. You have stepped up when I needed you, and even after all this time and all the drama in the past, you were still the guy for me. That is why if I'm gonna put anything on my body, it's gonna be about you. We are going to make an amazing life together because I love you."

Sam's stomach bottomed out for a split second before elation overcame him and he cradled her face in his hands. "I love you, too." Sam's vision blurred as he bent down and kissed her again, soft and slow, as happy tears trailed down his cheeks. "I love you."

Sam's fingers reached around the back of her dress, finding the zipper and bringing it down slowly while Wren discarded his bowtie, tossing it across the room. Her dress slid down her body, catching on her hips before pooling at her feet. There was no hurry as she removed his shirt this time, their motions slow and loving. Memorizing this moment, this core memory etched in their minds forever.

When the final article of clothing hit the floor, Sam sat back in the tattoo chair, and Wren climbed on top of him, straddling his lap. He kissed her gently, his lips cascading kisses along the column of her throat. When Sam reached the rise and fall of her breasts, he kissed both the hard peaks of her nipples as she lifted herself up above him, rubbing her already soaking wet pussy against the tip of his cock. Sam lifted his hips, answering her need with his own, his cock slipping into her. Wren held his shoulders and sank farther down his length, their eyes meeting with unwavering contact as he slid to the hilt inside her. Wren's head leaned back, a moan escaping her.

They barely moved together, rocking against each other. Wren wrapped her arms around his shoulders so that the front of their bodies pressed together, skin to skin. Sam had never felt closer to another human being in his life, and grasping her hips to bring them even more fully together, he felt her muscles clench around him. Her body shook, and her head fell back as she let out a cry of release.

Sam continued to grip her hips, moving her over him, picking up speed until his balls clenched in his body. He was so close, and as he held her against him, furiously pumping into her, the force of it shook him. He moaned her name over and over, jerking, and thrusting inside until he was spent. He collapsed back onto the chair, eyes closed and his hands no longer gripping her hips, but stroking them lovingly. When Sam felt her soft lips feathering kisses over his neck and jawline, he opened his eyes and gazed at her with all the love in his heart.

"That was wonderful," she whispered, running a hand over his chest and pushing herself to a sitting position, grinning down at him. "Now about my tattoo."

Sam chuckled. "Give me about fifteen minutes to recover, and I'll get you started."

She giggled, pressing a kiss on his mouth, and said, "I'm only teasing. We don't have to do it today. We've got the rest of our lives."

Sam loved the sound of that.

Chapter Twenty-nine

Wren got up early the next morning while Sam was still sleeping and drove up to her dad's place. She'd spent most of last night after Sam fell asleep thinking about the future. What would it look like now that they were in love?

Wren made a left onto her dad's driveway. There was a good bit of snow now on either side of the road, although his gravel driveway was mostly plowed. Her Rogue managed to push through until she reached the front of his house, spotting the smoke escaping the chimney.

Even if she hadn't seen the smoke, Wren would have known he was awake. Robert Little had woken up at six in the morning every day of his adult life, even on his days off.

Wren got out of the car and headed up the steps to knock on the front door. Her dad opened it with a cup of coffee in one hand and a confused look on his face.

"Wren, what are you doing here? I thought I wasn't going to see you until later on today."

"You are, but I was hoping you had something for me," Wren said.

"What would that be?" he asked.

"The letter from Sam," she said gravely, watching his face flush at the reminder of the contention between them. "Did you keep it?"

Her dad stepped back, making room for her to pass by. He nodded slowly. "I have it. Come on in."

She followed him inside, stopping to sit down on his couch.

"Do you want some coffee?" he asked.

"No, thank you," she said, clasping her hands in her lap. "I'm going to make some for Sam and me when I get home."

"Alright, let me go grab it then." He disappeared into his study, leaving her alone for several moments. When he came back with a box that she recognized, her heart thumped in her chest. It was the box she'd thrown away that had all her pictures of Sam in it. Not just pictures, but keepsakes, like every movie ticket stub. The flower from her prom corsage was in there. So many memories she'd tossed aside in a fit of anger.

"How did you get this? I threw this away when you weren't home."

"I took out the trash later that night, and when I saw it, I pulled it out just in case." Her dad shrugged, setting the box in her lap and taking the seat next to her. "After reading his letter to you—"

Wren groaned. "I can't believe you would read it!"

"I told you, I was worried you were planning on running away." Her dad stroked his beard, a nervous habit when he was uncomfortable. "What I realized after reading it, though, was that his feelings were real. Even though you seemed to have moved on, I thought if the two of you worked out eventually, you would regret not having the stuff."

Although Wren wasn't happy about his duplicity, she had never been a parent to a sixteen-year-old girl. If she'd been thrown into his shoes, Wren had no idea what she would have done.

"Thanks, Dad. I appreciate it." Wren gave him a hug, which he returned with a few hearty back slaps.

"I am assuming because you're asking about that letter that you and him have worked things out?" he asked.

"You would assume correctly."

"So, are we going to see him today for family lunch, then?"

Wren stilled, surprised by her dad's casual inquiry. "Do you want me to bring him to family lunch?"

"Well, if he's going to end up being a part of my family anyway, you might as well start bringing him around now so we can get used to him. Especially if the two of you are trying to expand."

Wren bent over with laughter. "Really, Dad? 'Expand,' like I'm a hot air balloon?"

"I'm just saying, I don't know what the heck is going on between the two of you, but what I do know is that a week ago you were talking about being impregnated and going at it alone. Now, you're back together with your high school boyfriend, and God knows what plans the two of you have for the future, but I am staying out of it. I am going to stay in my lane and mind my business."

"So, you wanna be surprised by our plans?" she asked, wondering how painful it was for him to say he didn't need to know.

"I figured when there's something to tell, someone will tell me."

"Then I guess if I'm bringing him to lunch today, I better go home and tell him so he can dress accordingly."

"Dress accordingly? We don't get all fancy for Sunday lunch."

"I know, Dad, I'm joking." Wren patted his shoulder and climbed to her feet. On impulse, Wren leaned over and hugged him. "Thank you very much."

"No thanks needed. I love you, kiddo. I'm sorry things got so messed up between us."

"It's okay," she said, releasing him to stand back up. "That's what life's all about, right? Second chances and forgiveness?"

"Whatever you say."

Wren headed for the door but stopped when her dad called her name. "I just want you to know that I will . . . try to like Sam."

Wren laughed. "That's all I can ask."

Sam woke up to kisses on his chest, and when he opened his eyes, he saw Wren hovering, smiling down at him.

"Good morning," she said.

Sam checked the clock and saw that it was after nine. He wondered why his alarm hadn't gone off, then remembered it was Sunday.

"Good morning," he murmured. "Come back to bed."

"I would, but every Sunday I have lunch with my family. And this time, you are invited to join us."

Sam sat up in bed, giving her wide eyes. "Did your father have a stroke?"

Wren laughed. "No. I think he's actually gotten softer in his old age."

Sam snorted. "I highly doubt that."

Wren's smile slipped a bit. "You won't come with me?"

"Hey, hey," Sam said, wrapping his arms around her. "I'm happy to go with you, but that means going home and getting cleaned up and changed. I don't think showing up to lunch with my night-before clothes on is going to cut it."

Wren's lips twitched. "He might definitely have something to say about that."

Sam gave her a kiss and got up out of bed. He headed for the bathroom to clean up and thought about how things had changed in the course of the last few weeks.

Wren loved him. They were together now.

It was a crazy miracle he didn't want to take for granted.

When Sam emerged from the bathroom with his tuxedo pants on, Wren was nowhere to be seen. He finished dressing, and with Duke by his side, went exploring the rest of the house to find her.

"Wren?" he called.

"I'm here." She was standing outside the spare room with the door open, looking at it.

"What are you doing?" he asked.

"Trying to imagine what the room will look like when I finally get furniture."

"How many rooms do you have?" he asked.

"I have a three-bedroom and a finished basement with a bathroom, but I think the previous owners used it as a hangout."

"Do you wanna show me?" he asked.

"Sure, come with me." She opened the other bathroom, pointing to the large barnwood-framed mirror and pedestal sink. "They'd done some updates before I bought it, but I honestly hate the sink. There is no linen closet or other storage in here, and that drives me nuts."

"I could help you fix that," he said, stepping inside the bathroom. He pointed to the open space in front of the toilet. "We could install shelves here for storage. Take out the pedestal and replace it with a vanity with drawers."

Wren grinned at him from the open doorway. "All good ideas. Wait until you see this."

Sam followed her to the end of the hallway past the primary bedroom to an open doorway. Through the door were stairs that took them down into a great open room with egress windows and a bathroom with a shower, sink, and toilet.

"I figured they must've had teenagers, and this was their hangout area."

"We would have killed for a place like this," he said, waggling his eyebrows.

Wren laughed. "Yes, but the difference is my dad would've never had something like this for us, especially not a place where we could invite members of the opposite sex."

"Touché." Sam walked the entire area, whistling. "You know, you could add two more bedrooms down here and still keep most of the space."

CODI HALL

216

"Why would I need two more bedrooms?" she asked.

"Well, your brother likes to hang out over here a lot. It would be nice for him to have his own room tucked away downstairs rather than a few doors down from yours."

"Fine, you aren't wrong about that, but I feel like there was something else on your mind when you suggested it."

Sam was afraid of saying too much and scaring her off, but he cleared his throat, going for broke. "You said that you wanted to be a mom. If it ends up being something you love doing, why stop at one?"

Wren watched him for several moments before she approached him, placing her hands on his chest. "You're getting a little ahead of yourself, don't you think? I'm not even pregnant yet, and you're thinking about more?"

"I'm only looking at the space and ways to better utilize it. A second child was just the first thing to pop into my head."

"Aha," Wren said, heading toward the stairs.

"I didn't spook you, did I?" Sam asked.

"No, you didn't," she said, stopping to turn his way. "I'm just surprised you'd think about having more."

"Technically, I didn't even know if I'd be able to be involved with this one, since we agreed you'd be doing it on your own. We haven't had a chance to discuss what changes for us now."

"Changes, huh?" she asked, coming back up the stairs slowly, looking up at him with interest. "What changes are you wanting to see?"

"Well, since 'I love yous' have been exchanged, I was thinking we could try out boyfriend and girlfriend."

"Wow," Wren said, her mouth twitching. "One 'I love you' and you wanna label it, huh?"

"Heck yeah I do," Sam said, wrapping his arms around her waist. "I want to lock this down before you change your mind."

Wren laughed. "I could be down with boyfriend and girlfriend."

"What about having a child that we share?"

"I still want one, and whenever it happens, it happens," Wren said, holding him around the waist. "I already burned the contract. As long as I'm with you, I am not in a big hurry. I want to enjoy this."

"In that case," Sam said, lifting her into his arms, "now that we've got that sorted, I figure you can move in with me next week."

"Moving all the steps up, are you?" Wren stroked his cheek with her hand. "If we're moving in together, you would be moving in with me. I own my place."

"That's fair," he said, kissing her. "Playtime is over. I better go get cleaned up and changed. I'll see you in a few hours."

"See you then," she said.

Once Sam made it home, it didn't take him long to get showered and changed. It did give him time to think, especially about how fast life could change. One minute he was a single guy, taking things day by day, and now his girlfriend was picking him up, and they were taking a ride up a mountain to her father's house. The same father who had threatened him with jail time years ago.

Sam was still dwelling on this when they took the left onto Wren's dad's driveway, the trees on either side growing denser the higher they went.

"Have I mentioned that I'm a little nervous?" Sam said.

"What are you nervous about?" Wren asked.

"We are going to your dad's home in the woods, and history shows he doesn't like me. Yet here we are, trusting that I'm going to make it out of this alive and that your dad and brothers aren't planning to murder me."

"It's going to be fine," she said, putting her hand on his knee. "My brothers don't have an issue with you. There will be lots of witnesses, and you forget that I am a trained police officer. I'll keep you safe."

"Are you sure none of your brothers takes issue with me?" he asked.

"I don't know for sure, but I think Pete likes you. Except for that whole thing about stealing his place to sleep."

"Great. I'm going to get murdered because you didn't want your brother sleeping on the couch."

"Will you relax?" she said, squeezing his thigh. "Trust me, everything is going to be fine."

They pulled up to the house and got out of the car in unison. Sam took Wren's hand the minute he rounded the hood, and they headed up the steps. She didn't bother to knock, simply opened the door and led the way inside.

"We're here," she said.

"Who is 'we'?" Luke asked, glancing away from the television.

"Her boyfriend," Wren's dad said, pointing at Sam. "Sam Griffin."
Everyone swung around to look first at Sam and then at Robert.

"And we're okay with this?" Garrett said.

"She's a grown woman who can make her own decisions." Robert scowled at each of his sons, growling, "Why do you have to be all up in everyone's business?"

Although it was subtle, Sam saw Wren's dad catch her gaze and wink.

Pete blinked. "Have we been replaced with pod people?"

"Where is Elizabeth?" Wren asked, trying to take the attention off them.

"In the back, watching something with Lukas," Luke said, barely glancing away from the TV. "She has a headache, and he was restless, so they went to lie down."

"And you didn't think to take charge of your son in order to give your wife a break?" Wren scolded, dropping Sam's hand and marching toward the back of the house without another word.

Luke looked at his dad and his brothers. "Am I the asshole in the situation?"

"Yes," all of them chorused, including Sam.

Luke climbed to his feet and followed after Wren.

Robert got out of his chair. "Time to get some more firewood." He motioned for Sam to come with him. "Let's go."

"Wouldn't you rather take one of your sons who are related to you and whom you love very much to do this chore that requires the splintering of wood with an axe?"

"Stop being a candy-ass and get out here," Robert said, opening the door and holding it for him. "If I wanted to hurt you, I would have done it when you walked through the door."

Sam looked at the other two men in the room, who raised their hands. Pete mouthed, *Good luck.*

Resigned to his fate, he followed Robert out onto the porch and down the steps. They crossed the yard to a large shed where wood had been stacked neatly inside.

"Hold out your arms," Robert said.

Sam did what he asked, and Robert started stacking wood in his arms.

"Now I need to say a few things to you, and then I don't ever wanna talk about it again. You understand?"

"Alright," Sam said.

"I realize that my actions when you were just a kid were not right, and I am sorry that I misjudged you. I was scared that you were going to ruin my daughter's life, and I acted out of that fear. I took your letter and hid it from her. I am sorry for that as well."

Sam stared at the top of the other man's head as Robert continued to load Sam's arms as if he wasn't telling him that he had derailed his entire life. He said it in such a matter-of-fact and casual way, like it hadn't altered the course of their lives. This rankled Sam, but it wouldn't do any good to hash it out more.

What else could Sam do? This was Wren's dad, and she loved him, warts and all.

"Thank you for saying that."

"So, we're good?" Robert asked, wiping his hands on his pants.

"Actually, I have a few things to say."

Robert looked to the sky. "Oh brother, let's go."

"I love your daughter, and I want to make a life with her, and that means I have to forgive you. So I do."

"That's it?" Robert asked.

"That's it."

"Alright, then let's go back inside. Start up the fire and make some sandwiches."

"Let's do it."

Chapter Thirty

The winter games kicked off with the goofiest race Wren had ever seen—grown men sledding down hills and tapping their partners in, only for those fools to slip into blow-up Rudolph costumes and race to the finish line in order to build a snowman.

All she could do was shake her head.

The crowd seemed to enjoy it, though, as all of Mistletoe was lined up along the route of the race, cheering on their favorite contestants.

At the center of Mistletoe Park where the games were being held, three large tents had been erected. Inside were different activities, including chainsaw ice sculpting, Christmas dessert contests, and of course the pie throwing. Wren planned on stopping by during Sam's shift as moral support.

After the race and a break for lunch, there would be a hockey game on the ice-skating rink. Then everyone would leave to get ready for the Christmas concert. It was the final event in a long Christmas season, and Wren was happy that she'd be here for it, even if she was technically working the event.

Wren saw Sam leaning against the fence, talking to his brother, Holly, and Merry. Wren approached them nervously. Although Clark had been an adorable kid, she hadn't paid him a lot of attention when she'd dated Sam in high school. As for Merry and Holly, they were sweet, but she'd heard the rumors about Sam and Holly, before she'd started dating Declan Gallagher.

Wren heard Millie calling her name and turned around, searching for her. Millie was walking away from a tall, fit man in a backward hat and glasses. Wren was positive it was Matt, the dreamy physical education teacher, but she waited for Millie to catch up before she asked.

"Hey, sunshine," Wren said, nodding to Backward Hat. "Was that Matt?"

"Yes, he's playing in the hockey game this afternoon and asked if I was going to come watch."

"And you said of course you were?" Wren asked.

"I did say I would stop by."

"Oh, very good. Noncommittal, letting him know who is in control."

Millie rolled her eyes. "Oh, right. How about you?" She glanced over to where Sam stood with his friends. "Why are you hanging over here instead of going to say hi to Sam?"

"Sam? Oh, I didn't even see him there. He looks busy, so I'll wait."

Millie crossed her arms over her chest. "What's up? Are you scared of hanging out with Sam's friends? Merry and Holly Winters are super nice."

"I'm sure they are, but I've also given them tickets for jaywalking—multiple times—so I doubt they will be excited to see me."

"That's your job, though. If they don't like you, then screw them." Millie linked her arm with Wren's. "Come on, I'll go over there with you. If anyone gives us any attitude, I'll throw something at them."

Wren laughed, letting her friend drag her over to see Sam. When he spotted her, his face split into a wide grin, a pair of dark glasses covering his fantastic eyes.

"Hey, gorgeous," he said, leaning over to give her a kiss. "How is protecting and serving going?"

"It's going," Wren said.

"It's Millie, right?" Sam said, holding out his hand. "I remember you from high school, but it just took me a minute."

"Glad you convinced this one to give you another chance, Sam," Millie said, ignoring Wren's dark look.

"We were just talking about the games. Apparently, Anthony and Pike got themselves into a tight jam over this afternoon's hockey game. They bet the opposing team a pair of snowmobiles for their boat?"

"So stupid," Merry muttered.

Holly shrugged. "Maybe so, but I can't stand Brody and Trip, so I hope Pike and Anthony kick their rears."

Wren felt Sam's hand clasp hers, and she blushed, loving the warmth of his touch.

"Speaking of activities," he said, hugging her, "I have to get back for my stint in the pie-throwing ring."

"I'll be sure to come by and check it out," she said.

Sam covered his heart with his hand. "Don't tell me that you're gonna throw a pie at me."

"Is there a reason why I should throw one at you?" she asked, rubbing her hand against his chest.

"You should never throw anything at me. I'm your boyfriend."

Wren cocked her head to the side, teasing, "I thought I read somewhere that throwing things at your boyfriend is a rite of passage?"

"You should be kind to me," Sam pouted. "I think I'm going to really get it today."

"We'll see," Wren said, giving him a kiss. "I'll come by in a bit."

"Alright, I love you," Sam said, jogging backward away from her. Wren thought that she would never get tired of hearing him say that.

"I love you, too," she said.

Sam sat in the chair in the pie-throwing area for what felt like hours. He was covered with everything from pumpkin to chocolate, and his hair was a mess of different textures. Thankfully, a sweet young woman with a wet towel came to him in between pies and wiped his face. His neck felt a bit crusty, though, and he couldn't wait to get out of there and take a shower. He'd had a coughing fit earlier when someone chucked a pie at him and he'd gotten globs of filling up his nose.

Although most of the women had left smiling after chucking a pie at him, there were a few who hadn't seemed at all appeased. Finally, there had been a lull in people looking to hit him with pies, and thankfully, he only had about fifteen minutes left in his shift.

The Winters clan stopped at the gate of the pie-throwing booth, various stages of amusement etched into their friendly faces.

"Man, you really got hammered!" Chris called out to him.

"It's okay, I mostly deserved it," Sam said, wiping a hand over his saturated hair. "You aren't thinking about getting me, right?"

The majority of them shook their heads, but then Sam caught sight of the devilish gleam in Declan's eyes. The big man reached into his back pocket and pulled out his wallet, removing a five-dollar bill from the black leather.

"Oh, come on," Sam groaned.

"I've been wanting to do this for a long time. I'm not passing up the opportunity," Declan said, studying the available pies.

"Is this seriously because I flirted with your girlfriend when you were first dating?"

"Yeah, a little bit." Declan selected a white mousse pie, holding it balanced on the palm of his hand. "Also, you are too handsome, and I think you need a little smear on your face."

Declan threw the pie, catching him on the chin.

"Weak aim, Gallagher," Sam said.

"We need to get in on this action," Merry said, grabbing a pie off the table and handing over her five-dollar bill to the attendant.

"Whoa whoa whoa," Sam said, holding up a time-out sign. "You are my sister-in-law. What are you doing?"

"This is for all the times I told you to stop flirting with my sister and you just kept going, mocking me."

"Man, Holly," Sam said, scowling at his friend. "You're getting me into all kinds of trouble!"

"Sorry," she said, laughing.

"Fine, whatever, but for the record, she flirted back!"

Merry let the pie fly, but it only caught his shoulder.

"Ha ha," said Nick as he handed over a five and picked up a pie.

"Wait wait wait! What did I do to you, Nick?"

"Nothing," Nick said, smirking. "It just looks like fun."

Nick's lemon cream pie hit Sam square in the face, the pan dropping to the ground and leaving behind yellow and white goop. The Winters family cheered while one of the attendants ran over with a wet towel, wiping away the goop from Sam's eyes, nostrils, and mouth.

When she finished cleaning up, Sam addressed the group with a sardonic expression. "Are we all satisfied now?"

"As your little brother," Clark said, digging out his wallet, "I feel like I should be able to hit you in the face with a pie." Clark pulled out his five, and he handed it over, weighing the pumpkin pie in his hand.

"Fine, little brother. Come on, let me have it!" Clark's pie caught him against the cheek, and pumpkin filling exploded into his ear and hair. A few people hung on the outskirts, watching, and Sam felt like yelling, *Are you not entertained?*

"Anyone else?" Sam asked.

"I think you've had enough," Chris said, giving Holly a stern look when she started rummaging in her purse.

Wren came walking in from the left, took one look at him, and burst out laughing. "Jeez, you really got it, didn't you?"

"I know." Sam hopped off the chair to greet her, leaning against the fence. "And I didn't even date half the women who showed up."

"I think they may have posted an advertisement after your announcement at the bachelor auction," Merry teased.

"Is your shift about done, or are we waiting on more angry women to get you?" Wren asked.

"Oh, the last five pies were just us having fun," Holly said.

Sam checked his watch and shaved off the last two minutes. He was tired. "It's two o'clock. I'm done."

"Let's go." He waved at the attendant. "Thanks for sticking with me."

The girl blushed, and Wren rolled her eyes. "Have you learned nothing?"

"What? I was just being friendly."

He came up to Wren and was going to put his arm around her, but she put her hands out. "No no, let's not do that right now."

"You don't wanna hug me?" he pouted.

"Not when you're covered with globs of gunk. I just got changed."

"Come on, I got some coconut pie on me that is calling your name. I think over here," he said, wrapping his arms around her as she squealed. He kissed her on her neck, cheek, and finally claimed her mouth. After a few moments of protest, she gave in, melting under his kiss and wrapping her arms around him.

When they pulled apart, they realized the Winters clan was still standing there, staring at them with wide eyes.

"Holy shit, he really does love her," Merry said.

"It's the end of the world as we know it," Declan deadpanned.

Sam would have flipped them off if Chris and Victoria hadn't been with them. "You guys are hilarious."

"Come on, kids, let's leave the lovebirds alone," Victoria said, shooing her brood out of the tent. Before she exited, Victoria pointed at Wren and said, "You and I will have to get together and chat if you're going to marry my adopted son."

Wren blinked at her. "We didn't talk about that!"

"Not yet, but I can always smell a wedding."

"That is the weirdest thing I have ever heard, Mom," Merry said, leading the way out of the tent.

When Wren and Sam were alone, he looked at himself in his cell phone camera and grimaced. "I think we need to get cleaned up."

"Hey, I'm all good with that," Wren said, feeling around her neck and cheeks. "I think you got a little in my hair."

"I probably did," he said, wrapping his arm around her waist. "Whatever happened to your baby grinch?"

"He got probation since his parents brought in everything he stole, and we were able to get the items back to the owners except for a few things he'd already sold."

"My crime-fighting Birdy," Sam said, kissing her forehead. "I feel the need for a dual shower. I don't suppose you could blow off work and come join me."

"That's not how my job works, but how about tonight after work we get dirty again?"

Sam grinned. "I'm all for that."

Chapter Thirty-one

B urglary in progress at the Wolf's Den."
Wren's heartbeat quickened as dispatch came over the radio. Technically, she was heading back to the station to clock out. It was Christmas Eve, and Sam wanted her to head over to the Winters to visit after she got off work, but there was no way she was going to let Quinton twist in the wind. Especially since he wasn't a fan of some of the other officers on duty.

She picked up her walkie off her shoulder. "This is Officer Wren Little; I'm headed that way."

"Thank you, Officer Little."

After the games, she'd had a few disturbance calls, mostly family squabbles, but the closer she got to the Wolf's Den, the harder her pulse pounded. She had so many questions about what she was walking into that she got back on her radio.

"Dispatch, this is Officer Little. Do you know how many suspects and if they're armed?"

Static erupted before their dispatcher, Lisa, got back on the line. "Single suspect is armed and behaving erratically."

"Thank you. Over."

Wren's stomach rolled and twisted as she pulled up front at the same time as Barret. She got out of her cruiser, leaving Duke in the back seat. When the dog started to protest, she firmly said, "Stay."

He quieted down, but as Wren joined Barret in front of the bar's double doors, she could feel the canine's heavy gaze on her back.

"I got your back," Barret said as if sensing her unease, and she nodded.

"And I got yours."

They headed to the front door, which was open, hands on their guns. Wren got a look at a skinny guy waving a gun at Quint, and rage pushed through the fear, tamping it down as she watched the bar owner's pale face.

"This is Mistletoe Police Department," Wren called out, standing on one side of the open doorway while Barret took the other. "Is everything okay in there?"

"No, everything is not okay," a high, shaky voice called, "and you need to leave."

"Do you mind if I come inside, actually?" Wren shot back. "I'd like to talk to you."

"We've got everything under control here. Once Quinton gives me what I want, I'll be on my way."

Wren nodded at Barret, who took off for the patio door. "And what is it you want? Cash? Booze?"

"I want the cash that's owed me."

"Well, if I put my gun away, could I come inside and talk to you unarmed? See if we can't work this out."

"Okay." The guy sounded young and inexperienced, but that could make him even more dangerous.

Wren holstered her gun and stepped inside, assessing the situation. Quint was on the other side of the bar with one of his bartenders. At the back near the rooms was one of the bouncers, and the other one looked like he had been knocked out cold near the door. Half a dozen patrons huddled in the back.

Wren stopped to check the bouncer's pulse; he was fine. Then she took a step forward, her hands in the air.

"I'm Wren. What's your name?"

The skinny guy was shaking. The gun in his hand was almost too big for his thin frame. He looked like he was on something, and Wren's heart skipped a beat. People on drugs were not usually calm and collected or playing with a full deck in these kinds of situations.

"Ivan," he said.

"Okay, Ivan, what is the money that he owes you?"

"I came in here and bought stuff from a guy in the back, and it turned out to be nothing," Ivan said, his gun hand shaking as he pointed it at Quint. "He slipped me a placebo or something, and I want my money back."

Quint shook his head. "I've tried to tell him we don't sell anything here—"

"The guy who sold you the drugs, what did he look like?" Wren asked, giving Quint a stern look. The last thing she needed was Quint aggravating Ivan and getting accidentally shot.

Ivan's eyes squinted like he was trying to remember. "Bald, with a tattoo of an eagle on his throat."

Wren glanced at Quinton, addressing him, but keeping Ivan in her purview. "Do you know anyone who fits that description?"

Quint nodded, his jaw clenched. "I know him."

"I'll get that information from you later." She turned back to Ivan. "I'm going to find the man who took your money, and we are going to charge him, but I need you to put down the gun and let these people go. They're not involved."

"I need the money," he said, almost in tears, and Wren realized he was coming down hard from something. Withdrawal could make someone do terrible things.

"I know you do, but right now I think we need to get you some treatment, and then we will take care of the rest." Wren held her hand out to him. "Okay, can you hand me the gun?"

Ivan's wide eyes slicked between her and Quint, and in that moment's hesitation, she froze. If he didn't drop the gun and swung it toward her, would she be fast enough to get out of the bullet's way? Would she be able to pull hers if he aimed for Quint? Would they know to contact Sam and tell him she was hurt?

Her chest seized, thinking of everything the two of them had left to do. She didn't want to lose him.

Finally, Ivan let the gun swing barrel down and handed it to her.

"It's not real," he said softly. "It's a water gun. I took it from my nephew."

Wren opened the top, and sure enough, there was water inside. She almost let out a hysterical giggle, but she was afraid if she let loose, she might weep instead.

Wren spotted Barret in the shadows by the stage and called out to him.

"Barret, it's clear." She read Ivan his rights, and as she put the cuffs on him, she glanced over at the bar owner. "I'm gonna need that name."

"I'll get it for you," he said grimly. "I don't want anyone doing that in my bar."

"Good to know."

As Wren helped Ivan out to the car, she realized that she had put herself, unarmed, in a situation that could've become deadly. As much as Mistletoe was a quieter pace than all the other cities she'd worked in, there was no guarantee that dangerous situations wouldn't find their way here.

"Hey, Barret, do me a favor," she said.

"What's that?"

"Don't tell Sam about this."

"Your secret is safe with me."

Chapter Thirty-two

Last night, Sam had noticed Wren was quiet when she got off work, and they swung by the Winters' to spend Christmas Eve with Jace and Clark. They woke up early this morning and got dressed to spend Christmas Day with Wren's family. He had no idea when she had had time to go gather up gifts, but as she placed them into the car, he stalled her with a hand on her shoulder.

"Are you okay?" he asked, staring into her dark eyes for any sign of what might be going through her head, but she just smiled brightly.

"Sure, I'm fine. Why?"

"You just seem a little distant today."

She shrugged, her tone cheery as she said, "No, I just have a lot on my mind, is all."

"Alright, well, if it's something that we need to talk about—"

"We don't," she said, standing on her tiptoes to give him a kiss. "Let's just go enjoy Christmas."

Sam let his concerns go as she took his hand and led him out to the car. The ride over was quiet, and when they arrived at the top of the hill, Lukas came running out the front door, talking a mile a minute about the presents he'd gotten. Sam and Lukas had hit it off the first time they met, and Lukas took both Wren's and Sam's hands and led them into the house, telling them all about his new Lego sets and tablet that Santa had brought him.

When they crossed into the house, Luke and Garrett were in the kitchen preparing food while Elizabeth sat in the living room with her feet up, a cup of tea in her hands. Pete set a plate of fruit on the side table next to her, and Wren almost snickered, wondering what in the world was going on. Luke had barely acknowledged how tired his wife was, and now all her brothers were doting on Elizabeth like she was a queen.

THE MISTLETOE MIX-UP
231

Robert was nestled in his chair with a cup of coffee in his hands, smirking when he met her questioning gaze.

"What's going on here?" Wren asked.

"Your brother offered to make Christmas dinner," Elizabeth said, beaming proudly at her husband, whose cheeks were flushed.

"And he enlisted my help," Garrett grumbled.

"Well, that's awfully nice. Should we be scared about possible food poisoning?" Wren teased.

"Wren, I love you," Elizabeth said, pointing her finger at her, "but if you ruin this for me, I will bury you in the backyard."

"I will keep my mouth shut and vomit silently when I get home," Wren deadpanned.

"Hey!" Luke stopped chopping and brandished his knife, waving it in their direction. "I'll have you know, I cooked for myself all the time before I met Elizabeth."

"Yes, but it wasn't any good," Pete said.

When Luke swung his way, Garrett leaped back with a yelp before unarming his brother. "Stop waving that thing around, you idiot!"

As the two elder Little siblings bickered in the kitchen, Robert kicked out as Pete passed by. "Leave your brother alone and go say hi to your sister."

Pete came and gave Wren a big hug, then shook Sam's hand. Wren made the rounds to her other brothers and then went to hug her dad, whispering in his ear, "Did you say something about taking care of Elizabeth?"

"I did, and I should have done it sooner. When your mother was pregnant, I always took care of her. I'll do the same for all my daughters-in-law and you, when the time comes."

Tears pricked Wren's eyes, and she hugged him again. "You might just make a decent husband out of Pete, yet."

"Not Garrett?" Robert teased.

"If he can find a woman to look past his hygiene, I'll be shocked."

Sam and her father shook hands, while Wren hugged Elizabeth, taking the seat across from her. Once she'd settled in, her sister-in-law leaned forward, eyes bright as she whispered, "I heard about the hostage negotiation at the Den last night."

"The what?" Sam called across the house.

Wren shook her head rapidly, signaling to her sister-in-law not to say anything, when her brother Luke piped up from the kitchen.

"Are you talking about the holdup at the Den?"

Wren groaned as Pete joined in. "I heard about it on the news. Apparently, some guy went in there with a gun and held a bunch of people hostage and was trying to get money."

"You were there, right, Wren? You talked him down?" Garrett asked, and Wren silently wondered how three semi-intelligent men could be so obtuse.

"Unarmed from what I heard," Luke said, frowning. "Which wasn't the brightest move. Brave, but stupid."

Wren swallowed as Sam turned to her with a thunderous expression. "I was fine. I had backup."

"So, you went into an armed situation and didn't tell me about it?" Sam asked, his tone dangerously calm and in drastic contrast to his blazing blue eyes.

"Technically, I did not," she said, smiling sheepishly, "because it turned out the guy was using a water gun. It just looked real."

Robert patted Sam's shoulder. "I hate to break it to you, son, but if you're gonna be a police officer's wife, or I guess in your case, husband, worry comes with the trade."

Wren jerked at the mention of marriage, but Sam was still watching her intently. "Who was your backup?"

"Barret."

"Why didn't you let him go in and de-escalate the situation?"

"Because I was the senior officer with more experience in high-stress situations."

Sam turned around and took three deep breaths before she heard him counting quietly.

"Hey, you're giving him the same headache that you give us." Pete laughed. "You're part of the family, Sam."

Wren flipped her brother off, and Sam stood up straight. "Excuse me. I'll be right back." He walked out the front door, and Wren watched out the door as he started kicking at the snow on the ground and cursing loudly and fluently.

"I remember the first time someone took a shot at me," her dad said, standing over her shoulder. "I didn't think she was going to let me out of the house again."

"I better go talk to him," she murmured.

Wren stepped outside onto the porch, coming up behind Sam and wrapping her arms around him. She pressed her cheek against his back and whispered, "I didn't want to tell you because I didn't want you to worry."

"How am I going to be okay with you putting yourself in dangerous situations, especially if we have children?" he asked, his voice gravelly. "Mistletoe is quiet, but the quietest communities can be shaken by violence every single day." His hands came up to cover hers, and he squeezed them. "I don't want to get a call that something happened to you."

Wren pressed a kiss into his back. "I can't promise you won't get that call."

Sam turned in her arms and held her tight against him, his body trembling. "I'm going to worry every single time you walk out that door, but my biggest issue is that you didn't tell me."

"I'm sorry," she said, rubbing her hands over his back soothingly. "I won't lie again, even by omission."

"Thank you," he said, cupping her face and kissing her softly, briefly. "I know you can handle yourself. I'm not saying you can't, but I don't want to be kept in the dark because you are afraid that I don't want you to be a police officer."

"So, you're not going to ask me to quit?"

Sam shook his head. "I am proud of you. You found something that you love, and I will support you in everything that you do." His hands slid back and cradled her head, his blue eyes boring into hers. "But you cannot treat me like some weak man that you have to coddle and protect his ego."

"I'm not treating you like that!"

"Good, because I'm not a guy who would be insecure about his wife's profession. I think it is sick as hell that you kick ass and you have a bullet wound to show for it." Sam kissed her forehead. "I have the baddest woman as my girlfriend. But yeah, if we are going to do this, then I want to be your equal, talking things through and sharing our fears and insecurities." He released the back of her head, sliding his hands along her body to her waist. "I want to be there for you, and I want you to be there for me, and I don't want anything between us but love and trust."

Wren swallowed, trying to push down the emotional lump in her throat, but it wouldn't budge. Snuggling into him and wrapping her arms around his waist, she mumbled against his chest, "I promise to always be honest with you no matter how scary the truth might be. I will always treat you like my partner, but more than that, you're my best friend, Sam." She pressed her lips to his chest. "My most special, cherished friend."

"Thank you." Sam squeezed her to him before kissing the top of her head and then holding her at arm's length. "Now, if you will, please go back inside and give me a moment to collect myself, because I am still processing you walking unarmed into a bar with a man you suspected had a gun."

Wren kissed him before doing what he asked.

Sam took another deep breath after Wren went inside, thinking that she was going to be the death of him, when he heard the door open. He turned around, thinking it was Wren again, but it turned out to be Robert. Wren's father walked down the steps to stand next to Sam, shoving his hands in his pockets.

"Merry Christmas," he said.

"Merry Christmas, sir."

Robert stopped alongside him, arms crossed over his barrel chest. "Are you gonna make her quit?"

Sam's jaw dropped for a split second before he protested, "No, I'm not gonna make her quit."

Robert nodded, still watching him intently. "What about marriage?"

"If she wanted to marry me," Sam said, acknowledging that this was Robert's version of the what-are-your-intentions speech, "I would marry her in a heartbeat, but she doesn't seem to want to go that route."

"It's my fault, really." Robert sighed, sounding defeated. "I was angry when her mother left, and I probably didn't set a good example of how to handle divorce. I should've dated. I should've moved on, but I was busy. I was working, I had the kids, and I didn't stop to think about it until all of my kids were gone and I was alone. And by that time, I was set in my ways. If a woman came in and tried to change things, how was I gonna feel?"

Now Sam was lost and had no idea where Robert was going with this. "Is there a point you're trying to make, because if you're asking for dating advice, I don't know that I'm the right person to come to."

"No, I'm not coming to you for dating advice, you idiot," Robert snapped, giving Sam's shoulder a nudge. "I am saying that Wren's views on marriage are my fault, and I've tried to fix it, but I think the only way she is going to change her mind will be because of you."

Robert reached into his pocket and held out a box to him. "Open it."

Sam did and found a beautiful princess cut diamond ring inside. His heart pounded at the magnitude of what Robert was offering with the ring, not just something that would be special to Wren but also his blessing. Sam wanted to say something heartfelt, but he knew the big man wouldn't handle sentimentality well coming from Sam.

Instead, what came out was, "It's gorgeous, sir, but I'm in love with your daughter."

"I know that, smart-ass. It's for her." Robert pulled the ring out of the holder and turned it so the sunshine caught the diamond, making it sparkle. "It was my mother's ring. I was saving it to give to Wren when she found somebody she wanted to be with, and I think that person is you. I am giving it to you so that you can change my daughter's mind and make her happy." Robert's face suddenly turned thunderous, and he growled, "Because if you don't make her happy, I've got a spot between two pine trees in my backyard just long enough for you."

Sam stared at Robert for several seconds and finally beamed at him.

"Thank you, sir, for giving me your blessing."

"Oh, for the love of God, it's a damn ring," the older man grumbled. "That ain't my blessing."

"I think we should hug this out," Sam said, holding his arms wide and taking a step toward Robert, who backed away.

"Get the fuck away from me."

"Another time, then, but someday you're gonna love me."

Robert just grunted. It wasn't a no.

Chapter Thirty-three

The family was sitting around the Christmas tree looking through all the presents and talking. Spiked eggnog had been passed around, and for those who couldn't partake, tea and hot chocolate. The dinner turned out to be really good with no upset stomachs. Wren suspected that something was afoot, though, because Sam had been extra charming today. Instead of being reserved and letting the rest of the family do all the talking, he had joined in, even razzing her dad several times; Robert seemed to take it in stride considering how he'd felt about Sam for nineteen years. To see him come around so quickly boggled Wren's mind.

Sam excused himself and went outside, and when he came back, he had one more gift that he placed on her lap.

"For you," he said.

She opened the small, flat box, and inside was a piece of transparent paper with a drawing of two hearts on it: one had the date they met nineteen years ago, and the other had the date of their first dinner after reconnecting. He'd taken her idea one step further by coloring in the hearts with watercolors in brilliant shades like a sunset. In addition, he included a small heart at the end.

"I figured we could always add in the last date when the time came," he said, and she knew he was talking about when she got pregnant. Wren's heart thudded in her chest as she stared down at the beautiful gift that had come from his heart.

"It's beautiful." Wren traced the outline of the hearts with her fingertips, imagining what they would look like on her skin, and her heart swelled with pride and happiness. This was something meaningful, something she could imagine putting on her body. The fact that Sam understood and had created something so perfect touched her deeply.

"What is it, some kind of drawing?" asked Elizabeth, craning her neck to see.

"It's my tattoo."

"You're gonna get a tattoo?" Pete asked incredulously.

"I am. I'm going to get *this* tattoo." Wren turned the picture around to show her family, and Pete was the first one to get up, truly studying the drawing.

"What is it?" he asked.

Wren shot Sam a warm smile. "It's the first time we met and the date we reconnected."

"Oh my gosh, that's so romantic," Elizabeth gushed.

Luke made a face. "Gross, that's my sister."

"I don't care that she's your sister," Elizabeth said, elbowing him in the ribs. "I think that's sweet." She turned to her husband with a scowl on her face. "Why don't you get a tattoo of our first date?"

"I should. At least then I wouldn't get in trouble for forgetting our anniversary," Luke said.

Elizabeth rolled her eyes.

"I think you should adjust the tattoo, Sam," Robert said.

"What do you mean, Dad?" Wren asked.

"I think you should have one more heart for the date you two get married."

Wren glanced at Sam, her gaze spinning around the room to the expectant expressions of her family members. Everything had shifted so completely, Wren felt like she was in a parallel universe. How could her dad have casually brought up marriage as if they hadn't recently had a conversation about her very strong feelings regarding holy matrimony. Was he messing with her or Sam on purpose?

"Will you excuse me?" she said. "I'm gonna go to the bathroom."

Wren went into the bathroom and took a deep breath. She couldn't believe that her dad had brought up marriage. After the conversation they'd had, he knew she was on the fence about it, and he'd thrown the possibility out like it was a certainty. Plus, getting Sam's hopes up?

God, how could he be so insensitive? She could just imagine Sam thinking that she had mentioned something to her dad, and her sweet, wonderful Sam would be elated, and then she'd have to be the one to burst his bubble.

What her father needed was a swift kick in the pants for interfering and opening his big, troublesome mouth.

There was a knock on the door, and Robert asked, "Peeing or pooping?"

"I'm not doing either."

"Well, then, open up the door and let your dad in."

"You wanna have a conversation in the bathroom?"

"Isn't that what you girls do? You have something serious to talk about, so y'all crowd into the bathroom and talk?"

"You are not a girl."

"Maybe not, but I wanna have a talk with you just the same."

Wren opened the door and let her dad in. "What do you want?"

"I just want to say that I know we had that talk last week about feelings and marriage and lifetime commitments." Robert leaned back against the sink, crossing his arms over his chest as he stared down at her. "You said you can't see yourself being married, but you are talking about putting a permanent mark on your body for that man. If you are that far gone, the least you could do is put a ring on your finger."

"Tattoos can be removed."

Robert scoffed. "Yeah, but it's expensive and hard and painful. You are thirty-five years old and have never gotten one. Now you are talking about getting one that marks your relationship with that man out there."

Wren copied his posture, crossing her arms and glaring at him. "Which is not as big of a deal as saying yes to the dress, and the cake, and till death do us part."

"Married or not, love is a big deal, sweetheart," Robert said, reaching for her shoulders and squeezing them. "You need to stop talking about all this stupid foolishness that 'you don't see yourself getting married because of your past, blah blah blah—' Kiddo, get over it. I made mistakes, your mom made mistakes, you've made mistakes. Learn from the mistakes and have the kind of relationship you want."

"That's what I'm trying to do, but everyone else keeps pushing," she muttered with no real conviction. The thought of walking down the aisle to a waiting Sam held some definite appeal.

"If you really don't wanna get married, that's fine," Robert said, reaching for the door handle and opening it. "But if you're just not getting married because it's something you've been telling yourself you don't want for nineteen years, you go out and you look at that man's face, because I guarantee you, he would marry you tomorrow if you said yes. That is how far gone he is for you."

Wren opened her mouth to answer, but he stepped out and closed the door before she could get a word in, jumping in surprise when he stuck his head back in. "Also, I'm not one to gossip, but I've heard a few things around town about Sam Griffin and women. So if you're the one for him and he's the one for you, I'd snap him up, because he apparently has a line of ladies waiting for him."

"To throw a pie in his face," she quipped.

"Oh yeah, I saw that." Robert smirked. "Stopped by between cutting ice sculptures to throw one myself."

"You were doing chainsaw ice sculpting?" Wren's mouth hung open when her father nodded. "Why didn't you say anything?"

"Because I didn't want any of you stopping by to watch in front of the whole town."

"You don't care about that kind of thing," Wren said, suspicions swirling through her. "Why didn't you want us to come see you?"

Her father's face turned beet red, and he muttered, "Because I had a date."

Now Wren had heard everything. "You had a date to the winter games? Who is she?"

"I'm not ready to talk about it yet," he said, trying to close the door on her, but she stuck her hand out, stopping him. "We're just taking things slow."

Wren laughed. "I want to meet her."

"You'll meet her in due time."

"No, I'm gonna walk out there and tell everybody that you are dating someone unless you tell me who she is."

Robert scowled at her. "If I tell you, you'll keep your trap shut?"

"Yes, I will."

"Fine. Margot Jenkins."

"Miss Jenkins." Wren mulled the name over before everything clicked into place. "My fifth-grade teacher?"

"Yes."

"You are dating Miss Jenkins?"

"Yes," he sighed. "I am dating Margot Jenkins. What?"

Shock rushed through her as she tried to picture her burly dad and the plump, sweet Miss Jenkins getting it on. "How long?"

"Six months or so."

Wren's mouth flopped open and closed several times before she blurted out, "You called her an uptight California interloper."

"That was back then," Robert said calmly. "Woman makes a mean pot of chili."

"Oh my God. Six months?! That's a long time, especially—" He gave her a dark look. "Especially for someone who is getting on in years," she finished.

Robert laughed. "Don't say anything. She's got grown children, too, and we haven't quite figured out what we are going to do."

"Are you talking about living together?" she asked.

"I don't know what we're talking about. All I do know is that I'm not lonely anymore, and she makes me laugh, and we have a lot of fun together. I just want to be happy."

"Me, too. I want you to be happy, too, because you deserve it," Wren said and kissed his cheek. You really were a good dad. You had a few hit-or-miss moments, but I'm glad you stuck around."

"Me, too, or you'd have been raised by your Uncle Floyd."

"Who is Uncle Floyd?"

"You don't wanna know," Robert said as he made a move toward the door. "Come on out when you're ready, but just remember you need to start living your life for you and not using all these excuses to hold yourself back."

"Thanks, Dad."

He exited the bathroom, and she stared at herself in the mirror for several seconds before holding her ring finger up, imagining the heavy weight of a band on it. It didn't terrify her. It didn't make her wanna run in the other direction as long as Sam was the one she would be marrying. If her dad could move on, even if it had taken him a little bit of time, maybe she could, too.

Wren stepped out of the bathroom, and when she came back into the living room, everyone was standing except for Sam, who was bent down on one knee. In his hand was a ring box, open to reveal a glittering diamond ring.

"What the hell?" she said.

"Your dad gave it to me," Sam said. "It was your grandma's."

Wren glanced at her dad with tears in her eyes, realizing that whole speech was to prepare her for this moment, because the two of them had colluded on the entire situation. While she should've been pissed off beyond belief, she was actually so filled with joy, she thought she would burst.

"You're really asking me to marry you on Christmas, in front of my whole family, with my grandmother's ring?"

"Yes, I am."

Tears pricked her eyes, and she glanced at her dad, who simply quirked an eyebrow at her as if to say, *What's it going to be, kid?*

"That is just the most perfect proposal I could ever imagine," Wren whispered.

The whole family sucked in their breath as she walked into the living room and held her hand out.

"You gotta ask me, though, 'cause I'm not gonna assume anything in this moment."

Sam smiled. "Will you marry me?"

"Yes, I think I will."

"You only think?" he asked incredulously, his eyebrows hiked halfway up his forehead.

"Well, I guess you better hurry up and get something planned before I change my mind," she said.

Sam climbed to his feet, slipped the ring over her finger, and he kissed her. "I'll get right on that."

Chapter Thirty-four

On New Year's Eve morning, Wren slept in, excited that for the first time in sixteen years of law enforcement, she had both Christmas and New Year's off. She got out of bed and went to use the bathroom, spotting a note on the mirror as she walked by. She pulled the letter off the glass and sat down to do her business, reading.

Good morning, Birdy.

I had to take care of something this morning, but your family is going to pick you up and bring you out to the Winters' farm for a New Year's Eve party. I love you.

Sam

What New Year's Eve party? She'd told Sam that she wanted to stay in and have a quiet New Year's. Instead, they would not only be with her family but also his surrogate family, and they would probably be on the road when all the drunk people were leaving the bars. This was the whole reason why she hated New Year's. She'd spent way too many nights filing police reports on crashes and drunk drivers, and she just wanted to chillax.

Plus, she wasn't drinking, just in case one of their earlier sexcapades had taken root.

When her brothers and dad showed up a few hours later, she was fit to be tied and told them, "You might as well leave, because I'm not going to any party. I want to stay home, veg out, and eat junk food."

"You can do all that after the party," said Elizabeth, who came around the back of Garrett's truck looking shiny as a new penny in a black dress that flowed over her burgeoning belly. She hooked her arm through Wren's and cajoled, "Come on, Wren, it'll be fun."

Wren groaned and went back inside to get ready while her family crowded into her living room. When she came down in a simple red dress and heels, her family applauded, and she waved her hand like she was Miss America.

"Let's get this over with," she said.

She rode in Elizabeth's van with her and Lukas while the boys rode in Garrett's truck. When they pulled up to the Winters' Family Christmas Tree Farm, she noticed the twinkling lights decorating the outside of the tree tent.

"Is that where they're having the party?" Wren asked. "It's eighteen degrees outside."

"They'll have heaters inside," Elizabeth said impatiently, motioning for her to get a move on. "Come on, come on."

Elizabeth got out of the car and retrieved Lukas, handing him off to his father. When her sister-in-law came around the car and took Wren's hand, pulling her toward the house, Wren stopped her.

"What is going on?" Wren asked, her gaze sweeping over the Winters' home. "Where are you taking me?"

"To get ready."

"I already got ready for the party," she protested, frowning in confusion.

Her dad cleared his throat and handed her a white envelope. "It's all in the letter," he said.

Wren took and opened the letter and started reading.

My Darling Birdy,

You're probably wondering what I'm up to. Well, the truth is, you told me to hurry up before you changed your mind, so this is me hurrying up. The Winters' agreed to let us have our wedding on their farm. I have all the papers, and they're ready to be signed. There's a nondenominational pastor waiting in the tent. All that's missing is you and me. Our family and friends have gathered to eat and celebrate with us. What do you say? Do you want to get married today?

I love you,
Sam

Wren wiped her eyes with the back of her hand and looked at her dad. "Is this real?"

"I got my dress uniform hanging up in the back, ready to go," her dad said, beaming. "The question is whether you want this to be real."

"Because if you don't wanna do this, I'll drive the getaway car," Pete broke in.

Wren laughed tearfully, going to each of her brothers and Elizabeth to hug and thank them before she stopped at her dad and gave him a hard hug.

"Did you help make this happen?" she asked.

"I had a little hand in it," he conceded, wiping away her tears with his thumb. "I wanted to make up for some of the wrong I did."

"You have, thank you."

"Come on. Your bridal party awaits."

Wren let Elizabeth lead her into the house where Millie and the Winters women were waiting for her.

Millie had a garment bag, and when she unzipped it, Wren gasped.

"It's just like the gown we saw at that bridal boutique when we went shopping for your bridesmaid dress for Elizabeth's wedding," Millie reminded her. "I thought since you loved it so much then, you might still love it now."

"You went all the way to Twin Falls to find this dress?"

"No, I looked online and found the dress and had it express shipped." Millie shrugged when the room full of women all stared at her. "It was cheaper than gas money."

Wren laughed, and suddenly she was surrounded. She was plucked, straightened, curled, and cinched up. She had enough makeup caked on her face to paint a canvas, but when they turned her around and Wren stared at her reflection, she didn't speak for several beats.

She looked beautiful. She looked happy. She looked ready.

Her dress was off the shoulder with long, gauzy bell sleeves and a beaded bodice that hugged her curves. The dress fluffed out into a ball gown style, and the snow boots they'd given her to wear to the tent were white with little seed pearls on them.

"And we know you're not gonna dance in heels, so I bought you a pair of white Hey Dudes," Elizabeth said, holding up the simple slip-on shoes with a grin.

"Thank you," Wren choked, tears welling in her eyes. "All of you."

"You are very welcome," Holly said, waving her hands in front of Wren's face. "No crying, or you're going to mess up your makeup!"

"Here is your 'something new,' a gift from Sam." Millie pulled out a velvet bag and opened it to reveal a white gold necklace with two hearts encrusted in diamonds. Holly took it from Millie and put it around Wren's neck, while Millie tossed her the 'something old and borrowed.' It was a pearl comb Millie's grandmother had given her before she passed. Wren knew how precious this was to her friend, and her eyes pricked with tears.

"Thank you."

"I'll put that in your hair," Elizabeth said, sliding it into Wren's updo of curls.

"And 'something blue,'" Victoria said, handing her a blue silk garter. "It's a tradition in our family, and since you're marrying my unofficially adopted son, that's what you are to me."

Elizabeth beamed at Wren. "I think that's everything. Are you ready?"

Wren nodded and they helped her out onto the front porch where her dad was waiting for her in his dress uniform. He held his arm out to her, and the other ladies rushed ahead, giving them a moment of privacy.

"You look wonderful."

"Thank you," she sniffled, trying the fanning trick Holly did to stop herself from crying. "I feel wonderful."

"In that case, we should probably get you down to the tent before your boy paces a hole in the ground."

Wren's heart beat faster the closer they came to the tent. The minute they crossed the entrance and she saw Sam waiting for her at the end of a white walkway, all her doubts melted away as she stared.

Sam stood in front of a white arch in a black tux, looking dapper and handsome. He froze when their eyes met, and he watched Wren walk down the aisle, his jaw slack, with Clark's hand on his shoulder. She finally got close enough to see the tears streaming down his cheeks, and her breath caught. Her own eyes stung again, and she was afraid that if she started crying, all the ladies who'd helped her get ready would pitch a fit about her makeup running, but she couldn't help it. While Wren had never imagined getting married until the last few weeks, she had to admit that Sam had put everything together exactly how she would have planned it. Simple. Intimate. Beautiful.

But the best thing of all was seeing the man she loved, the "player" of Mistletoe, with all his walls crumbling because he saw her coming down the aisle in her wedding dress.

It was the most perfect moment she'd ever witnessed.

"Who gives this woman?" the pastor asked.

"We do," her brothers and father chorused.

Millie and Elizabeth stood on her side, both beaming. Her father gave her hand to Sam, who took it. When Robert put his hand on Sam's shoulder, Sam leaned over and gave him a hug.

Wren heard him say, "Thank you," before they broke apart and Sam faced her.

As they stood in front of the pastor, Wren reached up and wiped the tears from Sam's cheeks.

"You're supposed to cry after the wedding," she said.

"Watching you come down that aisle was like seeing the sun crest the mountains for the first time."

Now her eyes were burning again. After they went through their vows and had their very first kiss as husband and wife, she pulled away and said, "You do realize I wanted to have a quiet New Year's Eve, right?"

"Yeah, I know," Sam said, bringing her hands to his mouth and kissing her knuckles, "but I figured this would be the best excuse for us to stay home on New Year's Eve for the rest of our lives and celebrate our anniversary."

Wren squeezed his hands, joy bursting in her chest. "Good thinking."

"That's why you married me. Because of my brains."

"Something like that," she said.

"Ouch, can I claim spousal abuse yet?"

"You might wanna wait until you see what I've got going on underneath this dress before you have me locked up."

Sam chuckled. "The anticipation is going to kill me."

Epilogue

TWO WEEKS LATER

"This is Jilly G, and you are live on the air."

Sam held the cell phone to his ear while he maneuvered his rolling luggage through the Boise Airport. "Hi, Jilly, I don't know if you remember me, but this is Sam. My nephew called in just before Thanksgiving, and you dubbed me 'Lonely in Mistletoe.'"

"Oh, the one all the girls couldn't stop talking about?" she said, laughter ringing in her voice. "How are you doing, honey?"

The fact that she still thought what happened on air was funny needled him, but watching his wife walking ahead of him in a pair of ass-hugging jeans took the sting out of it. "A lot better than I was after your show."

She had the nerve to *pshaw*. "You know how some of these live shows go. They can sometimes take a turn we weren't expecting, but I'm glad you're doing better. Did you ever find somebody? I know your nephew was awfully worried."

"I did, actually. An old girlfriend came back to town, and we got married New Year's Eve."

Wren glanced at him over her shoulder, eyes sparkling. Their whirl-wind romance had been the talk of the town, and people had started taking bets on how long it would last, but Sam was banking on forever. They'd spent the last two weeks moving him out of his duplex and into her house, and Sam had taken out a decent chunk from his savings to take his bride on a romantic honeymoon. When they got back, he would figure out what he wanted to do with the rest of it, but that could wait.

"Well, that was awfully fast! I guess the Jilly G Show did work its magic."

"Something like that," Sam said, rolling his eyes. "Anyway, I just wanted you to know how grateful I am, because if I hadn't come on air and listened to everything those women had to say, I wouldn't be where I am right now. Which is getting ready to board a plane with my beautiful bride and spend a week on our honeymoon."

"That's right! You tell the world that Jilly G makes magic happen."

"Yeah, you sure do." Sam paused just before security, his arm wrapping around Wren when she snuggled close. "Oh, by the way, I noticed you wrote an article for the *Mistletoe Oracle*, and you have a very distinct and interesting tattoo. I saw the picture. What does it mean again?"

"It means 'courage and strength' in Japanese."

"Yeah, that's what I thought you said. But actually, it doesn't. It means, 'I am loud and annoying.'"

Jilly G gasped. "No, it doesn't."

"Actually, it does. I had a friend of mine who grew up in Japan take a look, and he confirmed it." Wren giggled against Sam's chest, and he kissed the top of her head before adding, "It's a simple Google search if you ever wanted to check."

"I'm telling you," she said, her voice tight with anger, "I don't have 'I am loud and annoying' tattooed on my body."

"I tell you what? If you discover that I'm right, you come see me at Inks, and I will give you ten percent off a tattoo cover-up."

"I don't need that because I don't have that tattooed on me," she shrieked.

"If you say so, but, just so you're aware, there's a viral video going around with your tattoo as the main focus. Have a great night. Thanks for all your help!"

"What video?" She screamed so loud, he moved the phone away from his ear before he ended the call, chuckling devilishly.

Wren smirked at his amusement. "Do you feel better now?"

"Yeah, a little."

"To be fair, she wasn't the one who dragged you," Wren said, rolling her suitcase away from the sidelines and into the security line. "She just gave them the ammunition."

"It's the same thing I'm doing for her. She put the picture out there. I'm just sharing it with the world."

"I never knew that you were vindictive," Wren tsked.

"I like to think of myself more as Karmic."

"Okay, Karma," Wren laughed, stopping behind a couple and their young kids, "what's next on your list of things to do while on our honeymoon?"

Sam pulled Wren into him, kissing her in the middle of security and ignoring the stares of other travelers. For the next week, it was just the two of them in paradise, and he couldn't wait to soak up every minute of it.

"Make love to my beautiful wife as much as possible."

"Mmm," she murmured, wrapping her arms around his neck. "That is a good start."

About the Author

Codi Hall is the penname of Codi Gary, author of more than thirty contemporary and paranormal romance titles like the bestsellers *Things Good Girls Don't Do* and *Hot Winter Nights* and the laugh-out-loud Mistletoes series. She loves writing about flawed characters finding their happily-ever-afters because everyone, however imperfect, deserves an HEA.

A Northern California native, Gary now lives with her husband and their two children in southern Idaho, where she enjoys kayaking, unpredictable weather, and spending time with her family, including her array of adorable fur babies. When she isn't glued to her computer making characters smooch, you can find her posting sunset and pet pics on Instagram, making incredibly cringey videos for TikTok, reading the next book on her never-ending TBR list, or knitting away while rewatching *Supernatural* for the thousandth time. To keep up with all her hijinks, subscribe to her newsletter at codigarysbooks.com.

Podium

DISCOVER MORE
STORIES
UNBOUND

PodiumEntertainment.com